RANDOM HOUSE

LARGE PRINT

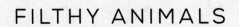
FILTHY ANIMALS

FILTHY

ANIMALS

BRANDON TAYLOR

RANDOM HOUSE
LARGE PRINT

Copyright © 2021 by Brandon Taylor
All rights reserved. Published in the United States of America by Random House Large Print in association with Riverhead Books, an imprint of Penguin Random House LLC.

The following stories have been previously published, some in different form, in these publications:
"Potluck," as "They Belong Only to Themselves," as an e–short story by Platypus Press; "Flesh," as "God is Not Flesh, But Air," in **Gulf Coast**; "As Though That Were Love" in **American Short Fiction**; "Proctoring," as "French Absolutism," in **Joyland**; "Anne of Cleves" in **Guernica**; and "What Made Them Made You," as "Grace," in **The Rumpus**.

Cover design and art by Na Kim

The Library of Congress has established a Cataloging-in-Publication record for this title.

ISBN: 978-0-593-41438-5

www.penguinrandomhouse.com/large-print-format-books

FIRST LARGE PRINT EDITION

Printed in the United States of America

10 9 8 7 6 5 4 3 2 1

This Large Print edition published in accord with the standards of the N.A.V.H.

CONTENTS

If you were of the world, the world would love you as its own.

—John 15:19

BRANDON TAYLOR is the author of the acclaimed
novel **Real Life**, which was named a finalist for the
Booker Prize and an Editors' Choice by **The New
York Times Book Review.** He holds graduate degrees
from the University of Wisconsin–Madison and the
University of Iowa, where he was an Iowa Arts Fellow
at the Iowa Writers' Workshop.

BRANDONLGTAYLOR.COM

POTLUCK

LIONEL HAD BEEN OUT OF THE HOSPITAL
for only a few days when the potluck invitation came.

The host lived in the first-floor apartment of a Near East Side duplex separated
by a tiny cul-de-sac from the wide-bottomed
cottages that fronted Lake Monona.

Noise of an undifferentiated party variety drifted out into the deep blue cold,
meeting Lionel under the sunroom window

where he had stopped to peer inside. He felt powerfully anonymous out there in the dark, looking in on all of them. That he did not recognize anyone apart from the host felt at once a comfort and a warning.

A rectangle of pale light unfurled down the stairs as the host pressed the door open on screeching hinges.

"Shit, it's cold out here. You walk all this way?"

Lionel climbed the stairs and tried to arrange his stiff face into a friendly expression, the effort of which made his scalp tingle. He had walked only part of the way, about ten minutes in all. The bus had dropped him on the other side of Orton Park. When the host realized that Lionel wasn't going to answer, he said, "Well, you're right on time."

"I didn't have a chance to go to the store—I just got back," Lionel said. The several pairs of shoes in the front hall indicated to him that this was not the small gathering he had thought it would be. It also indicated that he was **not** right on time, but he knew that already.

"Long trip?" The host wrapped his arm around Lionel's lower back and pulled at him until they were very close, at the threshold of the apartment, but not yet inside. "Good?"

"Couple weeks," Lionel said. "Sorry for not being in touch more."

"It's a busy time," the host said in a way that wasn't entirely **not** passive aggressive. Lionel turned his head a little out of reflexive guilt, and the host's dry lips grazed the corner of his mouth.

"Thank you," Lionel said.

"It's good to see you. Let's talk tonight. Catch up. It's been forever."

"Yeah, let's."

A few of the guests sat around on mismatched chairs and on the floor, holding plates of damp vegetables and grains. The improvised nature of the gathering diluted the strangeness he felt standing there alone, because although he was clearly a latecomer, the rest of them didn't seem to belong to one another in the way that friends sometimes could. There was no operating logic to their association that he could see. They were all awkward, anxious strangers in the host's living room. He waved to them, and they waved back. Their having seen him and his having seen them moved him.

Lionel felt alive, in the world.

The larger, noisier contingent of guests assembled their food in the kitchen. Lionel waited his turn, watching as they pirouetted and collided. They touched the smalls of each other's backs and shoulders. Men and women. They hugged and kissed and pressed against each other. Looped arms and hooked thumbs into each other's pockets. They poured wine and spooned things onto each other's plates. The loud **whack** of plastic trays and the tinkle of ice, the hiss of seltzer. As they finished and squeezed by Lionel, he saw that they were about his age, twenty-four, or a little older. They smelled like tobacco and bright, vegetal things—orchids, hydrangeas. They said **hey** and **hi** and **excuse me**, and he stepped back to let them pass.

When the kitchen was empty and everyone had settled down to eat, Lionel made his own plate of baked asparagus, brown rice, kale salad. He leaned against the flaking yellow counter and pushed the food around until it had all been drawn across and through itself. The kitchen was humid, redolent of people and their colognes, shampoos, lotions. But the open window let in a shaft of cold, clear air. The wind whistled as it caught stray openings in the screen.

"Lionel!" the host called from the other room. "Lionel, what are you doing in there? Come on!"

He felt silly being summoned. When he was in the doorway, the host clapped loudly in a way that made the overhead lights flicker brighter in Lionel's vision. His teeth hurt.

"There he is, there he is!"

The others did not clap, which made the host's gesture seem both pitiful and cruel. Lionel could see the full array of people who had come to the potluck. The chubby man on the floor between two chairs kept insisting that he was fine. A blond woman sat with both feet on her chair and a plate balanced on her knees. The host shared the chaise with a couple who looked like siblings, in matching black corduroy pants and gray socks. The woman had a messy topknot, and the man wore his scraggly hair down to his shoulders under a felt baseball cap. An androgynous person, tall, striking, with a platinum buzzcut and septum piercing gestured at a black woman in overalls with pierced cheeks. Some skinny gay men in Breton sweaters, one black-white, the other white-black, were flirting with an equally skinny black man wearing sunglasses. A woman in chinos sat scowling at the space between her knees. Their faces were a wall of pleasant, bland expressions, but then they sank back into their own conversations. The chatter rose above the low music.

Near the defunct fireplace, over which someone had mounted a set of steer horns, Lionel squeezed into an opening on the floor next to a man in a burgundy turtleneck. The man was densely, unnecessarily muscular and looked like someone who enjoyed being looked at and could hold eye contact.

The conversation was difficult to catch.

Everyone was talking in extended references to other moments, other events, other parties, and each reference, instead of drawing two things into relation, was instead the whole of the idiom, the entirety of the gesture. Which was fine, okay, he had gone to college with men who talked only in references to Will Ferrell movies and Adam McKay jokes. But he had not gone to these other parties. He had no way of getting inside the reference, the system. He laughed hollowly when other people did, though on a delay, but soon he grew tired of the feeling of falseness vibrating in his sinuses. The man next to him kept looking his way, and one or two times their eyes caught, and Lionel wondered at the feeling of recognition he experienced. The two of them were, by some strange bit of luck, on the outside of the conversation, though Lionel suspected that for the man this was intentional. He envied that. The way some people could choose to be in a moment with others or not. It was a choice he didn't have access to, personally. He always felt that he was arriving at the moment just as it was ending and everyone was moving on. He had no sense of timing. But the man's eyes kept catching him, and Lionel started to feel that the two of them, on the outside, had come to rest in their own moment. Their own tempo.

"I'm Charles," the man said eventually.

"Lionel."

"I heard. You're famous now."

"Well, he's like that. He thinks everything is okay as long as he can laugh about it," Lionel said. Charles raised his eyebrows.

"Is that right?"

"Yes," Lionel started to say, but then stopped because he didn't want to be considered a gossip, and Charles had leaned toward him slightly like gossiping was exactly what he had in mind. "He's funny that way."

"You a vegetarian?" Charles asked. The randomness of the remark, coming as it did from out of the ether, wrongfooted Lionel.

"How did you know? Something on my face?"

"Your plate," Charles said. "You're living that grain life."

Lionel, as though he hadn't made up the plate with his own hands, looked down and saw the food assembled there. The rice and kale mixed up. The stalks of asparagus. Oxidizing avocado chunks going soft.

"Guilty."

Lionel looked at Charles's plate. He had two fish portions, the kind with the head still on and the skin all crispy and brown. They looked like brim or something. Lionel had stopped eating meat the year before, when he was in the hospital. There was something so awful about it. Meat was so proximal to death, and he'd spent too much time looking at videos of the commercial food industry while he was in the private care facility. The kind shot on shaky camera phones and involving a lot of panting and rustling clothes, up-close shots of the cows pressing their snouts to mud-streaked bars or lying pathetically on their sides, suffering, with oozing sores and distended abdomens. He wasn't radically vegetarian. He possessed no militant energy whatsoever. But still he felt insecure about it, because the origin of his desire to forgo meat wasn't environmental or even about the animals, really. It was selfish. Because the thought of consuming dead things, when he had been so close to dying, when he had wanted to die, was too much. Lionel waited for Charles to say something dismissive about vegetarians, for that moment when people projected onto him whatever lingering guilt they felt about the consumption of meat.

He missed hamburgers terribly sometimes.

"How do you know our mutual friend?" Charles asked. "I don't think I've seen you at one of his dumb parties before." Lionel was prepared for the abruptness of the transition this time.

"We were in the same department," he said. He had known the host for several years, first when they were undergrad interns in the computer science department—Lionel from Michigan, the host from Arizona. Then both of them had been accepted into the same applied mathematics program at Wisconsin, and they'd been students together there for a few years, though Lionel was more pure math, while the host was working on applications to shielding and space exploration. They met for coffee and lunch after and before seminars and bonded over the fact that they hadn't been math prodigies as kids. They slept together that first, itchy summer, fresh from undergrad and waiting for their lives to change. The host was now on track to graduate early—his project had attracted interest from the Department of Defense, which wanted to turn it into a weapon to be deployed in foreign wars.

"Oh, you're a weird genius too, huh? That must be nice." Charles whistled in fake appreciation.

"Definitely not a genius," Lionel said. The word made him a little queasy. "I'm not in school right now, anyway. I'm on leave."

Charles spun his fork around with a flick of his fingers. The metal flashed as it moved across his wrist and came to rest right side up. He did it again, just like that, a neat little trick.

"Then what do you do?"

"I proctor exams," Lionel said.

"You what now?"

"I give exams for professors. I do entrance exams, too." Lionel's appetite shrank to a tiny white heat in the pit of his stomach. He was ashamed of proctoring only when he had to tell other people about it, and only when those people knew that he had once been a graduate student with good brain chemistry. He didn't think proctoring was bad, but he could see how other people saw him the moment they heard it and how they appraised his life as it was by the metric of what it had once been.

"You're pulling my leg. From math genius to proctor? Is that even a real thing?"

"It is," Lionel said. "It's what I do."

"How'd that happen?"

"I just sort of fell into it," Lionel said.

"Steep fall."

"Not as steep as you'd imagine."

Charles narrowed his eyes but smiled. Lionel felt a crackle of static between them.

"Is that your heart's desire? To proctor?"

"Is your heart's desire to interrogate strangers at a dinner party like a Chekhov character?"

"I don't know what that is," Charles said dryly, and Lionel snorted. The solidity of the sound startled him. Charles went back to spinning his fork.

Lionel resisted the urge to respond, grateful for the opportunity to drop down and out of the conversation. It was clear to him now, in a way that it hadn't been before, that he and every other graduate student depended on the currency of their university affiliations to get by in conversations. As though academia were a satellite constantly pinging, letting him know who and where he was. It wasn't until he had come out of that life that he realized he had no real way of relating to people without it. People looked at him differently when he didn't mention that he'd once been a student or that he had a university affiliation. They looked **through** him, but the worst part of it was that he sometimes looked through himself in the same way.

"You like it?" Charles asked.

"It gives me time to think," Lionel said. "It's funny. I used to think so fast. Like, sometimes, I felt like I was having six different conversations in my head, all at once. But now it takes me a year just to get to the end of one thought."

"If I were that in my head, I'd kill myself," Charles said. "Sounds awful. Jesus."

The acuity of the words stung Lionel right between the eyes. The air in the room was dense. His tongue felt heavy and numb. Something lodged at the base of his throat when he tried to respond. He coughed experimentally to see if he could clear it, but the hard knot of whatever it was remained stubbornly fixed. His neck bulged under his fingers. His skin was flushed and warm to the touch. He thought briefly that he was having an allergic reaction, that weird sense of driving panic and dry throat. His heart hammered along, and his eyes watered. Even the wool of his sweater itched and burned against his arms. He made another attempt at coughing loose whatever was in his throat. He beat on his chest to break up the tension, but there was no give.

"People **do** kill themselves," Lionel wheezed. "They do."

"Easy, buddy," Charles said nervously. He slapped Lionel between the shoulders. The jolt of it made Lionel's plate slide from his lap to the floor with a loud thunk. The wilted kale, coated in dressing, and the greasy avocado made a sad little pile.

The conversation, that wall of party noise, dropped away, and it was just the curious silence of the voyeur and the watched. Their attention felt like metal prods inserted into his joints.

"I need," Lionel rasped, but then he stood up on his gummy legs. He went around the back of the chaise, and the host reached for him. The others called out:

Is he all right?

If I had to sit next to Charlie—

Charles, what did you do?

First door on the right!

LAST FALL, Lionel tried to kill himself.

His attempt had not been subtle, so his father had flown in from his suburb of Houston and his mother had driven from her suburb of Detroit. They converged on him in Madison, furious and terrified as they reprimanded him for yet again being so careless with himself.

He was held in UW Hospital for a few days. **Held,** because he could not leave of his own volition. What Lionel remembered with great clarity was the pain in his lower back: a hot ache just over his sacrum that throbbed all night. The doctor frowned at his EKG. The nurses spent a lot of time monitoring his respiration rate and his blood pressure. They told him to calm down and to think positive thoughts. They asked him about what he did, what he studied, said that he was young, that he was healthy, that he was okay, safe. He didn't have to be so afraid. But his pulse stayed high, and eventually they had to give him a sedative, and he dropped into a blank void of sleep.

When his parents showed up, he was bloodshot and cold. His father guffawed and said, **You look homeless.** The doctor flinched at that, but Lionel knew he was only trying to make a joke. To be easy. His father was an engineer who worked in oil. He had worked on a new method to extract oil from shale. Before Houston his father had been in North Dakota, and before North Dakota he had been in Wyoming, and before Wyoming he had been married.

Lionel's mother cried when she saw him and asked why he had done it, but the doctor said, **We don't ask that here. That is private.** His mother looked at the doctor and said, **Nothing about my child is private from me**, and Lionel had wanted to say that his mother had taken the locks off his door when he was little and never put them back.

His parents left that first time, going back to his place to get his toiletries and a change of clothes. The doctor said Lionel didn't have to go with them when they returned for him if he did not want to. He could stay. Lionel asked the doctor about the pain in his lower back, and the doctor offered to give him Valium, but said it was habit-forming. **It's not that bad**, Lionel said then. The pain was all right. He could live with it.

A couple of weeks later, he checked into a

private care facility outside Detroit. The facility had large, rolling lawns. There were cedar and pine trees, trails to walk. They called it hiking, though it was really just walking to the top of a modestly steep hill and looking down at the facility. From that height, one could see black fencing around the perimeter of the allotment. The building itself was the typical modernist arrangement of interlocking rectangles, edged here and there with a touch of wood paneling. It was the type of modernity that was hostile to history, to time, seemingly without precedent but utterly referential, almost dully so. The kind of building one saw so often that it had become a kind of visual cliché for money, for comfort, for aesthetic consideration.

Lionel had nightmares in which he fell through a slot of air, and he'd wake into another dream about being trapped under a thick sheet of ice. He'd cut his way down through sequential layers of dreams, waking into steadily more dire situations until at last he woke from a too-high bonfire or from wolves chasing him or from feeling lost in the woods at the base of an erupting volcano. The tachycardia left him winded just getting out of bed. He spent his time reading or lying under the gravity blanket his mother had brought him. When he'd been there a few weeks, he got permission to open his window. An aide unlocked it and explained that there was no screen and that he should look out for mosquitoes in the spring. The delicate security bars were impossible to remove. **Unless you're really persistent**, the aide said with a wink. Even these had been designed. Their appearance. Their material. The interlocking mechanism that prevented their removal. All of it made to look **not threatening**. An **affirming cage**, Lionel thought. They wanted the people at the facility to feel **affirmed** by their captivity.

He was there for six months, and then they cut him loose. His mother wanted him to stay with her, but Lionel wanted to go back to his life and his research. He wanted to be himself again.

In Madison, Lionel was okay through the spring and the summer. He had a doctor, a routine. His leave of absence was ending, and he'd go back to the program in the new year.

He was not yet himself, but he was getting there.

Then, a couple weeks ago, he had been startled on the sidewalk in the middle of the afternoon by a crystalline image of himself stepping out in front of a car and getting obliterated. The next day, he checked himself back into UW Hospital to be monitored. When the sense of danger passed, when he no longer thought he'd hurt himself, he went home. And there was the invitation from the host. Like a call from the world he'd left behind.

People did try to kill themselves—some of them succeeded and some of them did not.

IN THE HOST'S BATHROOM, Lionel tried to be easy. His pulse thumped in his thighs, and he thought the force of it would make him slip from his perch on the edge of the toilet. The motion of it made him dizzy.

He hated that he had let Charles's remark, casual and dismissive as it was, jam him up. He'd let it rule him, but worse still, he'd let on how much it bothered him. Lionel stood, bent over the sink, and splashed cold water onto his face. The faucet handles screamed when he twisted them, and the head gave a jittery, anxious stream. He drank from his cupped palms, trying to get his pulse down. He found the water a little soapy, and the dizziness remained, that teetering, swaying sensation, as if his legs might go out from under him.

There was a hard knock on the door.

"Two minutes," Lionel said. He ran the faucet again to give the person on the other side the idea that he was washing his hands. His mother would have told him to comb his hair and said that he had the bad habit of letting white people see him nappy and disheveled. He always wanted to tell her when she got on him about it that white people were just people, but he knew that it was a naive and stupid thing to say, because white people were **white people**. Back in the care facility, his mother had told him that his aunts and uncles down home, which was what she called her own hometown in eastern Georgia, thought his current state was because he'd been ripping and running with all them white kids at school and math camp. His aunts and uncles saw his desire to kill himself as an extension of all those things they didn't like or understand—how he talked, how he saw things—and they blamed his father and his father's ways for that.

It was dumb.

It was pointless.

It was nobody's fault.

Things happened.

When he cracked the door open, he didn't immediately see anyone. It was only after emerging fully into the narrow hallway, lined with photos of the host and his family, that Lionel saw Charles leaning against a shut door with his eyes closed.

"You good?" Charles asked.

"Looks like I should be asking you that."

"I didn't want to come to this thing."

"Then why did you?" Lionel rested his back against the wall. Directly across from him was a photo of the host as a child, head thrown back in ecstasy. He looked happy. Pleased. A woman in white shorts stood next to a tall bush with a muted expression.

"Sophie," Charles said. "Sophie wanted to come."

"Which one is she?"

"The blond one."

Lionel turned his head enough to look through the kitchen doorway and out into the living room.

"The flexible one?"

Charles nodded. He pushed off the door and leaned against the wall. The kitchen light fell through the doorway into the hall where they stood, separating them.

"It's nice you do things for each other," Lionel said.

"I really put my foot in my mouth."

"I'm in one piece. You may continue with your conscience intact."

"Really, man, if I fucked up, you can tell me."

"In my experience, nobody wants to hear that they fucked up."

"We should probably go back."

"We?" Lionel shook his head. "You can do whatever you want. I think I'll hang out here for a while."

Charles sighed then. There, resting his cheek against the wall, he looked a little helpless. Lionel mirrored him, turning, resting his cheek against the cool plaster.

"You mind if I hang?"

"Suit yourself. Not my house," Lionel said, but then he saw it. Relief. Charles was shy too.

"Okay, tough guy."

Lionel felt their breathing sync. The eye contact had reached the point of being ridiculous, but it wasn't uncomfortable or uneasy. Lionel wasn't even sure if they were seeing each other anymore. His own eyes had gone slightly crossed, and Charles broke up into blurry segments. But they were in another moment apart. They had returned to their own tempo, just the two of them. Lionel felt free of other people's expectations for how he should act and be. He felt free of his expectations for himself.

It was like kindness, as simple as that.

They went back to the party. Charles stopped behind Sophie. She rubbed his arms. The host reached again for Lionel's hand and pulled at him.

"You okay?" the host asked. Lionel sat on the arm of the chaise. The host's hands were greasy from dinner, and he'd stretched his feet across the laps of the couple. They were leaning forward now, each of them having a different conversation with the androgynous person, talking over each other in a hash of references to Dostoyevsky and Planned Parenthood:

"People only **think** they like Tolstoy better, but he's basically J. K. Rowling. Dostoyevsky is the real genius."

"Like, we're this fucking close to being totally defunded. Skip a latte and make a damn donation, right?"

"Okay, but, like, I've tried. Where should I start?"

"Sure, but one person can't do anything

against the vast political machine of American empire."

"Honestly, I think telling someone where to start with an author is kind of a slippery slope to fascism."

"That's what they want you to think. Like, imagine if MLK had just stayed home because it was **hard**."

"I personally think **Crime and Punishment** is better, but hey, what do I know anyway?"

"I'm fine," Lionel said. "Just getting over a bug."

"You're not contagious, are you?" someone asked. Lionel looked up and saw that it was the chubby man from before, sitting on the floor next to Sophie's chair. "It's flu season."

"I don't think it's contagious," Lionel said.

"Good, because I don't have a great immune system, and, like, it's socially irresponsible to come out if you're not feeling well."

"Oh, 'social responsibility,' here we go," the host said, rubbing his greasy fingers across Lionel's back.

"It's not funny. I mean, not everyone has a robust immune system and—"

"Maybe if you ate more vegetables and hit the gym," the host said with a sneer. Lionel felt conflicted. The man was annoying, but the host was being unnecessarily mean, and Lionel sensed it was because the man was fat and because the host did not find him attractive.

"Plant-based diets aren't actually shown to have a significant protective effect against infections from viral vectors."

"Oh, right, yeah, totally," the host said, beaming, looking around the room for validation, and since it was his potluck and his apartment, people did go along with him, smiling thinly and humming in assent. The man on the floor turned red, but then shrugged.

"Speaking of vegetables, I should probably clean up my mess," Lionel said.

"No, stay," the host whined.

Lionel crouched near the fireplace, but his plate and the food had already been cleared away. What remained was a shiny streak on the scuffed wood flooring. Across the room, Charles had put his arms around Sophie. The two of them were looking at Lionel. Charles had leaned down to say something into her ear, and Lionel watched her eyes narrow fractionally. But then Sophie turned her head and whispered something back to Charles, and the two of them seemed to be chuckling. Lionel wished that the food was still on the floor. Then at least he'd have something to do with himself. Instead, he stood up and made his way to the kitchen. Maybe he could make himself useful, get started on the dishes.

Charles followed him, and then it was the two of them at the host's sink. More of the small fried fish lay on a plate nearby. Charles picked one up and chewed on its crispy fins.

"You didn't have to do that," Lionel said. "I could have cleaned it up."

"Figured it was half my mess, too."

"Sophie seems nice." Lionel ran water into a plastic cup. The sink was too full for him to want to actually help out. He'd lost his nerve or his charitable impulse or both.

"She's something else," Charles said.

Lionel was about to ask why Charles had followed him into the kitchen and why he was standing so close, when the host rounded the corner. He was a little surprised to see the two of them there, it was obvious, but he recovered like a cat shifting its weight mid-fall, and he reached around Charles to pull the fridge open.

"You boys want some wine?"

"None for me," Charles said, drawing his fingers cross his neck in prohibition.

"I'll have some," Lionel said. The host pulled a bottle of rosé from the fridge, then reached down by Lionel, right in front of his crotch, and pulled a drawer open. He extracted a pair of kitchen shears and winked at Lionel before he pushed the drawer shut, his thumb tracing the outline of Lionel's dick.

Lionel jumped at the contact though it was brief. It felt somehow like a threat. Or a promise.

The host snipped the cage over the cork and pulled it free with a pop that made Lionel's mouth water. He could almost taste the wine in the sound. Charles stood back chewing his fish and watching as the host made a big production of pouring Lionel a glass and handing it to him.

"Cheers," the host said.

"Cheers."

"Are you going to congratulate me?"

"Sure. Congratulations. On what?"

"I'm defending right before break," he said. "I'm a free man."

"That would explain the potluck," Lionel said.

The host nodded as he poured his wine into a mason jar. They toasted.

"Congratulations. You deserve it." The host smiled. His teeth were very white and straight in a way that suggested that they had also been very expensive. The wine was good, though there was something metallic to it. Then again, Lionel didn't know what constituted good wine. His face felt hot, though the wine was cold and crisp. He was a little embarrassed for the host, at how deep his need was and how clearly he displayed it. Lionel felt that in that position, he wouldn't have been so needy. If he were that lucky, if he were that fortunate, he would have played it cool. He would have worn his success easy. But when you won, you got to decide how you celebrated. And everyone else had to accept it, otherwise they were sore losers.

His doctors had tried to help him get out of the habit of basing his self-image on things like success and what other people thought of him. They had tried to help him develop a robust sense of self-value. But in the host's kitchen, he felt that old ego peek its head above the water and glare in judgment.

"You hitting the job market?" Charles asked. His voice cleaved through the kitchen, and Lionel regained some sense of equilibrium.

"Yeah," the host said, "I got a couple interviews."

"Anywhere good?" Charles raised his eyebrows like he knew what **good** was, but Lionel suspected that he did not. No one did. Partly because there was no **good** for mathematicians. You got a job in a university or you were a consultant. If you were lucky. If you weren't, you adjuncted at three separate community colleges and worked in the small, dark hours of the morning and the evening on whatever small corner of the universe you had carved out for yourself in your graduate studies, but with far fewer resources and far less time. And then, year over year, the light of your future dimmed and died like a far-flung star. In the end, you told people that you had **once** studied with a Nobel laureate. And that you had **once** given a paper at the same conference as Terry Tao. And that you had **once** been nominated for the Fields Medal. All of this while the people you went to graduate school with raced out ahead of you and solved the universe's deep mysteries. Your peers superseded you until you could hardly remember what they were like when the two of you had stood in their kitchen one snowy fall night drinking rosé and toasting their graduation.

Lionel knew and the host knew, and maybe, it was possible, Charles knew, too, that this was just polite dinner chatter. But it made Lionel feel worse. He sipped the wine, wishing in a cold, cruel part of himself that the host would fail his defense. But then Lionel ran over that thought with a bright white streak and erased it.

The host's lips parted and those great, expensive teeth of his flashed in the kitchen light. In the living room, the party went on. Voices rose and fell. And someone called for the wine.

"Yeah," the host said slowly. He put his hand at the small of Lionel's back, leaned over, and kissed him. His lips were animal warm. Startlingly so. He seemed feverish. The host withdrew and winked at Charles. "Maybe one day I'll tell you all about it." Then he lifted the bottle over his head and posed at the doorway.

There was a loud, shrill cheer. Charles turned to Lionel.

"You okay?"

Lionel set his glass on the counter. The host went out to adoring noise, and Lionel eased himself down to the floor. He braced his back against the cupboard. Charles took a seat opposite him, but sinking to the floor, he winced and hissed in pain.

"I know what that's like," he said.

"What?"

"I know a couple assholes in my program, too."

Lionel nodded, then shook his head. "No, he's not an asshole. He's talented."

"You can be both."

"If you're talented, don't you deserve to be an asshole?"

"I'm not sure that's true," Charles said. "But people seem to think it is."

"Maybe I'd be an asshole too if I hadn't gone on leave. If I were graduating early." But then Lionel didn't like how bitter he sounded, in part because it felt like giving the host credit or power over him. "Anyway, it's fine."

The wind through the screen chilled his neck. Charles rested the back of his head against the drawer.

"It's okay to be mad," Charles said.

"Mad about what?"

"Your life." Charles stretched his knee out gingerly and then rubbed it flat with his palm.

"Did you hurt yourself?"

"Overworked. It's nothing."

It was easy to see how Charles might have overextended himself. He had the kind of body you could only get at great personal risk. He was good-looking, in a way that seemed incongruous with ordinary life. Like the kind of attractiveness only people on TV or with large social media followings could have. But he looked pained, too. All that body had cost him something.

Lionel could understand that. The cost of the life you wanted. The way it could bound back on you. Extract its due.

The kitchen tile crackled, and they both looked toward the door. It was Sophie. She looked down at them. Her eyes moved quickly from Lionel to Charles, to his knee.

"Do we need to go?" she asked.

"It's all right," he said. "We can stay."

"It might be better if we iced it at home."

Charles inhaled and then said, sharply, "I'm not a pussy."

"Oh, brother," Sophie said. She pulled the freezer door open and stuck her head inside like she'd done it a thousand times before. She took out a blue ice pack, offered it to Charles.

"What the fuck am I supposed to do with that?" he asked.

Her eyes narrowed again, this time lighting upon Lionel. She dropped the ice pack in the middle of the floor, and it spun around on its back like a helpless turtle. They all watched it come to a stop.

"Maybe your new buddy can help you," she said.

"Easy, Sophie."

"You're so selfish."

"You're the one who wanted to be here. I'm here."

She said nothing after that, just watched Charles another moment or two. Then she went back into the living room, and Lionel felt he could exhale. All through that exchange, he had been holding his breath. And he'd seen them bare their teeth at each other. Was that what it meant to be with someone? Was that what it meant to care?

Charles stood stiffly. Lionel could hear his knee popping.

"What did I say about assholes?" Charles said, and then he left the kitchen, too, shaking his head as he went.

Lionel drank the rest of his rosé in peace. He brushed the ice pack with his foot, and sent it spinning around again. When it came to a rest, he spun it in the opposite direction.

EVERYONE WENT OUT into the backyard, even though it had started to snow; there was nothing to see but the glare of the lampposts through the trees and the bright blue light from the neighbors' shed.

They passed around a joint someone had brought.

"Analog vaping," the host said. "Love it."

Lionel reached out through the porch railings and combed through the fat flakes of snow that drifted downward through the night. Their delicacy as they melted made him want to cry.

The host smelled like wine and pot, sweet and a little musky. He squatted next to Lionel, and they bumped shoulders.

"Do you want to stay over tonight?" the host asked. "To properly celebrate." Lionel knew he meant **Do you want to have sex?** He asked it loud enough for others to hear, but quiet enough to suggest that there was some seriousness to the query. Lionel looked out at the other people's faces and wondered what they would do if he said yes.

"Hmm," he said instead. There, with their faces pressed close and the smell of smoke in his hair, Lionel felt that if things had been slightly different he might easily have said yes and let himself be pulled under. If only for the possibility that the host's good luck and good life might rub off on him.

Charles sat on a stool and Sophie leaned down against his back. She had her arms around his neck, but she was watching Lionel. She was not quite smiling at him. No, not that. But there was warmth beneath her expression. In the porch light, she glowed. Charles stroked her arm with his finger. They could go on forever that way, Lionel thought. They knew what to do to each other. How to be together. That business in the kitchen had been an aberration, or maybe just the prelude to this tenderness.

Sophie kissed the top of Charles's head and pulled away from him. She sat next to Lionel in her thick gray tights and corduroy skirt. She had a purple jacket over her shoulders and a green hat that someone had knit for her. As everyone had been getting ready to go outside, she had passed the hat around, clearly proud of it, like a family heirloom.

"Rough going at dinner. I see you and Charlie made up, though."

She propped her chin on her hand. **Charlie.**

"Yeah," Lionel said. "We're old buddies now."

Sophie's face shifted subtly under the porch light, like a figure from myth or a trailer for an ominous horror movie. Charles leaned forward on the stool and braced his arms on the banister. In the yard, the others had begun to spin in slow circles with their heads back and their arms out in Christ pose.

"He's good at enjoying himself," Sophie said.

"I'm afraid I'm out of my depth. Or maybe I'm too drunk to have this conversation."

"I just mean—he isn't always considerate of other people." She was amused as she said it, and Lionel relaxed. They squeezed together against the side of the house. Lionel felt he could breathe again. Sophie offered him her cup, and when Lionel hesitated, she clarified, "Water."

"In that case," Lionel said. The lukewarm water tasted vaguely like beer—someone had done a pretty halfhearted job of rinsing the cup out before refilling it or had simply refilled it without rinsing it at all. But he was aware, the moment he took the first sip, that he was powerfully, endlessly thirsty. He couldn't stop drinking. The water passed through his mouth and down the back of his throat, where it dissolved into nothing. He kept drinking to satisfy his dry tongue, and before he knew it, he had drunk all of Sophie's water. She looked at him in a way that was either impressed or annoyed. "Sorry."

"The hour of thirst is upon us."

Lionel offered to replenish the cup, but she shrugged and said it was fine. She'd brought a lightweight blanket out on the porch and draped it over their legs.

"I'm sorry if I was being bitchy before," she said. "In the kitchen."

"You weren't."

"I was, but thank you. I just hate when people lie about how they feel."

"You must be bitchy all the time, then."

"I consider myself an honest person."

"It must be nice to have a robust sense of yourself."

Lionel could feel through the house siding the pressure of Sophie's head turning toward him. He could tell, too, from the subtle realigning of her shoulder against his arm.

"Now, **that** was a bitchy thing to say."

"It's been a long few weeks," he said.

A kind of heat passed between them. Some kind of animal recognition. Sophie's eyes were blue. She had bleached hair, but it was luminous and healthy-looking. Her mouth was full and soft, and she had a small scar on her chin. It was an unfamiliar sensation—or, no, it was familiar, but not one he was accustomed to feeling toward women. It was not desire as he understood or remembered it, exactly, not a desire to have sex with Sophie or to see her naked, but he wanted to reach out and touch her and be touched by her. He wanted to feel her against him. She had a perfectly tranquil expression, and he felt he might tell her anything about himself if only she might ask. Under them, the porch boards were cold and drafty. Sophie shivered and looked toward Charles, severing the moment.

"Charlie said you proctor exams."

"Yeah—for the university. It's only a few days a week, though."

"That's cool," Sophie said, and Lionel rolled his eyes. It was the kind of thing you said when you were pretending not to find someone boring. They'd retreated to the inane chatter of dinner parties at last, the shuffling of banal bits of information like so much unwanted food on a plate.

"What do **you** do?"

"Oh, I dance. Since I was five. It's like the one thing I'm good at. Absolutely no money in it, but hey."

"That's a real thing. Dance. Like, an actual real thing in the world. That's art."

"Sure, yeah, thanks," she said. "Actually, Charlie's a dancer, too."

"Is he?" Lionel asked. Suddenly, the body made sense.

"We're in the grad program."

"How long have you been together?"

"Maybe eight months, something like that? I'm bad at this." She crinkled her eyes and shook her head a little. Charles was looking at them over his shoulder. Sophie waved at him, but Charles shook his head and turned back to look out at the yard.

"That's a long time," Lionel said. Eight months was forever. A whole life could change in eight months. Or end entirely.

"Is it?" Sophie asked. "It doesn't seem that way. But I guess time flies."

"Yeah. Unless you want it to."

Sophie looked at him sideways. "What are you trying to say?"

"Nothing. Well, nothing about you two, anyway," Lionel said.

Sophie watched for a beat longer, and she seemed to make up her mind about something. She said, "He was right. You **are** hard to talk to."

Lionel felt a frisson then, pleasure and discomfort rubbing up against each other. He hadn't registered it before, when she'd said that thing about proctoring, but he realized now that they had been talking about him. Lionel ran through what Sophie had said and done since coming to sit next to him, trying to find the subtext. But he found nothing. Just the jangle of her voice, and the warmth of her body next to his under the blanket. Her hand was on his wrist, and then it slid down until her palm cupped his. Her hands were cold, lightly callused, but strong. She flexed her fingers through his and looked at him directly. Lionel wanted to pull his hand away, but he did not.

"People are hard," he said.

"Spoken like a true introvert."

"If I were a real introvert, I would have stayed home. Which would have been the wiser choice."

"I think you really believe that," she said in open awe. "You must really be afraid of yourself."

Lionel shivered. He did pull his hand away from Sophie. But it was just as well, because Charles had jerked the blanket from their legs and whirled it around his shoulders like a shawl.

"Some of us are freezing our nuts off out here," Charles said to them.

"I tried to get you to sit with us," Sophie said.

"I didn't want to," Charles pouted.

Sophie made a condescending sound in the back of her throat, moaning in exaggerated sympathy. Charles stuck his bottom lip out.

"Sure you didn't," Sophie said, no longer mocking him. Charles stopped pouting, too, and there was a taut silence between them.

"I'd leave it alone if I were you," he said.

"Get real."

"Sophie," Charles barked. His eyes flashed, and his shoulders opened slightly.

Out in the yard, the people had begun to leap and clap and shout. The host stood up, leaned out over the banister, and hollered. The snow was falling fully then. And everyone was howling. Charles put his head back and belted out a forceful, vibrating call. Lionel watched the muscles in his neck bulge. His skin reddened. He was the last to stop. Lionel felt soaked through with his sound.

He could still hear it when they all went back inside, out of the cold.

LIONEL SAID GOOD-BYE to everyone in the front hall. The host embraced him for a long time, slid his hands up Lionel's shirt, and said, "I want you to stay."

"Next time," Lionel whispered back. He gave Sophie a short squeeze. They exchanged numbers and promised to text or call for lunch in the next few days. Charles gripped his hand very hard and pulled him in close.

"See you around, Lionel," he said.

"Good-bye, **Charlie**," Lionel whispered into Charles's ear, surprising them both.

Pleasantly buzzed, Lionel decided to walk home. The last bus was long gone, anyway, and the distance wasn't terrible. He'd had only a couple of puffs on the joint and the one glass of wine. He floated on a warm cloud.

Lionel lived on Hancock, so he cut a path through Orton Park. The playground looked a little sad and eerie. The swings moved in the wind. The gazebo had white-blue lights going, but snow had piled up to the benches.

The neighborhoods and their mismatched houses. Queen Anne and modernist and Dutch colonial, all mixed together, side by side. During his first year in graduate school he had taken a walk with a friend through one of the East Side neighborhoods, and the friend, from Denmark, kept saying, **You have turrets on one end and Frank Lloyd Wright on the other. It makes no sense. No flow.** At night, the houses made a kind of sense. As if they were embedded in a shared context.

Lionel almost missed the chatter of the party, missed talking to Sophie and Charles. **Charlie**. It hadn't felt **comfortable**, exactly. But he'd felt good talking to them. Sparring a little. It was easier to forget what lay in wait for him at his apartment: The dishes in the sink. The laundry he'd left. The dust covering all his possessions. Not for long— just a week and a half—but still. When he'd come home from the hospital, his apartment was stale and unfamiliar. Like it belonged to someone else. It had been the water sitting in the sink, he knew. The crusty dishes and soggy pasta. He'd done the dishes before the potluck, at least.

His phone vibrated, and he checked the screen. He did not recognize the number.

where r u?

Lionel looked up the long gray street. The little houses finally giving way to stone-and-brick apartment buildings. Near the capitol but not on the square. The snow had dampened the cuffs of his jeans and soaked through his socks. The drifts were high and thick. He checked the cross streets and saw that he was almost home. He had been walking for fifteen minutes without realizing how much time had passed. He texted his location to the number he did not recognize, feeling a kind of drugged, silly courage.

His phone pulsed again:

on my way

This was different. This was not a question but an answer. Something was on its way toward him, and he did not know what or who it was. He had texted his location as a joke, almost, but here was its echo, bounding back at him, and he felt a prick of something, a little bee-sting sensation at the base of his skull.

Then another text:

c u soon

Lionel went on walking, texting briefly:

who are you?

Another pulse, another text from the ether:

;)

Lionel looked behind himself along the street from which he'd come. He felt a pale version of fear. As if his whole body were numb, but trying to wake up, registering sensation only through a dense haze.

He kept walking. He would get home and forget about the potluck and Charles and Sophie. He would fold his laundry. He would get under his blankets and sleep. He would be okay. He would be fine, fine, fine.

Another text:

where are you? i don't see you

Lionel did not answer. He kept going. But then came a voice calling down the street after him. He did not turn, just crossed the street. The voice grew louder and closer.

He began to sweat. Heat covered his back
and his stomach. **Keep going**, he said to
himself. **Keep going**.

Lionel slid a little down the inclining
sidewalk. The ice was scratchy beneath the
snow, but then his soles found traction and
he righted himself. The voice was closer
then, but Lionel could see his building
nearby, right there on the corner. He had a
first-floor apartment. The light from the
center hall of the building projected out
onto the snow, a dull, yellow pool. He patted his pockets for his keys.

"Lionel!" he heard, the voice no longer
indistinct but clear and ringing through the
night: his name. Lionel looked up, and
there was Charles, at the boundary between
the light and the shadow. He breathed hard
and bent over, clutching his side. His hair was
damp, and beads of sweat had frozen to the
ends of his curls, glinting. It was strange to see
him here. Lionel found his keys in his pocket.

"Why are you here? How are you here?"

"You ran! Who runs?" Charles looked up
at him, his panting coming to an end.

"I guess I did," Lionel said. "I wasn't trying to. I mean, I didn't know I was running from you."

"I texted you!" Charles said. He was upright then. His hands rested on his hips. But his weight distribution had him favoring one leg over the other. Lionel remembered his knee and felt bad.

"Ah. That was you."

"Yes, idiot," Charles said.

"Where's your car?"

"Up the street."

"I guess that makes sense," Lionel said. His thighs burned and his lower back hurt. He **had** been running. Jostling himself through the thick snowdrifts. He felt very tired. And he wanted to be warm. "Do you want to come inside, then?"

"Sure," Charles said.

Lionel nodded but did not move right away to open the door for them. He looked down into his palm at his keys, which the hospital staff had returned to him a few days before, along with the rest of his possessions. They were light, cold against his palm. The apartment building loomed behind them. All he had to do was turn and put the key into the lock, but he couldn't. His joints wouldn't move. His muscles wouldn't budge. It felt too much after too long a night.

"Can you?" Lionel asked. "Would you?"

"You're such a little weirdo," Charles said. But he took the keys from Lionel's hand. He tried the first one, but when it wouldn't undo the lock of the main door, he turned back to look at Lionel. He tried another, still no luck. "You want to help out here?"

"It's the one with the red tape," Lionel said. A car passed on the street, kicking up gray slush into the air. Some of it landed near the rim of light at the edge of the yard.

Charles unlocked the door and the warmth of the lower hall wafted out to them. It smelled like boiled cabbage and floor wax.

Lionel stepped into the warm lobby and pointed down the long hall with its red tiles and row of dented gray mailboxes.

"The blue key," Lionel said.

Charles looked down at the keys, noticing that they were all different colors. Lionel had retaped them just the morning before, as a way of remembering which did what.

"Handy," Charles said. "Good system."

"It helps," Lionel said, but he could only lean against the wall by the mailboxes.

IN LIONEL'S APARTMENT, they took off their coats and boots. Lionel turned on the light, and the intensity of its sudden brightness made them both flinch.

"Sorry."

"It's okay." Charles sat at the tiny kitchen table, his mere presence making everything in the apartment seem small and ineffectual, like a child's toy house. Lionel felt shy about it now, letting someone see where and how he lived.

"Do you want some coffee? I only have cheap beans—they're a little old."

"Sure thing."

Lionel ran some water into the kettle and dumped the grounds into the French press. Charles's chair scraped back, and the boards strained beneath his weight as he walked through the apartment. His step had an uneven hitch.

"This where you live?"

"No, we just broke into a stranger's apartment," Lionel said.

Charles stood near his bookcase, dragging a finger along the spines of his books. His humming filled the apartment. He turned to Lionel.

"Are you nervous?"

"A little."

"Why? Because of me?" Charles came nearer to him.

"No, me. You, too, I guess."

"What about me makes you nervous?" Charles pressed him against the counter. Lionel felt himself receding.

"You have a girlfriend," Lionel said.

"I do."

"Okay." The electric kettle turned itself off. "I should pour this." Charles stepped back to let him pour the water into the French press. Lionel poured slowly, watching the level of the water rise higher and higher. It brought him pleasure to do such things, to pay attention to ordinary tasks. They watched it steep in silence. Charles made a big show of it, letting on how intently focused he was on the surface of the coffee, and the occasional off-gassing. Lionel depressed the plunger.

"Cream?" Lionel asked.

"No."

"That way is too bitter for me."

"Sophie too." Charles took a long drink from his coffee, which must have been too hot.

"I like Sophie," Lionel said. "She's really . . . nice."

Charles smiled. Lionel felt embarrassed, thinking of how they'd been a little mean to each other, and how that had bonded them in some way. He thought, too, with rising color in his face, of that moment when it had felt like he and Sophie might have kissed on the porch, when it would have been the most natural thing. He liked Sophie. He liked the idea of being her friend. But Charles was looking at him, and Lionel could feel that possibility closing off. Charles set the cup on the table.

"Where do you sleep?"

"I'll show you," Lionel said.

IN THE MORNING, Lionel left Charles in bed.

He rinsed out their cups from last night. Then the French press, which he took apart and cleaned piece by piece and put in the rack to dry. He pushed up the window and propped it open with an old ruler. The cold would help air out the apartment, that stale smell from having left it shut up for almost two weeks.

Lionel could still feel Charles's hands all over him, the sureness of his grip and the grinding pressure of their bodies coming together. He went to the bathroom to brush his teeth, to brush the taste of Charles out of his mouth. By the time he got to the front of the apartment, Charles had rolled over onto his back and was lying there naked, on full display. His body was magnificent. Edges and lines and clear definition. A thatch of pubic hair. His cock was uncut and of medium length, but very thick. Everything about him was proportional.

Lionel made more coffee, waiting for Charles to get up, wondering where he'd go after he left, wondering what had brought him here. But as he stood waiting for the coffee to bloom, staring down into its brown mass, the ruler snapped in half. He had used it for years with no problem. He'd had it since he was a kid, when he'd gotten it as a gift from his math camp counselor. All the lines were worn off. Now it had snapped, and for a moment the window hung suspended, as if its mechanism had magically repaired itself or gravity had ceased to function. Then it fell, slamming shut with such force that the glass broke. In cartoonish escalation, the shards fell down into the sink, shattering further. He felt something old and powdery land on his lip, but it was only a bit of dust, a flake of paint perhaps, from the windowsill.

"What are you doing over there?" Charles had come into the kitchen. Lionel turned to him.

"It's a mess," he said.

"What?"

"I don't know," Lionel said, but his heart was beating fast, and his hands shook. He could hardly hold himself still.

"Oh, shit."

"I'm fine."

"Sure."

"No, don't! There's glass," Lionel said. Charles had made to cross the room. He was still naked, barefoot. At Lionel's warning, he drew up short. Then he put on his boots, still naked, collected a dustpan and broom, and swept a few glass fragments from the floor. Then he leaned down to inspect what was in the sink, and whistled.

"You better get a new one," he said.

With the glass gone, cold air was swirling into the apartment. Lionel saw the air raise goose bumps down Charles's back and thighs, little ridges of flesh.

"Thanks," he said. "Do you think you got it all?"

"You might run a vacuum over it if you've

got one, but I think you'll live." Charles
leaned down to kiss Lionel then, gripped
the backs of his thighs and lifted him easily.

"Your knee," Lionel said.

"You're not a physio."

Lionel wrapped his legs around Charles
and let himself be carried back to bed.
Charles stomped in the boots.

"Stay," Lionel said later, when Charles
was getting dressed.

"Can't," Charles said. "I have to go."

"Stay."

"I'll be back," Charles said. He kissed
Lionel's forehead and then his mouth and
he was gone out the door. Lionel drew his
blanket around himself and lay down.

"I have to go anyway," Lionel said, and
the only answer was the quiet of his apartment, the soft rattle of snow striking the
kitchen sink.

LITTLE BEAST

SYLVIA HAS BLOWN UP HER LIFE.

She slices potatoes into screaming hot water and chants, "Take it back, take it back, take it back."

Out in the living room: regular thudding. She has agreed to let the twins have fries for lunch if they are quiet and good while they color. The boy's whine trails each of the thuds. She's been played.

Sylvia drains the hot water, and then

plunges the sliced potatoes into an ice bath. The water numbs her fingers and wrists. Starch turns the water hazy, and the potatoes go slick like something hauled out of the sea. When her hands turn white, she pours off the cold water and blots the potatoes dry. Then she rubs them down with salt and garlic butter she made herself. And into the oven.

She feels productive, virtuous. Her reward is to close her eyes for just a moment. She dips into the brief dark of her eyelids, feels that woozy elation like holding her breath and letting it go. She drifts, sways. She considers, not for the first time this week, Hammond, the breakup. The doomed trip they took up to see her mother last month, how they'd they fought all the way there and back. The farm had done nothing to ease their splintering. All they'd done was move the location of the argument, not defuse the argument itself. Then she'd left him and that was that. But now, standing in the kitchen, she considers the permanence of that choice and how easy it had been to make in the end. So swift. Like a bolt of lightning. There and gone, but behind it an acrid, burning trail.

But before she can conjure sufficient self-pity, something pulls at her shirt like she's been caught on a nail or stray corner. She cracks her eyes open and sees the girl, who's got the hem of Sylvia's shirt gripped tight. Sylvia smiles at first. The desperate tension of the girl's grip sends a little thrill through Sylvia's stomach. She feels **needed**. But then she spies the brown clay sticking to the girl's fingers. Flecked through with green and black. The girl shifts her hands around Sylvia's shirt, and the motion changes something in the air current between them. Sylvia catches the scent. Dog shit.

"What are you doing?" Sylvia asks. She marvels at the cool distance in her voice. How mature and far away she sounds to herself. The girl doesn't even seem pleased with what she's done. She's no gloater. There is that to say for her. The girl spreads her fingers and clenches them shut again like she's making a point.

It would be nothing, would take nothing, to rend this girl to pieces. Sylvia feels in this moment like the grandmother who is part wolf. She'd gobble the little girl down and keep her there. Instead, she takes the girl's wrist and leads her into the living room. The boy sits quietly with his coloring.

"Stay," Sylvia says to him when his eyes track toward them. She winds through the piles of toys and cushions. The living room resembles not so much a battlefield as one of those emptied-out neighborhoods in a dying Rust Belt town. There's a sense of order having been overrun by chaos and wreckage. Work for later. Before the parents return. This is what they have been doing while they have been coloring. The sliding door is cracked open. No doubt it is the opening the girl slipped through in order to find her little surprise. This, Sylvia thinks, is what they consider being quiet and good.

. . .

IN THE BATHROOM, Sylvia runs water into the sink while the girl stares ahead. No fear. No remorse.

Good for you is what Sylvia almost says.

The water steams as it collects, turning the mirror ghostly white. Beneath the fog, Sylvia: Raw eyes, oily skin. Frizzed out, frayed at the edges, stained. This is not the first mishap of the week.

The girl coughs and smears dog shit across her face. No reaction. Sylvia's fingertips sting when she dips the cloth into the water. She reaches over and takes the girl's chin in hand without pretense of being gentle or trying to explain to her in a child's voice why what she's done is wrong. Her knuckles pop a little from the suddenness of turning the girl's head, but when their eyes meet, she almost gasps at the lack of surprise or discomfort. It's more out of her own fear that Sylvia puts the hot cloth to the girl's face and wipes at the shit. Anything to get away from the dark of her eyes, like she's staring up out of some deep well. After a few moments, the girl fixes her eyes on the back wall in a stare so intense that Sylvia almost turns to look, but she resists. There's nothing waiting for her back there except floral wallpaper.

The towel gets most of it, leaving the girl's cheeks and lips flushed. Sylvia holds out her hand for the rest, and the girl squeezes their palms close until they're glued together in the brown mess. At close proximity and in the bathroom's humid heat, the smell is more potent. The texture is like wet sand, grainy and clumped. Sylvia can feel diffuse, solid kernels of something sticking between her fingers.

"Come here," Sylvia says, and she lifts the girl up over the sink. Before she can threaten to drop her in, Sylvia feels her throw herself forward. She plunges in up to the elbow. Sylvia tries to pull her back up and out of the hot water, but the girl flails and kicks as though she is being kept from the thing she desires most in the world. When Sylvia jerks her back one solid time too many, the girl screams with such fury that the room fills with the sound of her. It's a horrible, fierce sound. Sylvia's legs buckle. How can one tiny human make so much noise?

Take it back, take it back, take it back.

Eventually, the girl vents herself empty and goes limp in Sylvia's arms. She tilts forward like a little rag doll when Sylvia puts her on the edge of the sink, and so Sylvia has to let the girl's face rest against her chest. She pulls the girl's tunic up, and blots her dry. Then the girl rocks back and Sylvia catches her by the shoulders. It's then Sylvia remembers the shit on her own shirt. She works up and shimmies out of it using one hand. She feels greasy in the humid bathroom. The girl's eyes shift over her, widen slightly. The girl lifts her hand, the tips soggy and red, touches the bruise on Sylvia's side.

Sylvia growls.

IN THE KITCHEN, they all wait for the fries. The twins sit at the table with their coloring, the boy struggling to decide between red and blue to fill in the crude tree he's drawn and the girl staring at him hatefully. Sylvia would like to go over there and color the whole thing green. It's a disservice to let children go on thinking the world can be something it cannot. Her parents hadn't let her think that sort of thing for long— that life could be what she wanted it to be, that all she needed was to try.

"Sylvie," the boy says with his cheeks between his hands. "Hungry."

"Is that a whole thought?" she asks, and he frowns, folds his arms across his chest.

"Hungry."

"Five more minutes."

The boy licks his lips until his whole mouth is wet and bubbly with spit. Booger eater, she thinks. The girl cuts her eyes at him.

"Sylvie. Hungry," the boy says again.

The fries crackle and hiss on the sheet pan. Sylvia wedges them free instead of letting them cool and transfers them to a plate that she leaves at the center of the table. They sit in a steaming mound flecked with coarse sea salt and red-pepper flakes. She hoists herself up onto the counter and watches the twins watch the fries. The boy licks his lips again. He is first, of course he is. Boys are greedy, always taking. But the world will make a mess of this boy. He's all nerve and skin. Nothing between him and the outside. The food burns his fingers, and he drops the fries onto the table. He tries again, blows on one of the fries. Sylvia can see his mouth watering. He makes little chewing motions. Oh, he wants it bad. Like his father. Scratching at her bedroom door these last few nights. She has fewer reasons to say no, and the last time that she let him go down on her, he had seemed so grateful that Sylvia had only felt a little guilty and a little selfish. Impossible not to see the resemblance between their two wants.

Sylvia tucks her knees against her chest and watches as he tries and fails, tries and fails, burns his mouth and his tongue. But he keeps trying. Eventually, he gets it in his mouth and keeps it there, chewing it into white mush. He smiles at her broadly, shows his food.

"Good!" he says, as if approving of her. "Good! Like!" The girl, because she is smart, stabs a fry through with a crayon and blows on it. Then she shoves the whole thing into her mouth, crayon and all. She gulps it down. **Good for you**.

THEIR LUNCH doesn't take long, and then Sylvia puts them down for a nap. She takes a tall glass of cold water to the back patio, where she sometimes smokes at night and sometimes drinks the father's beer with the mother while they talk about the twins, about Sylvia's life, about the easiness of youth and no attachments. It's not a conversation, not really. It's a monologue on the mother's part, delivered from a cashmere throw and the blurry edge of late middle age.

Sometimes, the mother gets drunk and waxes philosophical about her **geriatric pregnancy** and how utterly sexist the terminology is, running through the litany of grievances she's stored up at the world these past few years, returning to them again and again like treasured anecdotes of some far-off life. Reliving the trauma of maternity leave the way some people relive the horrors of the Great Depression or the Jim Crow South.

The house, like all of the other houses on their street, is not old but has been made to look that way. Pseudo-Victorian splendor meant to communicate—what, exactly, Sylvia wonders. Comfort? Material establishment. It's a street of doctors and white-collar serfs. The father works at a tech company down on the square. The mother works in pharma. She synthesized some sort of filament as a graduate student. Did some kind of molecular geometric voodoo, and now they have this house and they have Sylvia, and due to modern technology, they have the twins.

They split the cost of Sylvia with Mac and Jill Ngost next door. For slightly too little money—it would be more in Manhattan, but what can she do about Wisconsin—she cooks meals and looks after the twins. The Ngosts don't have children, and don't expect Sylvia to clean, only to cook. Mac and Jill are

in their early forties. Jill is attractive, a bru-
nette. She is funny, and she tells stories that
always turn in unexpected places. She keeps
her lips over her teeth because she is insecure
about a gray, misshapen canine. There is no
reason that this tooth should have emerged
as it did from her gums. All of her other teeth
are beautiful and white. Mac is tall and dense
with what is either muscle or fat or both. He
runs up and down the street for an hour or
two in the mornings. Sylvia watches him
from her bedroom. He likes sweet things,
and is always willing to let Sylvia experiment
on him with her desserts. Last night, she
served a berry crumble with a jam she'd made
herself.

Tonight, for the Ngosts, she is making
some sort of soup. Lots of shredded chicken
breast, a stock from the bones and marrow,
a thick cream base, some herbs. French
bread from the market. She can see the soup
in her mind, the way it goes from clear to
creamy white. She can smell the celery and
the carrots, the onion and small pieces of
beet she'll julienne and sprinkle in. A bit

of cumin, not too much. The meat for texture. She will serve a salad with berries and apricots. Or, she thinks, she could leave the chicken out of the soup and serve them cream-poached fish instead. The soup in small bowls next to the beautiful salmon.

She imagines Mac and Jill, their faces warm with hunger and desire. Jill will give her a knowing look. She will reach across the table, squeeze Sylvia's hands. Her mouth will become a perfect circle. Mac will eat, but while he chews, his eyes will stay on her. She is certain of this, can already feel the long pull of his gaze at her body.

But it is Jill who sits at the center of this fantasy. She is its white-hot core. Jill, with her longer fingers and sensible haircut. Jill, the investment banker. Jill, the insatiable.

Sylvia presses the glass between her legs to keep it still. It's cold and slick against her skin. Her stomach aches. There is something moving through her, working its way up her belly and into her chest, coiling and uncoiling. She grips her knees and tries to calm herself.

Inside, Sylvia can hear the soft rumble of footsteps.

The girl.

Up the stairs Sylvia goes, passing the pictures of the family, how they seem to regress as she goes. The two children vanish, and the parents recede back through their years, gaining hair, gaining smiles, gaining happiness. A family blooms, uncles and aunts, sisters and brothers, grandparents. It's like tracing a muddy stream to its clear, frothy headwaters. At the top of the stairs, she pauses. The sound of footsteps farther ahead. Yes, the girl. Except she is in her parents' room. Sylvia rolls her eyes. She is still a little jagged, a little rough. She tries to conceal her wolf's teeth, the part of her that wants to reach out and snatch the girl and tear her to pieces.

Along the long hardwood hall, with its expensive rug thrown down the middle, more pictures. Upstairs, the home is shut-in and close. Downstairs, there are so many windows, so much clear light, but here it's a cocoon, a hollow. She passes the boy's room.

On the other side of his door, there is silence. He will not move until someone comes for him. It is his nature. The girl's door is ajar. Sylvia peers inside. Her low bed, her toys scattered everywhere. A lilac curtain thrown open. Pale light. Her sheets have been dragged from her bed. There is an ugly stain on them, something yellowing, already smelling sour. Sylvia will have to attend to this before the parents return.

She leaves the doorway and turns to the parents' bedroom. There, sure enough, the door is also ajar. Sylvia hears a repetitive creaking. She pushes the door open. The girl throws herself into the air, lands on her back, and bounds back up.

"What the hell are you doing?"

The girl does not answer. She uses the bed as a trampoline. The Martins have blackout curtains, and there's just a sliver of light coming in through the tiny space between them. Everything is all velvet upholstery. It's the sort of room that needs torchlight, which seems incongruous with the sort of brightness that overhead lighting offers. Still, Sylvia flips the switch, and the room is bathed in a harsh white light.

The girl is naked. There are scratches up and down her arms, around her back. Her face is blank. She's lands on her back, climbs to her feet, leaps again into the air, getting God knows what all over the duvet and pillows. There are twigs and dirt in her hair. How has she done this to herself? She looks like a wild thing.

"Little beast," Sylvia says. The girl makes no attempt to stop bouncing. Sylvia grabs her bare ankle. The girl begins to scream, to screech, to holler, to tear at Sylvia's hands and arms and face. She is strong, and it takes all of Sylvia's strength to hold her down, to shake her into stillness. "What is your problem?"

She gazes up at Sylvia, and for a moment Sylvia thinks she can understand the girl. She knows what it is to be trapped inside a thing, inside a life. She knows what it is to want to tear a hole in everything. But still there is something else. This girl seems bound by nothing at all, except for the moment by Sylvia. There is nothing that can keep her inside herself. It's the kind of life Sylvia would like to live, but she knows it's the kind of life that is impossible because the world can't abide a raw woman.

"I know it's hard," Sylvia says to the girl. "But you have to try."

The girl lies on her back, as if the words have passed completely over her. In the light, Sylvia can now see that there are bugs, small green grubby things, among the tangled blond hair. Sylvia can smell the urine. It's dried in ugly patches on her thighs. She is never like this with her parents. With them, she's quiet, almost sullen. It's only when they leave that she gets unhinged this way. Sylvia thinks that she should say something, but it feels somehow like a betrayal.

"You have to try," Sylvia says.

SYLVIA SITS on the edge of the tub, pulling her fingers through the girl's hair, freeing bits of detritus. Where has she gotten this filthy? How she has managed to get herself into such a mess? The girl fidgets in the water, reaching for her bath toys, moving away when Sylvia's hands snag on tangles. She has already been still for longer than she likes, and Sylvia can feel the energy coiling inside her like a snake about to strike.

"Where did you get all these things?"

"My closet," she says, the first words she has spoken all day. "I keep them in my closet."

"Why?"

The girl shrugs and the bugs writhe as they drown. Sylvia rinses her fingers in the water and goes back to soaping the girl's hair. The bathroom is the same plush velvet as the bedroom. There's an insulated, womb-like quality to the acoustics. The light is comforting in its haziness.

"Why do you live with us now?" the girl asks. Sylvia considers her answer to this question. She could give the kind of gummy non-answer that children chew on for years before realizing there's nothing to it, or she could say the truth of it, but that might involve having to answer more questions, worse questions.

"Well," Sylvia starts. "I broke up with my boyfriend, and I needed a place to stay, so your parents are letting me stay here."

"Why?"

"Why what?"

"Why do you break up?" The girl turns to look at her, her eyes wide and blue.

"Oh, that's a boring story," Sylvia says. "Nobody wants to hear that story."

"I do," the girl says. "I want to hear."

"Well," Sylvia says, scooping up handfuls of water and letting them drizzle into the girl's hair. "He was not well. He was sick. And I was sick. And we weren't very good together."

"You're sick?" the girl asks.

Oh, yes, Sylvia almost says. **I'm fucking sick.**

"Just a little bit—I'm getting better."

"What's wrong?"

"Hard to say," Sylvia says. More water drizzling down the girl's face, across her cheeks. There's shampoo in her eyes, and it must burn, but she does not look away from Sylvia. How does she explain it? To this child? To herself? To Hammond—oh, Hammond.

Hammond is probably in their apartment—no, his apartment—pulling his hair out. She left him. She waited until he went to sleep that night, then packed her things and left him. She couldn't be with him, couldn't lie next to him, because she sensed in him the same thing that was knocking around inside her. The same looming, wild, stalking thing that moves behind her at every turn and corner. Something furry and evil that followed her off the mountain and all the way up here, to this city full of polite, clean people.

She left him—no note, just the careful packing away of her things. She left him.

"Grown-ups get sick sometimes, and nobody knows why and nobody knows how to fix it," Sylvia says. "And you try your best not to get anyone else sick."

The girl sneezes. The sound is scraping and rough in the bathroom. Sylvia tucks her hands under the girl's armpits and lifts her out. "All clean," she says. She wraps the girl in a towel and leads her down the hall to her bedroom. Leaving her there, Sylvia returns to the bathroom and lets the water out of the tub.

She runs some water to rinse the soap down the drain. Bugs twitch on the bottom of the tub, and Sylvia picks them out one by one, along with the twigs and the pieces of leaves that have not been washed away.

She flushes the black things down the toilet and goes downstairs to clean the living room. The parents will be back soon. In just a couple of hours. And then she'll slip from this house to the next like a ghost, like a phantom in the middle of the day.

As she cleans, she hears the girl upstairs, thumping around.

FLESH

IT WAS THE CLASS FOR STRAGGLERS.

Charles shucked his joggers so that he could pull yesterday's sour tights over his underwear. He squeezed two cold drops of Visine into each eye and blinked hard as he considered the black athletic brace in his bag. But he left it because if he couldn't get through a class, he had no business dancing at all.

He was against the back wall with two of the younger male dancers, Viktor and Ben. They were about sixteen and had been homeschooled from first grade. They wore wooden crosses under their Lycra shirts and talked about vacation Bible school. Once, Charles had come into the changing room after rehearsal and found them taking pictures of each other with their tights rolled down to the tops of their hips, flexing their chests and stomachs. They were startled to see him and quickly assumed a posture of boredom, their eyes cast down.

Now the two of them were doing mirrored stretches, pushing and pulling each other. They had turned it into a kind of strength contest and each struggled mightily to knock the other boy over. Their skin was taut but oily, the corners of their mouths boiling with angry acne. Their foreheads were spotted with a flora of sores and inflammation. But both of them had large eyes and emitted an intense freshness that made Charles feel ancient at twenty-four.

Charles got out the elastic, looped it over

his toes, and flexed until the burn subsided. He switched feet. The boys were talking about the afternoon rehearsal for Farnland's piece. Charles bristled. He was never going to be a beautiful dancer—this had never been a mystery to him. He was too tall, for one thing, and too slow for another. No matter how hard he tried, there was always something rough and unfinished about his dance—which was one thing if you were doing contemporary, but Charles had too much self-respect to consider himself a contemporary dancer. He had been classically trained, or whatever passed for classical in Maine, and he had certain ideas about what that meant.

They watched him as he changed shirts. They were hairless, those two, not even a faint blond fuzz, as smooth as marble. He felt their disgust. Their horror. They saw what their future might entail when they thickened and coarsened and their bodies turned them into men.

· · ·

THE INSTRUCTOR for the late class was Farnland, an ancient choreographer about whom there were rumors. But there were always rumors about what happened in private rehearsals and masterclasses. What people said and did in the steam room or in the evening sessions when they drilled and drilled because the instructor had been shot down at a bar the night before. Everyone talked about everyone else, passed around gossip about hands lingering, rising, falling, searching, coming to rest in inappropriate places for beats of time too long. All of it allusion and reference and innuendo. When asked to confirm, though, no one had anything to say, because, hey, letters of rec, hey, new works choreographed, credit given or credit withheld. A million ways to get even or pay off. Everyone wanted their pound of flesh one way or another.

Charles and the others set up the barres, locking down the wheels so they'd stay put. He found himself near the wall of windows that looked out over University Ave. The world was all brightness and snowmelt. His eyes stung a little. His head throbbed. He was stiff and sore from having slept in Lionel's bed. He could smell himself, sweat, garlic, and sex.

Farnland clapped them to attention and gave the accompanist a flick of his fingers. Late class was in the small studio, with the terrible acoustics and the electric keyboard. When the music began among the echo of Farnland's harsh claps, there was a tinny reverb to it.

They began their warm-up.

"Long, yes, longer, longer," Farnland called. "Think long, beautiful, easy, easy, that's it."

Charles stretched until he could feel something solid shift upward in his back. It felt good, that hollow click in his spine. Then up, and back, his foot sliding forward, careful with his arm, not dead weight—floppy noodle, as his earliest teacher had called it. His waist burned where the tights cut into his skin and against his hip bones. That felt good, too. His body hummed to life.

"Pliés," Farnland said. "And I want them **deep**."

Charles thought he'd barf, but he held his guts inside as they all sank into plié.

"Lot of shallow graves today."

Charles looked out over the rows of barres: dancers in leg warmers and joggers, jackets and quarter-zips. He felt at once relief and also distress at not seeing Sophie. If she could have seen the state of him, looking hungover and tired, it would have obviated a need for a discussion about what he had done with Lionel.

As it was, now he would have to talk. Use words. Say things. They were honest and open about the people they slept with. But whereas Sophie found this easy, and at times pleasurable, Charles found it difficult. He didn't like talking about the time he'd gotten his dick sucked at a party they'd both attended, or the time he'd done speed at the club they visited in Chicago, or the time he let one of the girls from the drama department think he was her boyfriend in order to score a meeting with her cousin, an agent who was coming through town.

Charles always felt dirty, implicated. The act of telling her held a mirror up to what he'd done, which was ordinary and base and simple and just the kind of thing that people did with one another or to one another, but somehow, in the duplicating that retelling required, it became something else. When he could see himself, really see himself, he didn't like what he saw.

"Charles, are you with us or not?" Farnland's voice carried through Charles's thoughts, and he found himself in the wrong position, completely out of the music's course.

"Sorry," he said, but Farnland gave him a long, exasperated look. Among the many lines and heavy folds, there were two bright blue eyes, as cold as the sea. Farnland gripped Charles's elbow and one of his hips, putting him into position as if he were a small boy. Charles absorbed the dry hardness of the touch and let the humiliation settle into the pit of his stomach.

"Are the rigors of second position too much for you?" Farnland asked. "Do you need a moment to prepare?" Charles was close enough to see the hateful moisture at the corners of the man's eyes. There was a flicker of true sincerity in his voice, as if he truly believed that Charles found second position difficult.

"Sorry," Charles said.

"Don't be. It's fine. We all make mistakes," he said with as much patience as scorn. "We'll take it from the top, if that's okay with you."

"That would be wonderful," Charles said through a tense jaw.

"From the beginning, then, Magnus," Farnland said, nodding to the slim pianist.

The music started up again, and Charles sighed. He assumed a slouched, grumpy first. He could hear his knee click. The cartilage felt hot, like a delicate, burning fiber trapped under the bone. But when Farnland's eyes came in search of him, his body had already slipped into the stream of the combination and was, for a moment, beyond reproach.

"Dismal, dismal," he said.

Charles shared his barre with Mats and Alek. Mats was light-skinned with blond and brown curls. He had a boyish face, but his body was all mean, tight lines. He could jump to Jupiter, yet his quads were humble. Alek was self-conscious about his chipped front tooth and tried to conceal it by talking as little as possible, which made him seem shy or nice. Alek was a ferocious, expressive dancer with the kind of timing that made his dancing look totally effortless.

"Long night," Mats said.

"The longest," Charles droned, drawing his body up. His knee popped as he slid his foot forward and then flexed. It didn't hurt, exactly. It wasn't **pain** in the true sense of the word. It just burned, like a low, simmering flame. And just on the one side. He could see through to the end of the pain, its temporary nature. And this was a comfort. It hurt only on certain movements. Certain configurations of tension. For example, reversing the position, sliding the leg back and flexing the other way, was totally without discomfort. He logged this information, storing it for when he would need to compensate. His body was a long tally of adjustments and allocations. He could feel, though, his feet coming to life. The muscles warming as they stretched.

Charles had once seen an X-ray of his foot. He had let the back of an ax drop down carelessly, and his grandfather had needed to drive him to the emergency room. The doctor said that it wasn't broken, just bruised very badly. She showed Charles the film of his foot and said that he was lucky. Because the foot was one of the most complicated structures in the human body. **They're never quite the same. All those little bones, you see. They don't ever heal right.** And he'd marveled at the ridiculous architecture of the foot, his foot. He had seen all the little bones, the way they fit together. He was already dancing by then, but it hadn't occurred to him until that very moment, the doctor outlining the shape of his foot with her finger, that if he hurt himself, he'd never dance again. Until that moment, he'd been content to do as he always had. Working on the tree farm to pay for his lessons and studio time. Doing handstands to make the men laugh. Suspending himself from the monkey bars at school. Running barefoot in the locker room over slick floors. The world had not seemed dangerous to him until that moment. That was the blessing of certain childhoods. The illusion of your invincibility. Your safety. Some people didn't know the danger they were in until years later, looking back. That was a kind of blessing, too, in a way. The ignorance of your own peril.

"You smell like hell," Alek said. "You smell like—"

"Something awful," Mats completed. Their voices were complementary: Mats very low, Alek higher, a dull tenor.

"Generous," Charles said. Mats yelped briefly. Farnland turned to them.

"Is there something so funny about our

fundamentals?" He let his arms hang down, his head tilted to the side. His mouth was furious.

"No," Charles said, squaring up his shoulders and facing ahead. "Nothing funny at all."

"No," the other two said.

"Oh, good. I'd hate to miss out."

Charles was not as afraid of him as he had been of other ballet teachers. There was something truly terrible about that species of human. They were farsighted by nature, seeing not what you did, only what you might do or, more often, what you might do wrong. The moment you completed a gesture, they were already looking ahead to the moment you made a mistake, and it was that fear and frustration that drove them to punish you. Again and again you drilled, again and again you dipped and turned and spotted and turned out and rotated and lifted, and higher, please, higher!, until their voices were as much a part of you as your own interior static. Charles saw Farnland for what he was, though: a preening, declining old man with a mean streak. They gazed at each other then, caught in a bitter contest of wills.

At a party the previous year, Charles had seen Farnland whispering in Viktor's ear, his hand at the small of Viktor's back, pulling at the oversize burgundy silk shirt he wore. Viktor with a plastic cup of champagne, giggling, his hand on Farnland's chest. Charles had seen it, and the Farnland had seen him see it. But what was there to do about it?

"Nothing to miss," Charles said.

"He hates you," Mats said with glee. "He hates you so much."

"You run over his cat or what?" Alek asked pointedly. "Keep me out of the splash zone."

"Maybe he wants to fuck," Mats said.

"Oh, most definitely," Alek said.

"And to skin Charlie alive. Maybe it's a Buffalo Bill thing. He wants to **wear you**."

"I'm not his type," Charles said, but then, his eyes falling on Viktor at the front of the room, he felt a bit of regret.

"You did show up late."

"Smelling like last night's garbage."

"It wasn't garbage, trust me," Charles said, turning to look over his shoulder at Alek.

"Oh, Sophie is going to love that."

"Say more. Don't leave us hanging." Mats moaned.

"Don't tell me about Sophie," Charles said to Alek. "You don't know anything."

They lapsed into silence. Charles could feel Alek's pointed stare, the heat stabbing him between the shoulders. There was a time during the summer when Alek had made a go at Sophie, all earnest kisses and declarations. They had gone to a movie and then a concert in the park, standing close together, she wearing one of Charles's old flannels and Alek holding on to her hand as they swung around in a slow circle. Then they had drunk beer in the woods around a fire as the air was settling down and getting cooler, and Sophie had been on Alek's lap. Charles came to the same gathering with a friend, and at first Alek blushed when they saw each other, but then he wrapped himself around Sophie.

You can't hold on to her, he had wanted to say to Alek then. The world had blasted away every other part of her life: her parents were dead, her sister was dead, nothing remained to tether her to the world as they knew it. She had only herself and dance. Alek could never hold on to her. No one could. Charles felt proud of her talent. Not that it had anything to do with him. But he felt proud that he could recognize it and what it meant. Yeah, there would be shitty years of auditions and open calls. But nobody who watched Sophie dance could say she didn't have real charisma. She danced in that way that made it seem natural. Improvised almost. But never sloppy. There was a through line, and you could follow it no matter how complex the combination. She had the same thing Misty Copeland had, which wasn't pristine Russian technique, but substance. And he felt like he knew that about her. That his talent was for recognizing her talent and knowing he'd get out of her way when the time came.

Sophie had lifted herself from Alek's lap and spun herself around, letting her arms rise above her head. She swayed to the music, animating the song, some formless acoustic indie number full of haunting melodies and high, piercing voices, by a band with a name like a ghost story. And then she left Alek and came toward him, skirting around their other friends, dancing, smiling, until she wrapped her arms around him.

"Hey," she said, "I missed you."

"Hey," he said, "long time no see."

"Long time," she said, drawing out the first word, letting it turn indistinct and gravelly at the back of her throat. "What're you doing here?"

Charles sighed and shrugged. The air had smelled of pine needles and burning wood, which made him think of home in rural Maine, and all those hours of light, and the water, so much of it everywhere, lakes and rivers and streams and creeks. So much water.

"Oh, you know."

"I know," she said, and there was a smile, a smile for him.

"Come over tonight?" he asked, letting himself pout a little. She looked up at him with a shocked expression, because they never made designs on each other this way, never intruded when the other was out, never asked unless there was a necessity. He knew that he was doing too much, changing the rules of the game, but he'd hated the satisfied look on Alek's face, so sure of himself, so **pleased**. He half expected her to turn him down, but she sighed and rolled her eyes.

"I can if you want," she said.

"I do," he had said, realizing he meant it, because as he said it, something in him hurt, and for a dancer, pain is always the way you know something is true. "Yes, I want you to."

"Okay," she said, and she kissed his chest and went back to Alek. That poor fool, though. If he got hurt, it was only his fault because he should know the score, and besides, Sophie was an adult, free to come and go as she pleased. She made dates. She messed around. It was known.

Alek still resented him, even now. It was obvious in the way he had suggested that Charles had been out rolling in garbage instead of being at home with Sophie. But it was really, truly none of Alek's business, so Charles put a little smugness in his turnout, let his hips roll and snap as he lifted into the air.

He wouldn't be bullied.

AT THE END OF THE CLASS, Charles was putting his arms into his flannel when Farnland approached him.

"Charles," he said. "A word."

"All right." Charles was soaked with sweat. Pins and needles ran down the outside of his leg to his toes. The afternoon light was brilliant through the windows. Their shadows stretched across the floor.

"You were late. You smell like a distillery. And you dance like a bowlegged ox."

"That's more than a word," Charles said. He did try to look apologetic.

"You are setting a **terrible** example. Think of the younger dancers," he said, and Charles flinched. "You are a senior member of this program. Don't make me regret fighting for you."

Think of the younger dancers, Charles repeated in his mind. Think of those young boys in their silk shirts at parties, with no one to look out for them, being given plastic cups of champagne. Think of the giddy high of being with people who understood what you did and what you loved instead of being shoved into a locker by a bunch of lacrosse jerks who got drunk on their dads' boats and drowned on lazy summer nights. Think of those poor young dancers, aching knees and throbbing feet. Their eyes stinging with sweat. Think of the young dancers. Charles clenched his jaw and squared his shoulders.

"I do think of them," he said.

Farnland sucked his teeth, the most ungraceful gesture Charles had ever seen

him make. He looked at his fingernails as if
Charles were worth less than what prospec-
tive dirt might be found there. He deserved
that, he thought. Fair enough.

"Your knee?"

"Can barely feel a thing," Charles ground
out. In truth, he should have listened to
Sophie last night and gone home to ice it.
He had no business running through the
snow after Lionel, and now dancing on it.

"You're listing," Farnland said. "No way
you're making it through rehearsal tonight."

Charles had been **selected** by Farnland
to dance in some Balanchine rip-off. It was
all cheap schmaltz and **feeling**. Neither
classical nor contemporary. It existed in that
middle ground of hazily choreographed
vaporware. He would not have considered it
had Farnland not mentioned to him that his
former apprentice ran PNB and would be
interested in seeing some of Charles's tape if
it included parts of this new work. It was a
blatant quid pro quo, Charles knew. Don't
say anything about fondling the little boys
and he could have a chance to dance for

PNB, which was not a **great** company, it was true, though it was a little better than he could otherwise reasonably hope for. But the knee, which had started to burn at the start of fall, now throbbed regularly.

"Maybe you should take it easy. Lay off," Farnland said with real human kindness in his voice. Charles watched Farnland's hand rise just a little, like he meant to reach out for him. Charles shifted away at the thought of that touch, and Farnland's hand fell back into place.

"I'm fine," he said. "I'm more than fine. I'll live."

"We can get Viktor to dance for you. It's no problem. He'd probably love it. No need for you to make it worse just for a rehearsal."

Charles cleared his throat and stood a little taller. He summoned what heat he had left burning in him and bore down on the choreographer.

"It's mine," he said. "I'll dance it."

"You could have a long career, Charles. Teaching. Dancing isn't the only thing." The choreographer slapped Charles's thigh with the back of his hand—"Think about it. Don't be dumb. You know how many teachers end up gimps? And why?"

"I'm doing your faggy little dance. Ease off."

Farnland wet his lips as though he had received something appetizing. Charles watched his eyes go glossy and distant. It was the same expression that came across Farnland's face during rehearsals when he watched Viktor shadow Charles, learning the overly emotive choreography of the middle section. It was supposed to be drawn from **The Four Temperaments** but lacked that piece's emotional reserve. On Viktor, Farnland's choreography was hectic, scattered. On Charles, because he lacked Viktor's speed, it had a certain gravitas. Or so Charles liked to think. But during rehearsal last week, he had looked up to see Farnland watching Viktor as he made some adjustments to the ending combination. That same distant, wantful gloss of the eyes, the subtle shifting of the lips as the music wound up to its slow conclusion.

"Well, just remember, we're all after the same thing."

"Right. **Pathos**."

"Fucker," Farnland said, but then he smiled, showing Charles his teeth, gnarly and green-yellow. Charles smiled back. **Pathos** was what Farnland had called his "dumb number." It was, he said often during rehearsal, art's most noble pursuit. One evening, one of the other dancers had jokingly said, **What about ethos?** And Farnland, from a seated position, had flung a hard-shell water bottle at her head. Then he'd shouted them all down for ten minutes about making snide little remarks and the terrors of their generation. What did any of them know about art? About anything? Charles half wished that Farnland would make a scene now. That he'd do something.

But he didn't. Farnland waved him off and pushed out into the hall. The noise from the class next door, the music, filled the room briefly, and then was gone.

Charles flexed his fist and worked over his knee. Little old man, full of spite. But Charles had done nothing to stop him.

· · · ·

CHARLES CUT THROUGH THE
courtyard, scattering a group of smoking
students. They trailed white smoke, legible
in the piercing daylight. His sweat had turned
to a chalky crust, and he could feel it breaking up when he moved, cold sneaking in
against his skin. The class had done its work.
His muscles were warm, and he felt pliant,
alive. He'd pulled the brace on to give his
knee some relief. On the other side of the
courtyard, he slipped into the dance library.

Sophie often haunted the upper levels of
the library in the media room, looking over
old choreography. She could have streamed
it on her phone in high definition, but she
liked browsing through the years of archival
footage, poring over little-known, minor
dancers, taking bits here and there from
everyone like a magpie.

He found her sitting on the floor with an
enormous album covering her entire lap.
She was running her finger up and down
the list, deciding which to take out. She

leaned down over it, exposing the tender white nape of her neck. He kissed her there before she knew he was present, and she jumped, screaming.

"**Shh,**" he said as he crouched. His knee crackled like static.

"You are a menace," she hissed, her eyes flashing.

"What are you looking at?" He sat down to take the weight off.

"Old shit." She handed him the book, the pages yellowed, little black disks tucked inside plastic wrap, neat type glued next to each one. "God, you stink."

"I had practice."

"That's not practice smell," she said. "That's not practice smell at all."

He squeezed his legs together, thinking that might help, but she just snorted at him. "Where's your phone?"

"I don't know, dead probably," he said, looking but not looking at the album.

"I called you," she said. "After you left last night."

"Oh, well, it died, so."

Charles felt her staring at him very intently. There was no anger in the gaze. She knew the truth already, where he'd gone and what he'd done—there had been no mystery to it—but what she wanted was confirmation of the act. Say it: **I went home with Lionel.**

"What?"

Sophie leaned back onto her hands. She arched her back and let her head hang. "You're such a shitty liar," she said. "Why must you lie?"

"I'm not."

"How boring, Charlie."

"I'm sorry for boring you."

"How was it?"

"How was what?"

"Jesus, Charlie." Sophie stood up and stretched, at first one way and then another, making her body as long as she possibly could. She was full of lines. Everywhere she turned, a line, a new way forward. The tips of her fingers were on a line from her shoulder: arms straight, legs straight, toes pointed even in the large boots she wore.

"It was fine," Charles said at last.

"That's disappointing, isn't it?" she said, and she wrapped her arm around herself and rotated her hips. "All that work for 'fine.'"

"All what work?"

"Well, picking a fight with me. Finding out where he lived. Going there. All that work."

"We didn't fight."

"Didn't we?" she asked. She was looking out the window. That hadn't been a fight. That hadn't been an argument. They'd just been standing in the corner after Lionel left, talking quietly, and she had said: **Go, you obviously want him. Go.** And he had said, **No, I don't, stop being ridiculous. We're here. We're having a good time.** They'd even left together, she and Charles. They had gone down the porch steps in the freshly falling snow, with the world perfectly still all around them, gone to the car and smiled at each other.

But on the way, she started again:

"I saw the way you looked at him."

"I didn't look at him in any way."

"I saw it," she said. "I saw it and I knew."

"What does it matter?"

"It doesn't. I don't care what you do. But don't lie to me about it."

They'd gone back and forth like that all the way to Sophie's apartment building, and when she asked if he wanted to come up, he said he'd go home and sleep, that he was feeling tired and a little drunk, and she said he shouldn't drive in the snow that way, and he'd just sat there behind the wheel, the car idling, issuing exhaust into the night, until she got out and shut the door not hard, but firm, which to him had seemed sadder than anything else in the whole world, that she wasn't even mad, that she was just concerned for him, and he was about to go do something shitty. But then she was gone, and he was in the car, and he texted Lionel at the number he'd watched him type into Sophie's phone and had committed to memory, as if he knew even then what he was going to do.

Charles looked up from the album, and Sophie was sitting on the table with her legs crossed, looking back at him. The light, a sea of white in the window, lay over her like a shroud, a veil.

"I'm sorry."

"It's fine—are you going to see him again?"

Charles thought of Lionel, his body not full of lines but yielding edges, curves. He seemed as if he'd bleed into the air around him. Last night he'd put his hands all over Lionel, gripped and tugged and pulled and sunk ever deeper. This morning, when Charles left, he had kissed Lionel and said he would be back, which at the time seemed like something to say. It was what you said after you slept with someone: **See you around, see you next time, I'll be back.** It didn't mean anything. But now, with the question put to him this way, he felt unsure what he'd meant by that—**I'll be back.**

"Maybe," Charles said. "Maybe not. It doesn't matter." He snapped the book closed and got up to hand it back to her. She took it from him, but he didn't let go right away, so they were connected through the book.

He stood between her open knees, holding the book, feeling its weight and the tension of her hand on the other side of it. He leaned down, kissed her softly.

"You stink," she said.

"I know—do you care if I see him again?"

"No, Charlie. I don't. But if you do, don't lie to me."

"Okay," he said.

"I do like him," Sophie said after a moment, and it startled Charles.

"How? You don't know him. I don't know him."

"There's something good and wounded about him. Like you." Sophie rolled her shoulders and smiled. "I like him."

Charles knew what she meant by that, how wounded and small and good Lionel seemed. Last night at the potluck, he had glimpsed some vast, open hurt in him. At the moment in the hallway outside the bathroom, Charles had seen how easy it was to hurt his feelings, to sting him. Now Sophie was accusing him of having the same quality, and Charles resented it.

"I'd say he's more like you," Charles said. "You're the damaged one." He playfully dug his finger into her side, and she slapped his forearm hard. The pain of it felt like a kindness.

"And what do you think you are?" she asked, wrapping her legs around his waist. They were alone in that corner of the library. It would have been possible, so very possible, for them to slide into one another, and Charles did feel something like thirst burning at the back of his throat.

"You calling me fucked up?" Charles leaned over her, and she just shrugged. She was utterly unintimidated by his size.

"Hardly a novel insight." She put her head back and closed her eyes. She slid her thighs against his hips, and Charles got hard.

"This morning," he said, "his window broke. Just dropped out of nowhere, apparently." Sophie hummed in pleasure. "He was so freaked out. Like, totally melting down. So I cleaned it, swept the glass, you know? And it was the weirdest thing. I don't think I've ever seen a person more exposed."

Sophie's eyes were still closed, but she had stopped humming. Charles stood there, her legs still wrapped around him, and he wondered if he should withdraw or continue. She crossed her ankles behind him, and pulled at him slightly, and he almost fell over onto her. He braced himself with his palms flat on the surface on which she was resting. She was warm and close.

"What then?" she asked.

"I picked him up, kind of like this," he said, "and I took him back to bed."

"You fuck him?" she asked.

"I did."

"And you liked it."

Sophie's eyes slit open, glossy and bright. She arched her back slightly. Charles dipped his fingers between her legs and she sighed.

"I don't like telling you this."

Sophie touched his wrist gently, then, having located it, wrapped her fingers around him. She drew his hand up to the top of her tights, and then down into the space between her legs. She was damp and warm there, and she breathed out when his fingers entered her.

"What else?" she asked. "Tell me what else."

She rocked against his fingers, and Charles thought of the morning, of Lionel's kind eyes, of the way he'd shivered and clung, of how gentle, how sweet. It seemed a great betrayal to share that with Sophie now, but it was as though she could skim his thoughts, read him.

"He asked me to stay, this morning," Charles whispered.

Sophie made a small, uncomplicated sound of pleasure, and she neatly plucked Charles's fingers from her. She drew up straight and smiled at him.

"Don't hurt him, Charlie," she said. "He's a good boy. He's not like us." She climbed from the high table, adjusted her tights. She collected the book.

Charles could smell Sophie and himself and Lionel.

"My shift is starting," she said.

"I'll walk you over."

"That's chivalrous," Sophie said. She had pulled on her coat and her hat.

"It'll just cost you one espresso." Charles squatted briefly to get a knot out of his thigh. The brace held his knee securely. He stretched, and there was another solid pop in his spine. He felt loose.

"Your body sounds like an old man."

Charles put her in a light headlock as they descended the stairs. They went out into the cold together, already talking about something else entirely.

AS THOUGH

THAT WERE LOVE

THE SWOLLEN RIVER, THE SOFT ICE, the world coming back to itself.

On Tuesday, as was his habit, Hartjes went to the small grocery store on the corner and bought ten apples and three bananas. There were places in the world where one couldn't get apples year-round or get bananas in the middle of the winter. There were places in the world where you had to wait for the seasons to change, and where seasons didn't mean just the state of precipitation but also commerce, industry, economy. Apples in February were a sign of good fortune, or that misfortune lurked elsewhere. The cashier grinned and chirped as he weighed the fruit.

That Tuesday made four weeks since Hartjes's mother had died suddenly. He had not seen her for seven years. Francisco, his stepbrother, had told him over the phone. At the time of her death, his mother had been living in the same narrow town in south Alabama, with its Catholic church, remarkable only because it did not also have a Baptist church. She had lived there all the years of her life, in and among a rotating series of trailers and cars that Hartjes had been spared only because he'd been sent to live with his grandparents. Then his mother married Francisco's father, also named Francisco, who had a better job and a small house, so Hartjes went to live with them. Hartjes had not remembered giving his mother his number. That's what he had been thinking when Francisco told him—shouted, really—as if trying to breach the actual raw distance between them, "She's dead, she's dead." The other thing that Hartjes had been thinking of was how much like a man Francisco sounded—it startled Hartjes to hear him that way.

They had last spoken on the night Francisco left for trade school in Georgia. They were in their room, Hartjes lying on the bed, Francisco stuffing clothes into a garbage bag. It was hot, their shirts sticking to their backs. Francisco sat on the edge of the bed, looked over his shoulder at Hartjes, and said, "I'm out of here, kid." Hartjes shoved at him and said, "Shut up," because it made him feel good. Francisco stood up, hoisted the black bag over his shoulder. He leaned down and they knocked fists. A friend of his gave him a ride to the bus depot, and then total silence until he called to say that Hartjes's mother was dead.

"Oh," Hartjes had said that Tuesday on the phone four weeks before. "Oh, all right." And then Francisco had hung up, and that was that.

The apples were not for Hartjes. They were for his friend Simon, who lived in the country. They were not for Simon, either, in fact, but for Simon's goats. The goats were named Helena, Maria, Bertram, Vicky, Dude, and Guy. Helena was a boy goat, the others were girls. Simon had named them before he knew their sexes, after picking them out at two different farms three years or so before, when they were all babies and awkward, barely weaned at all, when it was still possible to mistake a boy goat for a girl and vice versa if you didn't know what you were doing.

Hartjes cut the apples up for the goats and fed them from the sloping front porch. They had grown accustomed to his way of doing things on these Tuesday visits, and they formed a neat little line and filed up to him one at a time to receive from his palm a chunk of apple. He patted their sides, felt the bristle of their fur, watched the tufts of steam issue from their nostrils. The horizontal bars of their pupils shivered. Their eyes were pale blue. He fed them from a plastic bag, lifting chunk after chunk until they were all gone, and the goats, brushing his palms with their tongues, nipping at his fingertips, gave up on him. Off they wandered to find food elsewhere.

At the kitchen table, Simon sat with his skinny legs crossed, reading the paper. Hartjes came in through the side door (the front door had been bolted for as long as Hartjes had known him). Simon did not look up. He was a tall man, very pale, with thinning white-blond hair. He was just shy of middle age, a little under forty. Hartjes was younger, twenty-five. Two years before, they had met at a party, as people do, and they had fucked three times on three separate occasions, each a little worse, not to any degree that would have made any of the individual incidents awful, but when taken together they represented a doomed enterprise. A year earlier, after the last time they'd had sex, Hartjes said it would be best if they were just friends, and Simon said, "Sure, okay, sure." But it was clear even then that Simon expected that Hartjes would change his mind, and sometimes he grew irritated that it was taking so long.

"It's getting warmer," Hartjes said after he had washed his hands and sat down with a glass of water.

"So it is," Simon said from behind the paper.

"And the river's thawed," Hartjes said.

"So it is."

"And then I decided to kill myself," Hartjes said.

"So do it," Simon said, not letting Hartjes have the satisfaction.

"Some friend."

"I can get you a rope."

"Only if you cut me down after," Hartjes said, putting his head on the table, which smelled like ground pepper and flour.

"Har-dee-har-har."

Hartjes looked up and saw Simon watching him and beyond Simon into the front hall, where the stairs ran up to the second floor. There were pears in a bowl on the table. Hartjes put his cheek against his forearm and gazed out the window over the sink, into the tall pine trees and the gathering dusk. The kitchen was warm. The goats had come around the house and were trotting around the backyard, Guy and Bertram chasing two of the fatter hens. Simon lifted a cigarette from the ashtray and lit it.

"I just hate the spring," he said.

"Well, with luck, we'll all freeze to death long before then," Simon said, knitting the paper together and apart.

"What are you reading about over there?"

"War, famine, misery, and two for one at the co-op."

Hartjes felt little kick in his gut. "What's two for one at the co-op?"

"Apples," Simon said, lowering the paper so that Hartjes could see his expression.

"They charged me full price!"

"Racists."

"It's probably about class," Hartjes said grimly.

"Oh, it's about class, is it? I was raised poor, don't you know. Maybe they'll give me the two-for-one."

"I was raised poor. Poor me," Hartjes said.

"Yeah, but nobody expects me to have been raised poor. But look at me now. I live in a manse."

"You live in a shotgun house on a county road."

"A manse."

"My mother died, did I tell you?"

The paper rustled, lowered. Their eyes met. Simon's expression narrowed briefly, and Hartjes could see the momentary flutter of his concentration changing focus. Whatever was in Simon's mind slackened. Hartjes wondered if it was fleeting pity or something else. Simon raised the paper. Hartjes felt relief to have a barrier between them again.

"Oh, well, sucks for you, pal."

Hartjes felt a nudge on his thigh from Simon's foot, and he reached under the table and caught it. He ran his thumb down the instep, dug his fingers there, where a foot was tender and vulnerable, and Simon let out a low groan that turned, suddenly, into a startled cry.

"Serves you right," Hartjes said a little

more pointedly than he meant, but then, to make up for his roughness, he stroked Simon's foot, passing his palm back and forth along its length, up to the ankle and then down, pressing with his palms to get at the stiffness in the sole. Simon leaned back in his chair and let Hartjes work on his feet. The kitchen was quiet except for the crackle and snap in the wood-burning stove and sometimes the sound of Simon's bones popping. Hartjes felt own his body loosening up, could feel himself growing closer to Simon the longer he touched him. The opening of Simon's shirt, the blue flannel unbuttoned, sagged like the tongue of some loyal animal and revealed the smooth, pale white of his throat and chest. Hartjes wanted to want him, the same way he wanted to see the rise and swell of Simon's chest, the firm clench of his stomach, and to feel hot all over with need and the slick, gathering wet that sluiced the glide into desire. He wanted it all, yet what he felt, what he really felt in the seat of his body, where his soul nestled and hummed, was the companionable happiness that came with friendship. But he could see hunger in Simon's eyes, hunger and other things, other shapes of feelings that he wanted to ask Simon about but couldn't bring himself to. Simon put his hand to his own throat and worked the shirt open more, ran his hand up his neck and to his mouth and then back down through the shirt, popping the buttons open so that his white undershirt showed, and then lower into the front of his pants, like he was searching for loose change. But Hartjes just kept at his feet, his thumb between the two toes, clean and white, and his fingers on the heel, making the foot arch, bend until he could feel the tendons stretching. He sank lower in his chair, spread his thighs, and let that brace him. Simon groaned and grunted and sometimes lifted his hips or shivered as if he were cold. Hartjes gripped Simon's ankle and held it as tight as he could. And then he let go, and Simon, having slid low in his chair, seemed to surface in himself, his eyes glossy, his breath ragged. It had been enough for him to watch Simon abandon himself. It had been enough to cause it, to see it, to be a part of Simon's desire, so that even if Hartjes could not bring himself to want it, he could at least enjoy the sight of Simon wanting, needing. He was hard. They both were hard, but what was to be done for it? **Let it rest**, he thought. A thick blue vein throbbed at the base of Simon's throat, pulsed when Simon swallowed. His chest was red. His throat was red. He was watching Hartjes, and Hartjes watched the animal part of Simon submerge itself into the icy pool of higher brain function.

"It's always like this," Simon said a moment or two later.

"It's not," Hartjes said. "It's not like anything."

"What is it with you? Why is it always so hot and cold?"

"It's not anything, Simon. It's not."

"Okay, champ." Simon got up from the table. He buttoned his shirt. Blue light from the window fell across him. It was the part of the day when even the ugliest things were beautiful. "Are you staying for dinner?"

"I'd like to."

"All right."

"Do you need help?"

"Do you need help, he asks," Simon said, shaking his head. He had buttoned his shirt and stuffed it into the front of his pants. He brushed the back of his hand across his mouth and sniffed hard. "No, it's just stew from last night."

"I wasn't joking earlier, you know, about my mom. It seemed like you thought I was joking."

Simon lifted a heavy red pot from the fridge and set it on the stove. He put his palms against his lower back and stretched. He pressed the knuckles of his left toes against the floor. "I didn't think you were joking," he said after a moment.

"Well, all right, then."

"Don't get mad about it. What do you want me to say?"

"I don't know. What's to say?"

"If you have something you want me to say, then I'd like to hear it."

"Forget it."

"No, not forget it. Say it. Say words, Hartjes. Words."

Hartjes leaned back. The fire on the stove spat as moisture from the skin of the pot evaporated or dropped into the flame. The blue veil of night had passed and now it was dim in the kitchen, so that the only light was from the stove. Simon reached for the switch on the other side of the doorway.

"No, it's fine."

"I don't know what people say in moments like this—you didn't love her, did you?"

"No, I guess not, probably not," he said.

When Hartjes was ten, he'd gotten himself stung by seven wasps at his aunt Lora Anne's house, and his mother had said, "That's what faggots get." It was a story he had learned to tell white people with some degree of exaggerated gravity, and it had paid for his college, because white people had a vast hunger for the calamities of others.

When he told the story at parties, he took his time: His mother and the other adults had been reading and rereading with increasing levels of despair and also hysteria a suicide note found in the hand of Lora Anne's youngest son, an aspiring rapper and barber, who had shot himself once through the temple on the banks of the creek because he had been diagnosed with, among other rumored things, pancreatic cancer. Lora Anne was a preacher and drove miles upon miles to preach in nondenominational churches. Hartjes and his eleven cousins had been running around the rusty swing set, trying to coax it back into life, when out the wasps had come, and Hartjes, being slower and clumsier, had tripped and made himself an easy target. They'd stung him and he'd gone screaming into the house, and his mother had said it.

"Then what am I supposed to say? I'm sorry?" Simon asked.

"I just didn't want you thinking I had lied about it, that's all. I didn't want you thinking it was a joke or that I'd made it up just to have something to say. I just wanted you to know that. I wasn't complaining." Hartjes drank the water he had been nursing, which was lukewarm now and tasted faintly of metal from the pipes.

Simon hummed. He stirred the stew, which smelled to Hartjes like tomatoes and pepper, with the musky scent of venison. When Hartjes let his chair rock back and forth, balancing himself with the wide set of his feet, it sounded like a swinging door. His hunger felt distant, like it belonged to someone else.

Sweat collected against his forehead, and he wiped at it. The skin at the lower part of his spine was hot and dry. His eyes were stinging. Near the back door, Simon had put three red clay pots on a low bench. The bench had been a pew at Saint Anne Lutheran Church before the church had burned to the ground. Simon used to go out to the blackened ruins to sit in what was left of its pews and gaze out into the valley of pine and cedar and oak trees, the wind on his face and the scent of soot rising all around him. When he was out there, he told Hartjes as they twisted the pews from the foundations into which they had been bolted, searching for one that wouldn't crumble to ash, when he was out there, it seemed that the whole world went away, all his problems, all his needs—hunger, pain, money, viral load, all of it. Hartjes could understand that. He could understand how a person could get to needing that, stillness in the world. Simon and Hartjes had rescued the pews and scraped them down to their bones, and then they'd polished, coated, and lacquered them until they were smooth with a rich stain. All that work to use them for indoor plants: large, leafy green things with heads like that of a Saint Bernard or a Newfoundland, lolling in the winter light.

SIMON AND HARTJES ate their stew on the porch in the cold. Simon turned his portable space heater on its back under the slats of the bench, and the two of them sat with their legs tucked under them, though for Hartjes it was a struggle because he was thick through the haunch and some fifteen or twenty pounds heavier than Simon. Night had fallen by then, and the world was a smooth black sheet. Across the road and across the fields, they could make out the yellow-orange light in a house as narrow as Simon's. The yard was patchy with snow and ice. The goats had bedded down in their pen in the back, though sometimes their calls lifted up and swept overhead like the softening static at the start of a radio station.

More distantly, Hartjes could hear whining, baying, and felt a flurry of homesickness. When he had lived with his grandparents during the murky middle years of his childhood, he had raised three dogs into brilliant hunters, Gristle, Bone, and Marrow. He had run his hand along their spines, teaching them to be still, to be quiet, to wait. He'd felt their hearts beating, slowing, growing inured to the length of time it took for the world to show its belly. They had been mutts when he found them, three butterscotch pups clinging to life, drenched in ants and beetles. But he'd rinsed them clean and loved on them the way nobody had loved on him. He had taught them to hunt, to be keen and swift as they stalked and waited. He'd taught them to fetch at first with dolls and dummies filled with clay and rocks, realistic weights, and later they'd brought him the real thing, ducks wet and warm with blood. Pheasant. Squirrel. Whatever Hartjes trained his rifle on, they pinned and cornered and stalled. They could tree anything, the three of them, even turkeys, frothing with rage, bodies humming, ready to take flight. But the dogs calling in the distance were not his dogs. The dogs baying in the distance slept inside and ran from their shadows. Gristle, Bone, and Marrow would have eaten those dogs alive, because Hartjes had loved them enough to teach them how to fight, how to maim, how to kill, and the people here, in this place, let their dogs sleep in their beds, as though that were love.

They ate slowly because the venison was hot. Hartjes dug his spoon into the soft potatoes and the carrots. A light dangled overhead, and in the surface of the broth he saw their shadowed, inverted selves. Hartjes had on his flannel coat, and Simon had wrapped himself in a green wool blanket. The heater, on its lowest setting, droned like cicadas. There was just enough heat to remind them how cold it was. Simon's spoon clacked against the side of his bowl. He coughed into his shoulder. Hartjes studied the flaking skin along his jaw, the rosettes of sores spotting his cheeks and the primitive cliff of his forehead.

"Do you ever get lonely out here?"

"You ask that every time."

"Because you never answer," Hartjes said.

"Sometimes. It's not so bad."

"You ever think about moving back to town? You could probably get an okay amount for this place."

"Yeah, I think about it."

"But you won't."

"No, probably won't. I came out here to get away from all that, I guess."

"It's not exactly a metropolis you're escaping," Hartjes said.

"It's not about the size of the place. It's about . . . hell, I don't know. I guess it's about living on your own terms. Setting a limit for yourself. Being about something. In your own way."

"In my own way," Hartjes said, singing the words to the melody of some song from years before, on country radio, that had at that very moment surfaced in his memory.

"Do you ever get lonely?"

"Sure, I get lonely," Hartjes said, rocking them a little on the bench, his shoes scraping across the grit on the porch. "I get mighty lonely."

Simon nodded but didn't say anything. They ate quietly. The venison had cooled a little. Simon got up to bring them beers. It was the first one of the evening for them. They popped the tabs and toasted one another, toasted their loneliness.

"So, your mother died," Simon said. "Do you want to talk about it?"

"No, I don't suppose I do."

"People die."

"Such are the facts."

"How did she die?"

"Francisco didn't say."

"Francisco. It's a family affair."

"Please don't start."

"I didn't know you were talking to Francisco."

"I'm not."

"So no teary reunion between brothers after all these years."

"I guess we're all cried out," Hartjes said. The beer was cheap and weak. Hartjes burped and wiped the foam from his lips. He saw, briefly, the outline of Francisco's face: the somber brown eyes, the patchy beard, the flat, crooked nose, and the chipped tooth from the time they'd gone rolling down the hill, punching and kicking at each other. They were all cried out. Francisco had caught his face on the edge of a large rock, had almost sliced his lip right from his mouth. He had blamed Hartjes. It had been his fault. That's true. It had been his fault for provoking Francisco, calling him Franny, delighting in the rage that had swelled his boy chest and sent him hurtling at Hartjes. Franny, Franny, Franny. Hartjes had been the younger one, but taller, so people mistook him for the older brother.

"Family isn't everything," Simon said.

"No, it isn't," Hartjes said. "Do you want another beer?"

"It's my fridge," Simon said. "You can't offer me something that's not yours."

"Oh, and I guess you're the one who bought it? I guess you're the one who always buys it and stocks it so you don't run out."

"I didn't ask for it, Hartjes."

"You never ask for anything except what you know I won't give," Hartjes said, but he regretted it a little. He saw Simon flinch and then go still. Simon drew the blanket around himself.

"Well, all right," he said.

"I'll get that beer," Hartjes said. Simon was looking at the trees.

Hartjes stooped low in the kitchen and tore two cans from the plastic yoke. He held them in his palm, which was wide and paler than the rest of him. He counted the containers of food, the vegetables, the soups, the stock, the meat tumescent in its plastic wrap. He saw the jars of moonshine, the bottle of wine from two weeks earlier with a plastic stopper jammed into its neck, and gelatinous cubes of gristle and fat, which Simon used for broth and for taste.

The light was off, but they had left a candle going on the table. He turned in Simon's kitchen and looked back through the house into the living room, where the furniture slept like guests and where the windows were filled with the soft white glow of distant stars. He hovered near the window by the stairs and pressed his face into the bristling curtain, inhaled its dust, and closed his eyes. There had been a time when Hartjes hated the dark. No, it wasn't hatred. It was fear—he was scared both of what he couldn't see and what might see him. He touched his lips to the cold glass of the window and summoned the clearest image of his mother he could bear to hold in his mind, as though he were laying her within the glass itself, passing her off to the house like a benediction.

The thing that he never told anyone at any of the parties in college or elsewhere, the thing he had told Simon on the third

and final night they'd slept together, was
that his mother had been furious at him
because, two days before that afternoon at
his aunt's house, she had caught him on top
of Francisco in the church bathroom. He'd
had his hands around Francisco's throat,
and Francisco had been kicking silently
under him. It had started because Francisco
had let him into the bathroom, said, "Hey,
come in, pee, it's fine," and it was the first
brotherly thing Francisco had said to him
since they'd been living together. It made
Hartjes feel wanted. So, with them pissing
into the toilet, hitting one another with
their spray, Hartjes said to Francisco,
Do you want to play Mercy Me? And
Francisco, shaking off and tucking back
into his slacks, had shaken his head,
and Hartjes said, **Me first**. Then he
wrapped his hands around Francisco's
neck, and Francisco squirmed and said,
You didn't wash your hands, and Hartjes
said, **Shut up**. Mercy Me was a simple
game, a stupid game, one they'd all played
in the woods and in the sheds on the farm,

putting their hands around each other's throats and squeezing slowly at first: softly, then firm, digging into the soft fuzz at the nape of the neck, until the other boy beat your chest, until his face went red and he opened his mouth and gasped, **Mercy, mercy me. Have mercy on me.** In the bathroom, the spaces between his fingers still sticky with piss, he squeezed Francisco's throat gently, the same way he first held Gristle, Marrow, and Bone when they were first born and he sensed that he could, very easily, destroy them. It was love to choose otherwise.

In Simon's bed, telling the story, he'd tried to be jokey—"You should have seen her face"—but there was nothing funny in it. She had flushed with anger, with fear, and she'd pushed Hartjes to the side. He'd clipped his head on the edge of the window. She pulled Francisco, coughing, wheezing, up from the floor and beat his back hard and fast. She'd said, "I love you, are you okay, I love you." She had wrapped her arms around Francisco while Hartjes sat there holding his head. He had felt like he was full of wet sand. And Simon had rolled on top of him and kissed him and said, "Are you still waiting for her to turn to you, too? To say she loved you? You gotta let this go, man. It's done."

Hartjes had wanted to say that if it was easy to get over your mother discarding you, then the whole world would be a different and stranger place. That hurt had a weight to it, a gravity as essential as the Earth's, and it was a kind of natural law that kept them all doing as they should. But he just kissed Simon's throat.

But now she was dead.

It was a different thing to speak ill of the dead.

In his family, one did not speak the name of the dead after they had been buried. It was a summons. A beckoning. And who knew what the dead might take with them when they left again. When his grandfather had died, they had burned not only his possessions but almost everything he'd ever touched, all of it that could be burned. What made no sense to burn—the tools, the guns, the tractors, the car—they wiped and cleaned. They laid it all out on the benches and worktables in the back and scrubbed everything down with alcohol and bleach, with oil and polish, wiped and wiped as if that might erase history, time, possession. His family took down all his grandfather's pictures, stored them away.

When a person died, anything at all might be a way back, an anchor, a reason for fitful sleep. His grandmother had kept something, her wedding ring, and she woke every night for a month with his grandfather's ghostly image standing beside her bed. And finally, as she took the ring off and slipped it into a sock and buried it in the yard, she said that, looking at him, at that sad look on his face, that expectant look, she knew that she had to either join him or let him go.

ON THE PORCH he gave Simon his beer, but he wouldn't let go when Simon tried to pull it loose from his hand. Simon snatched again, and Hartjes held on tighter until he saw Simon bare his teeth, the slick, pointed canines. His eyes narrowed. The vein at the base of his neck bulged. His skinny fingers were strong. The beer sloshed. Hartjes let him have it.

"Fucker," Simon said under his breath. Hartjes sat roughly on the bench. It rattled under his weight.

"Work tomorrow," Hartjes said.

"He's getting back on his barge," Simon said, drinking.

"Call me Huck Finn," Hartjes said.

"You ever get sick of it?"

"No," Hartjes said. He worked construction down on the river, where they were putting up a new footbridge. His own job involved the careful freighting of materials onto the platform where the crane rested on the water. There were times when he thought he'd get sick from the motion of the barge, the constant shifting underfoot. There were times when his hands hurt from lifting and pushing and turning, tightening the straps until they wouldn't give, tightening them until it seemed impossible that anyone would ever be able to set them loose again. Days when his back ached and his stomach hurt and his hair was peppered with grit, when his eyes burned, and his nose burned from the stench of oil and of the river, which was dying a slow, choked death via a series of minor diversions. But then, on bright winter days, he'd look up and see the geese tracking across the sky, moving up there free as air, and he'd think that there was something beautiful left in the world. And he could go on like that, as long as there was something beautiful to look at. He sweated through his coveralls, through his flannel, into the white mud that caked his gloves and his sleeves. And he thought about those geese, thought about the ice breaking up and the slow green-black water that moved beneath it.

"Flowing and flown," he said under his breath.

"You went to Cornell," Simon said. "You went to Cornell to work construction on a river."

"I went to Cornell to get out of Alabama," he said with no irony, with no regret.

"All that trouble, for nothing," Simon said.

"I like it," Hartjes said. "It's only nothing if you expect something better. I never wanted anything."

"Except to get out."

"And get out I did," Hartjes said. He nudged the knob of the heater, and more dry heat radiated under them. "Do you know those people?"

The light of the house across the fields had deepened into a marigold color. Simon squinted.

"Big fields make for good neighbors," Simon said, biting at his thumbnail.

"There were houses like this in my town," Hartjes said. "Little specks out on the dirt roads."

"Rural America. The heartland."

"Dixie," Hartjes said with a low growl.

"Mine eyes have seen the glory of the coming of the Lord," Simon sang.

"Ein feste Burg ist unser Gott," Hartjes said, and Simon's chest rattled. "I, a Catholic, go to the trouble of learning your Protestant hymns and this is what I get."

"Protestant hymns. Okay, Martin Luther."

"Was that racial?" Hartjes asked, extending the joke perhaps a note too far, but Simon doubled over and howled between his knees. "Faithful are the wounds of a friend, but deceitful are the kisses of an enemy."

"Kisses? Are we kissing now?" Simon leaned over and kissed Hartjes on the mouth. His breath was hot and frothy from the beer. His eyes were glazed. Hartjes had not kissed anyone in more than a month, and the suddenness of it made him dizzy. He didn't know what to say, so he put his hand on Simon's knee, and Simon kissed him again.

"Simon," Hartjes said.

"It's not so bad. You can't catch it from

kissing." Simon's lips were dry. His eyes were hazy and blue. Hartjes held his hand.

"I'm not stupid. I know that."

"Then kiss me. Be merciful. Be good to me. Kind to me. Kiss me."

"Simon says kiss me," Hartjes said, putting their foreheads together. He peeled some of the wool from the blanket.

"You are a cruel person, Hartjes."

Hartjes kissed him. It was quick, there and gone.

"Are you satisfied?"

"You're cruel," he said, and Hartjes kissed him, and he said it again each time until their lips were warm and close and puffed from kissing.

"I'm getting cold," Hartjes said.

"It's warm inside."

"That's a lie."

"It isn't. Come in and find out."

"Simon—you know I can't."

"Why not?"

"I have work in the morning."

"Come inside. Just for a little while. Come inside."

Simon stood up. He stumbled a little and then stooped, the blanket still around him. He flicked off the heater. And he stuck his hand out. He would not be denied. Hartjes could see that. There was determination cut deep in the grooves of his face. He looked handsome again. The light from the moon was in the snow, and the world was impossibly bright.

"Okay," Hartjes said. "Just a minute."

They got up and went along the porch around the house. Hartjes shuffled near the doorway. Simon jerked his head impatiently. Hartjes crossed the doorway and stepped into the kitchen. His steps were heavy. They climbed the stairs, and with each footfall Hartjes could feel his body contracting. He felt hot and damp under his arms. He wiped at his brow with his sleeve. The pictures on the wall didn't belong to Simon. They had come with the place, and Simon left them up because he said he liked them and they had lived here longer than he had and what right did he have to usurp them. Spiderwebs billowed against the wall. The staircase felt dusty and grim. At the top of the stairs, Simon groped for the light, and Hartjes knew that if he made an excuse right then, right at that very moment, he might get away. He might yet manage to extricate himself. But he did not. Simon found the switch, and the hall was suddenly yellow, like sepia. On the small tables were minor trinkets, crosses and portraits of saints, delicate painted women, martyrs, beads and pearls. A nest of sacraments, antique brushes, and burnished jewelry.

The light in Simon's room was almost blue with cold. Hartjes dropped his jacket on the floor. He got into the bed and Simon climbed in next to him. Then on top of him. Simon's hard hands scraped over his chest and stomach, started to go lower. Hartjes reached for them sharply, and in retaliation Simon latched onto his neck. The damp, persistent heat of it. Hartjes closed his eyes. Simon kissed and bit a path upward until Hartjes had no choice but to kiss him back. Hartjes closed his eyes and put his arms around Simon, held him close. He rocked their bodies together, and then he rolled onto Simon and pressed him flat into the mattress. He could give Simon this, he thought. He couldn't want him back in the same way, but he could give him this. Hartjes kissed him rougher and more deeply, pressed Simon flatter. The bed shook a little. Simon moaned, but when Hartjes wouldn't let him draw any fresh breath, he bucked. Hartjes held on, his own breath sour and hot now, their mouths fighting. Hartjes pushed at Simon, felt the terrible weakness of his limbs.

At first Simon punched at his chest. He fought. He twisted. He kicked. He tried to get out from under Hartjes, but Hartjes wouldn't let him. Hartjes ran the seam of his palm along Simon's throat, felt the muscle of it jump and squirm like the backs of his dogs. No fur. Just the slippery animal surface, the gooseflesh, the chilled skin waiting. Hartjes squeezed, felt the muscle contract. Simon wheezed, gave a bronchial cough. Simon stared up at him. Hartjes could feel Simon getting hard and then going soft. He could feel the wet warmth cooling against his stomach. He could feel Simon twisting and writhing and trying to scrape something out of this. But he held on. The tiny vessels in Simon's eyes thickened. The circles of his pupils shrank, opened, shivered in the blue of his irises. Simon turned red and his cheeks swelled like he was holding his breath.

Hartjes tracked back through the hall and down the stairs and into the living room, where the light was on. Hartjes stumbled on the foot of the stairs. The living room was the same sepia shade as the upstairs, had the same blue-and-gold wallpaper that had faded with time. The light had been off. He and Simon had climbed the stairs in darkness.

It was a trick being played on him. He gripped at his head and beat the hard fat of his palms against his skull. He should never have said anything about his mother. He should never have gone up those stairs. It all felt so impossible—that his mother was dead, that he'd hurt Simon, thinking he could give him what he wanted, that he stood now under a light that he had seen Simon turn off. None of it made sense. But that was a kind of sense, too.

Hartjes turned in a slow circle.

Hartjes held his breath.

Hartjes waited.

The quiet of the house droned. It gave no answers. The light overhead did not flicker. It did not waver. It was steadfast. The faucet dripped. The candle had burned itself out. Their bowls were on the counter. Everything was as it should have been.

Upstairs, there was a thud like footsteps.

Hartjes went to the front door and pulled and pulled at the bolt. It would not budge. He pulled harder. It would not budge. The door itself was so thin and shabby that Hartjes felt he could have jerked it right off the hinges, but he didn't. He kept at the bolt, pulling on it, but the bolt just rattled and spun, and when Hartjes pulled on the knob, it twisted uselessly.

There was quiet upstairs.

Hartjes got the door open. The cold was

on him right away. He had left his coat upstairs. At his car, he looked back toward the house. Two lights, the first floor and the second, burned like one yellow column.

In Simon's window, a shadow passed back and forth as if pacing. In the cold, Hartjes watched the shadow glide across the curtain like the second hand of a clock, the persistent beat of its passage. Then both lights went out, and it was impossible to tell the shadow from the rest of the house. And overhead, the tips of the trees brushed the night sky like the wingbeats of a thousand starlings.

PROCTORING

LIONEL ALWAYS FELT A KIND OF secondhand embarrassment when he proctored exams. It was like visiting a friend's house during a family function: everyone behaving in a formal, context-determined way that at once applied to you as a guest but also did not apply to you, because you were not family, so the level of artifice was clear, yet you weren't supposed to comment on it.

The department head was teaching an

advanced seminar on early modern French history. Lionel's job was to write the prompt for the essay on the board, wait the two hours for the students to fill their blue books with everything they knew, and then deposit the blue books with the departmental secretary. It was as easy a chain of events as he could have asked for.

He was late getting to the room in the basement of the art library and found the fifteen white boys clustered in the hall, some standing and leaning against the wall, others on the floor, shuffling note cards, flicking them front to back. Their anxiety scuffed up the quiet. He let them into the room and wrote the prompt on the board:

French Absolutism

Then he wondered if he should have waited for them to seat themselves and put away their study materials. So he erased his writing, turned to them. He pulled up the PDF with the class roster and instructions and saw that he was supposed to have them sign in. But he had not gone to the departmental office to pick up the slip for them to sign.

"Does anyone have . . . ?" he motioned as if to write on air, and one of the students, tallish in some sort of gray sweatsuit, ripped a sheet of paper from his notebook and held it out between two fingers.

Lionel took the sheet and then, realizing he'd forgotten to bring a pen, looked up and scribbled in the air again. The same boy rolled his eyes and offered Lionel his pen. Lionel took it, wrote the name and number of the course across the top of the sheet, then drew a line down the center and wrote two column headings: **name** and **student id #**.

The boy wrote his name with a scratching swiftness and handed it over his shoulder. He wrestled himself out of his sweatshirt. His hair was oily and dirty blond, and he had greasy pit stains on the T-shirt he wore underneath. He had what looked to be four-day stubble. He stretched in his chair. The paper went back and up the next row, but then one of the boys said, "Uh, this isn't like, secure."

"What do you mean?" Lionel asked.

"Our ID numbers. Like, they're right here. I could take a pic and use them." The boy held the sheet up and gestured at it with his pen.

"Do you plan to take a picture and use them?"

"No, but I could. That's the point. This isn't secure. This is kind of a violation of privacy."

"I see your point," Lionel said. "But, honor system, right? Nobody steal anyone's identity."

There was a petty, pitying kind of amusement in the room at that joke. But the boy with the security issue wasn't pleased. He squinted down at the sheet of paper and said, "Do you mind if I don't? Like, I don't feel comfortable."

"Sure," Lionel said. "Okay. Whatever you want."

The boy signed his name and passed the sheet to the next boy, who looked at it for a moment while holding his ID card aloft in his right hand, as if making up his mind about whether or not to write down his number. Lionel felt like he had lost some control over the room, like he'd just failed a test of his own. But after a moment the boy did write down his name and number, and the paper went on, with people adding their details, until it was clear that the only person without an ID number was the boy who had complained. Lionel refrained from pointing out that this was as identifying as putting your information down in the first place, but people were allowed their convictions, and he could respect that.

When he had taken the sheet back, he wrote **French Absolutism** on the board again and said, "You have two hours. Good luck."

They put their heads down over their blue books. There were five rows of five desks each, and the boys had spread out across the room in a weird sequence. One row was filled entirely, then the next left empty, and then a couple in the third and fourth rows, and the last row also filled. It was like a riddle or SAT question: 5, 0, 2, 3, 5. Out of habit, Lionel shifted the numbers around, first in increasing order, then decreasing order. He calculated the sum, the average, the sum of squares, the sum of cubes, the standard deviation. He leaned against the table at the front of the room, running the numbers through a string of permutations. It made him homesick for math—for the library where he'd worked through his first-year coursework in the graduate program, going through two or three legal pads of calculations a week, checking his work against WolframAlpha, graphing ridiculous functions and sending screenshots to the friend who had hosted the potluck last night. He missed the cramped TA office the math department had provided to him and the others who taught Calc I, and if they were unlucky, remedial algebra—those sullen, unhappy faces of the probationary students who didn't know even the most basic of things. Lionel longed for that period of his life, when he made grilled cheeses and sat in the back patio of his building, trying to solve the problems that were sometimes pinned to the bulletin board in the department office. That smell like burning coffee when someone had left the machine on in the shared kitchen, the hum of the big printer and scanner. He missed the long talks with his advisor, Dr. Lauk, who had taken Lionel in after that summer program because Lionel was also interested in complex differential geometry, though Lionel didn't like analysis and had struggled through his analytic geometry class. He even missed the mean, brutal hours of Dr. Nonan's seminar on geometric isoforms and topology, the one class where he had gotten the minimum required B.

Lionel remembered staring at the grade with great incredulity. No one in grad school got Bs unless something had gone wildly wrong. He remembered being summoned when that fall semester's grade posted, and hearing Dr. Lauk say, with kindness that verged on condescension, "He can be a challenging instructor. You'll do better next time." The implication being that Lionel must retake the course and get an A because the subject matter intersected so deeply with his advisor's specialty. There were moments in the spring semester when Lionel wondered if it was for his own benefit that he was retaking the class or if it was because he was being moved around a chessboard he couldn't see, his graduate education a pawn passed between two egos. But even that he missed—the messy, ridiculous departmental politics, the rituals, all of it.

But in his second year, Lionel had tried to kill himself. And now that was over.

The boys wrote furiously. Lionel checked the time on his phone, then checked Instagram and Reddit and Twitter. He read a long thread about Wisconsin electoral maps and how Madison had recently been redistricted. He thought of the conversation he had overheard last night about Planned Parenthood being defunded. It often happened that two things that seemed unrelated in Lionel's life were actually connected in the larger context of the world, and a network revealed itself to him in random, strange ways. Usually mediated via the internet, via social media, via

someone saying something to someone at a
dinner party, not even directly to him or
about him. He was aware that he lived, in
that way, amid the great matrix of the world's
concerns.

He put his phone away, but then it pulsed
and he took it out again.

lunch?

The text was from Sophie. The sudden
shame made him dizzy. Because, of course,
Charles had shown up at his apartment.
Why else all those looks, that run-in outside the bathroom—what else had all that
meant if not **I see you. I want you.** What
else could all that have culminated in, if
not Charles standing in the falling snow,
taking the keys from Lionel's hand, and
letting them both inside? And Lionel had
done it, knowing that the moment he followed Charles in, he was saying good-bye
to Sophie and whatever friendship she
might have had for him.

Lionel stared down at his phone.

u there?

Proctoring.

sounds terrible. lunch?

Maybe not a good idea.

why?

A pause. Then another vibration.

charlie? i know, it's cool

Jesus Christ. He stared down at his phone and tried to figure out what that could mean: **I know.** What did she know? How did she know? What did she mean by **It's cool**? How could this be possible, unless Charles had told her, or unless it had been as obvious to her as it had been to him last night. Charles materializing out of the snow, breathing hard at his doorstep. He could see it, Sophie watching the whole thing with a detached ease, a calm paid for by who knew how many other similar events. There, he thought, was a truly horrifying possibility: that he was nothing more than another bit of local weather for the two of them, and that what felt to Lionel like the edge of some great change, a sign of his reacclimation to people, to the world, to the easiness of friendship, was nothing but another thing to them, one more thing that happened and was now over.

She **knew**, Lionel thought with sinking fear. She knew. **It's cool**. Lionel envied her but also felt humiliated—what to say? Best to say nothing.

it'll be fun. i'll buy

Coffee?

! ! !

even better! come to the café!

One of the students coughed, and Lionel looked up sharply. The boy with the security concerns was staring at him. No. The boy was staring beyond him at the board, at the question that was not a question. **French Absolutism**. Lionel felt sorry for him, because he looked like he was drowning and he knew it.

Poor kid. Lionel wanted to lean over and ruffle his hair, to say it would be okay, that no matter what he wrote in the blue book, it would be okay, that this was temporary and at the end of the two hours it would pass, would collapse down into the general topography of his life, and he'd forget this panicked, drowning feeling. The guy licked his lips and put his head down—back to work. Lionel glanced at the clock over the door.

There was time.

AFTER THE EXAM, Lionel took the fifteen blue books up the stairs to the history department's office. He gave them to the departmental secretary, a broad, bland-faced woman with a skin tag like a perpetual crumb at the leftmost corner of her mouth.

The secretary took the papers, shuffled them, and stared at Lionel reproachfully. He shrugged uneasily at her, signed the form saying that he'd done what he'd been asked, and left.

The look, he suspected, was because he'd had to cancel the last several proctoring appointments with the history department when he had been in the hospital. He could still hear her voice, scratchy on the phone, when he called to say he wouldn't be able to make it. "Your generation is killing this nation with your carelessness," she'd said, and hung up on him before he could respond. He'd stood in the reception area of the psychiatric care facility, staring at his reflection in his phone screen, thinking, well, maybe that was true, maybe they were killing the country and killing the world, but they were also killing themselves, and what would it list on his death certificate as cause of death, if not carelessness, misadventure. It was a serious thing to kill a world. He'd stood there with the clipboard of paperwork in his hand, had only called her because the act of lifting the clipboard to sign his name had brought to mind the fact that at that moment he was supposed to be somewhere else, on campus, giving an exam instead of admitting himself. But she didn't care about that, and he didn't blame her. He'd caused a mess. She was entitled to her feelings.

Lionel knew the café where Sophie worked—he avoided it because it was popular with undergraduates. It was crowded, noisy, the last place you could get any work done or be alone with your thoughts. But when he arrived via the seldom-used entrance from the adjoining library, he was surprised to find it empty except for Sophie and another barista. Sophie sat at a table near the window, looking out. Lionel wondered if she was looking for him—the window faced onto the quad and the usual entrance—and the thought touched him. But when the door shut behind him, she looked up and frowned in mock surprise.

"You have your tricks," she said.

"Some."

At her table, he unwound his scarf and unzipped his jacket. She reached out and stuck her finger through a hole in the collar of his shirt. "What happened there?" she said. Lionel pulled his chin back and looked down as she traced the hole, then flattened the collar with a little pat. "There we go."

"Oh, thanks."

"Do you want something? To eat, to drink?" She had gotten up, rested her knuckles against her hip. She was wearing black tights and a sweater the color of weak tea. Lionel found it a little hard to make eye contact with her. He pressed his hands to his cheeks.

"Oh, I'm fine. Well. Yes. A coffee," Lionel said, and when she returned a few minutes later with the coffee in a small carafe, he asked, "How much do I owe you?" She slapped his arm. She had already touched him twice. It felt like he was racking up a debt he wouldn't be able to repay. Yes, she'd said she knew about Charles, but about what did she know? Did she know the whole of it? About this morning, too? The more he let her touch him, be kind to him, the worse it would be when she found out everything. The harder it would be to salvage anything like friendship.

"I can afford a cup of coffee at least," she said. Lionel could feel the small mound of his wallet in his pocket. "Next time's on you."

"Is it always so busy?" Lionel asked. Overhead, Christmas music was playing. It was only November.

"Very funny." Sophie said. "It's our slow season, I guess. The calm before the storm."

"Finals."

"Bingo. You must get busy, too, around then," she said.

"I don't really know. It's my first finals season as a proctor," Lionel said. The coffee burned his tongue.

"You proctored today, right? What kind of test? Can you say?" She leaned forward with her elbows on the table. Her eyes seemed lit with real curiosity.

"History," Lionel said. She had a mole on her neck, black as a pupil. She had bright blue eyes. She had painted her fingernails pale matte pink. The tips of her fingers were cracking and white. She caught him looking at her hands.

"If I don't paint them, I chew," she said a little self-consciously. She pulled her hands away and put them behind her knees. She'd put her feet up on the chair again. "You were saying . . . the history test?"

"Oh, yeah. There was this one kid who was really up my ass about **security**. He acted like I was spying on his data or something. They all have to write their student ID numbers down to sign in. As protocol, I guess."

Sophie nodded like it made all the sense in the world, and Lionel wasn't sure if she was nodding because she thought the student had a point or if she agreed he'd made too much of it.

"But after that, it was fine. I just had to write the words 'French Absolutism' on the board and wait until they were done."

"Wow. What if they have questions?"

"I think that's why they don't have the history TAs do it? Because they might give them information they're not supposed to have? They pick a total idiot like me."

She gave him a look. "Weren't you, like, doing NASA research as a **child** or something? You're not an idiot."

"No, that's not me. I'd make a terrible engineer," Lionel said too seriously. "I did go to math camp, though. Guilty by association."

"**Math camp?** That's not just a movie trope?" Sophie made a show of leaning forward, putting her chin on her palms.

"Oh, yeah. Absolutely. I went for, like, twelve years. The last as a counselor."

"Holy shit. What's it like?"

Lionel swirled the coffee in the cup, aware of the gesture as he performed it, knowing that it had little utility, that it was something performed to make him look a certain way, pensive, thoughtful.

He'd gone to math camp in Tennessee, and they'd slept in cabins and showered in groups of three. They roasted hot dogs. They ran through the woods, getting welts on their legs, getting bitten by mosquitoes. They went home covered in new bumps and scrapes. One kid got his eye knocked out during a game of handball, which was why they no longer played after that year, fourth grade. But they also learned how to calculate their location based on the stars. They learned to calculate time from the angle of the sun. To calculate the distance between them and a summer storm by counting the seconds and the flash and the bang. They learned how to eye metric conversions. They did dumb little games and experiments like dropping bowling balls and baseballs and eggs from the roof. They swam and calculated distances from the opposite shore. They wrote letters home to their parents. They fished and threw back. They hiked and kept little journals of things they saw and would tell their friends back home. They hid under the covers and traded Pokémon cards and Game Boy cartridges. They practiced kissing when all the lights were out, and their bunks filled with their humid breath.

And at the end of summer, they went home and were alone. And sometimes things happened to them that they didn't tell anyone about.

"So, yeah, it's like camp," he said. "You must have done dance stuff, growing up, right?"

"No," Sophie said. "My grandma couldn't really afford intensives, could barely afford class." Her laughter was husky, and Lionel felt stupid for having said what he did.

"I'm sorry, I didn't mean that. I'm an asshole."

"You're probably just middle class, right?"

"Guilty again," Lionel said. "My dad's an engineer and my mom's a nurse practitioner."

"**Leave It to Beaver** over here."

"No, it's not like that," Lionel said. But it was true. It was all true.

"Don't be ashamed. It's okay. Everyone's so weird about money and stuff. Like there's something so noble about being poor. But having cash growing up, you know? That's good. It's good your childhood didn't suck."

"Yeah. They were good people. They tried with me," Lionel said.

"Then why all the shame?"

Lionel pressed his tongue to the roof of his mouth. The coffee had cooled. He drank to give himself something to do, and Sophie went on looking at him.

"I think I feel sorry for them," he said. "Because they got me. Instead of a real kid."

"What are you, Pinocchio or something?"

"I was such a weird kid. I mean—**math camp?** Kind of says it all."

"You're not as strange as you think you are, I bet," she said.

"Well, for my sake, I hope that's true. That would be a vast improvement in my circumstances."

Sophie watched him then, and he wanted to retreat from her. To hide from her probing gaze. He made a silly face and asked, "Is there another hole in my shirt?"

"So you wrote 'French Whatchamacallit' on the board and just hung out for two hours?" Sophie tucked her chin between her knees. It was the same posture she had assumed at the potluck, and it brought to mind the cold of the time they spent on the porch after dinner, how close they had gotten, her hand in his palm, the gritty texture of the porch. He swallowed the coffee. Felt his nasal cavities fill with heat and a burning smell.

"Yeah—like I said, even an idiot like me couldn't mess it up." Sophie narrowed her eyes at him and reached for his mug of coffee, as if she'd read his mind, and he pushed it gently toward her until she drew it back to herself. She drank from it, and Lionel felt a thrill of pleasure in his stomach, the idea of her lips touching a place where his lips had been, and there was something like a presentiment or a premonition or some other ephemeral, fleeting thought, that Charles had been a similar kind of conduit. A thing that they had both touched and been touched by, and he got a little hard remembering it, Charles sliding into him that first time, the awful discomfort of it, the smell like sweat and breath and piss, but it wasn't just remembering that Charles had fucked him, it was remembering it while sitting here with Sophie, and thinking that Sophie, too, had fucked Charles.

She drank from his mug, and he felt exposed.

"Tell me about last night," she said calmly. "Was he good? Did you like it?"

"The potluck?"

"Charles," she said, her lips tracing his name.

Lionel closed his eyes and saw Charles before him, how beautiful his body was, how solid, how real, how warm. He felt dizzy again, as if his center of gravity had shifted violently and suddenly upward. He gripped the underside of the table. Opened his eyes. Sophie was watching him, her lids low, lips parted just so.

"He came to my apartment. I thought— I don't know what I thought, but apparently, he was calling my name and chasing me and I ran."

"You ran?"

"And kind of slid? By the time he caught up with me, I couldn't really use my keys. But he helped me."

"You poor thing," she said, and she meant

it. She actually meant it. Lionel's mouth was dry and he motioned for the cup back. She shook her head, refused him.

"But then he came in. I made coffee, we talked a bit."

"What did you talk about?"

"That's so funny," Lionel said. "People say that, **We talked**. But I don't remember a single thing we said to each other. He asked, **Where do you sleep?**"

"**No.**"

"He did."

Sophie put her face behind her hand and shook her head. She groaned.

"It was nice, actually."

"Are you with someone?"

"No," Lionel said. "God no."

"Why not?"

Lionel considered the question. Then he unbuttoned his left sleeve and rolled it up to his elbow. His forearm was covered in a network of scars, culminating in a series of deep gouges near his wrist. His forearms were paler than the rest of him, except for this cluster of keloids with their tannish, reddish undertones. And sometimes, in the winter months, they grew dry and rubbery.

Sophie took in the view and Lionel watched her for the usual choreography of sympathy and disgust. She reached out and brushed her fingers across his arm and made a low, appraising hum. He could barely feel her touch. With the keloids, it was either too much sensation or nothing at all. Sometimes they burned powerfully or throbbed so much he couldn't sleep. His doctors had said that it was a real pain, but also not a real pain. They stopped short of saying it was psychosomatic. They didn't like that term, because it implied an unreal element, no matter how careful they were about contextualizing their comments.

"What happened?" she asked. "If that's not too personal?"

"I tried to kill myself. Which, I guess, is a little obvious. But I made a real hash of it. My roommate found me. Then I did some inpatient stuff. And some outpatient stuff. Not a lot of room for extracurriculars."

"Sounds like a lot."

"Yeah, last year, I was just . . . in this bad way. I felt really unsafe. I felt so sick, all the time. Like, really sick. Like my heart was going to jump out of my chest. And I couldn't sleep. Couldn't eat. Couldn't think. That was hardest—the not thinking. My mind wasn't even empty, just hazy. Like standing in a room you know perfectly well, but you can't see anything because it's full of this burning smoke. It was just. Impossible, and I was so scared—like this was going to be my life, I was never going to be okay again. I wanted some relief, I guess. I wanted to get out."

"Did you always struggle with that stuff?"

"No," Lionel said. "Well . . . yes? No and yes. I was always anxious. But the first two years of grad school were really hard, brutal. And I found it really hard to cope. It's like when a plane descends, you know? Gradually, down through the clouds, and suddenly you can't see anything? Except, with a plane, eventually you see the city. There was no city for me."

"Oh, Lionel," she said. She rested her

palm in his palm again, and he squeezed. It was the first time he had told someone about it. The whole of it. His throat was hot from talking and from trying to make himself known to another person. He put his head down on the table but went on squeezing Sophie's hand. She threaded her fingers through his.

"Anyway. I was okay until last week."

"You went back?"

"I had this feeling—this totally random sensation. It was kind of a thought and kind of not a thought. A voice, maybe? Something."

"What did it say?"

"You'll think I'm nuts," he said dryly. "If you don't already."

"Then you've got nothing to risk."

"That's true. It said—or showed me?— this image of myself, stepping out into traffic. I was on a sidewalk on my way home from the grocery store. And I was waiting for the light, and there were these cars coming on, and it just seemed possible to step out there and get swept away. It felt so real, for a minute I thought I had done it. But then I was just standing there on the sidewalk. And the cars were going by. And it was so cold. So I checked myself in."

"I think I know what you mean," she said.

People sometimes thought they knew what he meant, but what they usually meant was that sometimes, in their own lives, they had been disappointed. They had been a little unwell in totally manageable ways. What they meant was that they had suffered in the small ways that everyone suffered. But Sophie set the mug down and stroked his wrist as though she were stroking the head of a small animal.

"My parents died. And then my sister, a few years ago, died. Overdose. And sometimes, I think, **Fuck. Enough.** Or sometimes, it's like, **Why not make it a full set?**"

"Yeah," he said.

"I used to purge. Everybody thinks it's about being skinny and being light for ballet. They think it's to look a certain way. But I think most of us purge because of the control. Like, there's a moment when you go from feeling full and awful to feeling clean and clear and bright. There's just a moment, right before you get it all out, before you're burning up and convulsing, when you feel something go **ping** and you know it'll be all right. That's what it's about. That little **ping** of clarity. Anyway, I used to purge. When I lived with my grandma. All the other girls in ballet did, too. It's not special or anything, but I did. And then I got these awful ulcers. And I couldn't dance because I had no energy and my vision started to get weird? I felt like my body was betraying me."

Lionel sat up then. Sophie's thumb traced his knuckles.

"Then my sister died, and I thought, I can keep doing this or I can try to fucking live. Really live. Dance is awful, don't get me wrong—if your foot is too big or your shoulder doesn't bend a certain way. There are fewer than zero jobs. And everyone is on coke or a serial rapist. But when I'm dancing, sometimes, I feel that little **ping**. I know where I am in the world. I can feel myself. And, like, yeah, my technique is not classical. Come on. I learned to dance in Arkansas. But as long as I can dance, I'll be okay. I don't need ABT. Or Royal Ballet or anything. I just want to dance for as long as I can."

"It's your something," Lionel said.

"Everybody deserves a something, right?"

Lionel nodded, and Sophie blotted the corners of her eyes with a sleeve.

"Okay, so. Don't think you can distract me with all this blubbering. Tell me more about you and Charlie last night."

Lionel put his hands over his face. He could smell Sophie's lotion. The coffee. His own breath.

"You're relentless," he said.

"I just like to know things. I hate secrets."

Lionel felt exhausted by the prospect of telling her more of the seedy details from last night. But also by the prospect of convincing her that he'd already told her all there was to know. There was nothing interesting left except the petty details of how their bodies had been arranged and what it had felt like.

But she seemed keen to know exactly that, and Lionel shook his head.

"You don't want to know," he said.

"I absolutely do," was her reply, but then there was a solid bang at the window between their heads, and they looked out into the dim, late-afternoon sun. A snowball had exploded against the glass. Sophie leaned back and squinted. The world had attained a patina of blue light. The blue hour was upon them.

"It's Charlie," she said.

"Oh no."

The door opened and admitted a wave of cold, dense air. Lionel did not turn but instead watched Sophie's eyes course over his head toward the front of the café. "White Christmas" was playing, the version Lionel recognized from childhood, by the Drifters. Charles came strolling through the café, and Lionel could almost feel his body heat.

"Look what the cat dragged in," Sophie said. Charles braced himself on the table. He was soaked. The tips of his curls were beaded with something chalky: sweat or shampoo that he hadn't washed out entirely, melting snow. Charles hung his head, his expression hidden from Lionel, which was just as well, because Lionel felt at that moment that he probably should leave. He pulled his scarf free from the back of the chair and turned to take up his coat.

"I'll let you guys be," he said.

"No way," Sophie said. "You stay put." He felt her foot then against his knee, keeping in place. She smiled at him, but it was not a joke. Then she turned to Charles and asked him if he wanted some water or a coffee. Charles said that he wanted an espresso, with a tonic back. She made an elaborate bow at him and got up. Charles took her chair, and when she was around the corner, when they could hear her tamping out the used coffee, Charles turned to Lionel.

"What's all this?"

"She asked me here," Lionel said. "I'm not trying anything."

"That is so typical of her." Charles shook his head, leaned back in the chair. "She's playing a game. She thinks everything is fucking hilarious."

"She said she knew already. About last night."

"Yeah, I told her earlier—sorry if that was supposed to be a secret or something," Charles said. Lionel watched his lips shape into an amused smirk, the little dimple in his right cheek appearing, then vanishing.

"She seemed fine with it."

Charles turned and gripped the back of the chair, gave his body a hard wrench. Lionel's breath caught at the mobility of his joints. How easy it was for him to attain such a ridiculous position. The espresso machine hissed.

"You all right?"

"I can go if you want."

"No, don't. She'd just make a whole case about it," Charles said. "Better to let her have her way."

Sophie returned with the espresso and the small glass boot filled with tonic water. Charles shifted over to the empty chair closer to the window, away from Lionel, and Sophie reclaimed her seat. The small espresso cup was a deep caramel color. The crema was beautiful, perfect, and Charles sipped it to test the heat. Sophie had her chin on her palm, appraising his reaction. They had a whole routine down. One that excluded Lionel, made him feel extraneous, with his collar with the hole in it and his scarf and his anxiety. He rolled his sleeves down and buttoned them, and in the process drew Sophie's attention. Not in any obvious way, but he could feel the tension in her gaze shift slightly in his direction. Charles had seen him naked, of course, and had touched him. But that touching and that seeing had been focused in its particulars. They hadn't talked about their bodies, only used them. It was different in the café.

He had that feeling again, the one like watching an intimate function at a friend's house, the way two people who loved each other shared a context that had nothing to do with him. He was stupid for staying, for listening, when Charles and Sophie told him to stay put. He should have listened to himself. After all, his duty was to himself. Like that old line from his doctors: **Your duty is to your health. You owe yourself that much.**

"I think I should bounce, you guys," he said. Charles did not look at him. Sophie frowned.

"Didn't I say to stay right where you are?"

"It's getting a little weird, Sophie, isn't it?" he asked, trying to be funny, but sounding only desperate to himself.

"No," she said.

Charles knocked back the entire boot of tonic.

"You don't have to prove anything to her, Lionel. If you want to go, you can go." Charles pointed to the door over Lionel's shoulder.

Sophie turned her head then, and she put her arm around Charles's neck in a gesture that was at once playful and threatening. She was smaller than he was, but her arms were taut and strong. She clenched and

Charles reached down, lifted her up, and settled her on his lap with no more effort than moving a coat from a chair.

"Behave," Charles said.

"**You** behave," was Sophie's reply, but Lionel did see her arm slacken. "Where did you go earlier?"

Charles sighed. "Rehearsal. For the spring shows."

"Who's choreographing?"

"Farnland," Charles groaned, closing his eyes.

"I don't know they let him choreograph still. After the **incident**." She said the word with cartoonish exaggeration, turning to Lionel and giving him a very pointed look.

"It wasn't an incident," Charles said. "Come on. Don't spread rumors."

She looked at Lionel. "Farnland—**allegedly**—had an affair with one of the high school boys."

"Sophie, be serious."

The tension in the conversation cut against the casualness of their physical closeness.

Sophie's arm dangled around Charles's shoulders. He had one arm wrapped around her waist, holding her steady, but with his free hand he swirled the espresso, breaking up the crema. Their limbs were loose and relaxed. But it was clear that this was a thing they disagreed about, and not for the first time, which made Lionel wonder why Sophie had brought it up in the first place. In front of him.

"I'm just reporting the facts."

"You mean gossip," Charles said.

"Why'd you go with him, anyway? You could have danced in the stupid classical piece with the rest of us. You don't even like contemporary."

"It's **neoclassical inspired**, for one thing. Don't be a bitch about it."

"Ah, yes, his Balanchine homage," Sophie said.

Charles closed his eyes again. "And for two, he asked me. Plus, he knows that guy in Seattle."

"PNB? You were serious about PNB?"

"I need a job, Sophie."

"Or it's back to the paper mill," she said, slapping his chest. Then, looking back at Lionel, she said, "Charlie comes from paper folk."

"Why are you being such a bitch today?" Charles said.

Sophie got off his lap. The table rocked from her motion. "I'm not," she said. "You're the one who intruded on my coffee date with Lionel."

"Oh, I'm **intruding**?" Charles made a big show of looking between Lionel and Sophie, and Lionel once again pulled his coat from the back of his chair.

"He's fine, actually," Lionel said.

Sophie ignored this. "Yes, you're intruding," she told Charlie. "We were having a very intimate conversation before you arrived and invited yourself."

"About what?" Charles asked, looking directly at Lionel then. "What were you talking about?"

"Lionel's proctoring. He did a history test today."

"About what?"

"French something-something," Sophie said.

"Absolutism," Lionel said.

"What's that?"

"I don't know. I just did the test," Lionel said. "And then collected the blue books."

"And that's so important?"

"For some people, you know, tests are everything," Lionel said. He stood up, looped his scarf around his neck. "I didn't mean to make a mess here."

"No, stay. I'm being a dick. I'm just burned out," Charles said.

"Yeah, he's being a dick," Sophie added.

They were both looking at him then, each of them knowing something a little different about him. He should go. He should leave. But they were looking at him as if they wanted him to stay, really wanted him to sit with them, and it had been a long time since Lionel felt that anyone really wanted him around or needed him. Distantly, remotely, he felt a click, a little alleviation of pressure in his head. Something had been determined. Something was now opening. He sat again, and at that very moment, he felt one foot glide along the outside of his right leg. And he felt a reassuring pressure against his left ankle. They were both touching him. They were both moving against him.

"All right," he said. "All right."

FILTHY ANIMALS

MILTON AND NOLAN STEW IN THE MUSKY heat of Milton's basement, sipping lukewarm coffee from styrofoam cups. Upstairs, Milton's parents watch the news and clear away the remnants of dinner, their footsteps and the clattering of dishes in the sink like thunder. Nolan's busy on his phone, trying to find out what their other friends are doing—there might be a party later. Woolly

Christmas garlands and old coats peer at them from corners.

The night is just getting started, but Milton is already a little drowsy. Low music plays, a riff on a riff on a riff of some song by the Cardigans, sped up and looped infinitely over a soft electro-synth.

"You drowsing or what? It's all this sleepy-ass music."

"I'm good, I'm good," Milton says, and tries to sit upright on the beanbag chair, but it's seen better days and he almost dumps himself on the floor.

"How are you this wasted already?"

"It's my birthday," Milton says. "I'll do what I want."

"Tate and Abe say there's a burner on the hill."

"Bet."

Burner means that there will be ten to fifteen people they vaguely know and kerosene-soaked rags torched in metal barrels. Cheap whiskey, cheap beer for the Christians. Coke, molly, and weed for the true believers. Heavy bass pumping from the mudder trucks—Kendrick and Luke Bryan in some kind of awful mash-up like a diversity poster. Tommy Boy cologne, white polos, Wallabees, and dark denim turned white in the crotch and ass from wear. Exhausting.

"Unless you wanna waste a good high in your fucking basement," Nolan says, his gaze leveled on Milton.

"It's whatever."

"You're such a little girl sometimes."

Milton shimmies his jeans up over his basketball shorts and pulls on a gray sweater made for him by his grandmother from the wool of Sturdy Matilda, her bossy ewe. "Get up, lazy."

Nolan is already dressed in his jeans and eye-searing orange hoodie. They're almost the same height, and people sometimes mistake them for siblings. Nolan is beige and drenched in freckles. Milton has only one black grandparent, but Nolan calls him a **pale-ass nigga** just the same. Milton doesn't see a resemblance except for the parts of them that aren't white.

On his feet, Nolan punches Milton in the gut, then bounds up the stairs. Milton stomps after him, grabbing at his heels. They emerge into the back hall, and Nolan jerks the door open and sprints out through the garage to the safety of the driveway. Milton catches sight of his mother in the living room.

"Where you boys off to?" The gentle music of her voice makes Milton shift awkwardly near the door. He rests his hand on the outside knob. She's folding a thick blanket.

"The hill, I guess."

"Make sure you're back before too late." There's something else, he knows, but she won't bring it up.

"All right, yes, ma'am," he says.

"Milton," his father says from the kitchen. The news plays through the ending credits. **Wheel of Fortune** will be on soon. His father's tall and solid. He watches Milton over his glasses and that long straight nose of his.

"Sir?" Milton asks. Nolan kicks a pinecone

from foot to foot at the end of the driveway. Milton waits for his father to say what he needs to say.

"Having a good one?"

"Yes, Pop," Milton says. "I am."

"Get back safe."

"Yes, Pop."

"Milton."

"Yep?" Milton puts his forehead to the white grain of the door. Nolan's on his phone in the yard. His father twists a white towel around the inside of a glass bowl, though it must certainly be dry by now. The opening music of **Wheel of Fortune** enters the living room, and the glow from the television illuminates the side of his mother's face. Her pale brown eyes are on him, too. He thinks for a moment that they're going to stop him. It's his birthday. **Let me have this one thing**, he thinks. This one thing. Before it's all gone. His eyes sting a little.

"Have fun."

"Thanks, Pop," Milton says, and he gently taps the door with his fist. His mother smiles at him and turns to the television. His father goes back through the kitchen doorway. Milton shuts the door behind him, lets it click firmly, and steps out into the cold.

IT'S THE VERY BEGINNING of November, and the early-evening sky is the color of crushed lilacs. A thick forest of pine trees encircles their subdivision, and beyond that, in the distance, is the shadow of the mountain, one of those low hills at the cusp of Appalachia in northern Alabama. Standing in his driveway, Milton cranes his neck back and stares out over the top of his house and the next and the next, all the way into the city that has been built into this mountain, its lights like a string of pearls. Wood smoke crests on the air. He's trying to fix the image of the mountain in his mind, because soon he'll be halfway across the country, shoved down into a valley.

After winter break, Milton's parents are sending him to what they are calling an "enrichment program." For the entire spring, he's going to be on a small farm in Idaho, trying to make something of himself. No phone. No internet. Nothing but the hard slopes of the hills and what he imagines to be the vast plain of the sky, studded with stars, streaked with clouds. They have been disappointed with the shape his life has taken, and this is their last attempt, they say, their last big effort. Milton doesn't know what they want from him. He's seventeen today, and he feels that he should have more control over his life than he has. Nolan's got it easy by comparison—his parents give him whatever he wants.

Last week, on Glad Hill, he and Nolan got popped buying the pot they smoked earlier. Tate and Abe had said that this was it, this was the end of high cotton, and Nolan had shrugged. Nothing came of it, of course. No charge materialized, because it turned out that the cop who'd busted him had beaten a domestic charge the year before, thanks to Nolan's dad. The thing that bugs Milton about it is not that Nolan gets off all the time. Nolan complained about his dad after the fact. **He said he loved me,** Nolan said. **They don't give a shit.** It gets on Milton's nerves. Nolan wouldn't enjoy being treated like an animal circling his parents' love like a too-small enclosure. Milton would just like a little elbow room.

On the night Nolan got popped, the same cop delivered Milton home in the back of the cruiser, but didn't turn the lights on. Instead, he sent Milton out into the cool night on unsteady legs, tipsy and a little queasy. His parents looked at him as though from a precipice and shook their heads. No, that's it, Milton. No more chances. How many times was that already since spring? Four? Five? No, Nolan wouldn't like it one bit, parents whose love had a long, reproachful memory.

Idaho had materialized as a vague threat in September, and that threat had grown ever more solid until they came into his room a few days before and laid it all out for him. His father had put the pamphlet in his hand. Milton had taken it, though he couldn't meet their gazes. His room smelled damp on that day. Outside, he could hear music from a few houses over. Maybe it was best that he got some time away. That he spent some time on his own, learning how to be a man on his own terms. To see what the world would hold for him if he kept on this way. But Milton had wanted to ask them, What way? Because he drank? Because he smoked? Because he ran with Nolan and Tate and Abe? Because he'd stopped going to church? Because he stopped praying? He had sat clenching the slick, laminated pamphlet, its cover featuring a tough-looking boy with a white line down his face, on one side smirking, sneering, mean, and on the other a stern, hard gaze. But Milton couldn't tell which was meant to be the before and which was supposed to be the after. He'd stared at the pamphlet, thinking, **What's so wrong with me?**

They said they'd write him letters when he went—or his mom had, anyway. His dad said nothing except that he expected him to do something with this chance, not to piss it away.

Fucking Idaho.

"Come on," Nolan says.

Milton squares his shoulders. He hasn't told Nolan about Idaho or the camp yet, but soon he'll have to. After Thanksgiving break they'll have finals, and then Christmas vacation, and then it's Idaho. He shoves his hands in his pockets. He can hear how pathetic he will sound if he's like **I have to tell you something** or **There's something I gotta say**. Like he's about to ask Nolan to prom or to the fucking movies. There's no way to get into it that isn't dramatic or stupid. It's all like showing off or making a scene. He can't get it out and downplay it at the same time. So he keeps it to himself. He'll text or something on the way to the airport. That's when he'll say it, when there's no turning back, when the suddenness of the information will flash and disappear in the same instant. Easy. Simple.

The homes in the subdivision are all the same two levels, squat in the front and narrow in the back. They're in shades of pale blue and ecru, with hunter-green shutters.

Even the mailboxes are the same matte black plastic at the ends of the driveways. It's a wonder that they don't all wander into and out of one another's homes by accident, so remarkably identical are these houses, and as they wind past them, Milton wonders, as he always does, if each house harbors some better, happier version of himself, and if so, who does that make him, on the sidewalk with Nolan, if not the failed twin—the bad news come to rest at the door of his true self, the real Milton, the one not meant for Idaho in the spring.

"You on one tonight," Nolan says. "You could have stayed in your basement."

"I wish you would drop that," Milton snaps.

"Titty Baby's all upset."

"Stop pretending to know shit about how I feel," Milton says. They're outside Hank Dayton's place at the edge of the subdivision. Hank's beat-up Chevy drips oil onto the pavement.

Nolan frowns, then scowls, then takes a step toward him.

"This is the shit I'm talking about," Nolan says as he sticks a finger directly into Milton's chest. "Just what is up your ass?"

"I said I'm good." Milton pushes up against Nolan's finger, and Nolan shoves him. Milton shoves back, and they grip at each other's shoulders, their feet shifting for purchase. Their shoes scrape across the pavement, and Nolan calls him a pussy, a fag, a bitch-ass nigga. But the heat has gone out of the grappling, and they're wheezing for breath by the end of it.

"You lucky it's your birthday," Nolan says. He spits thick and white down between his knees. Milton finds his breath more easily than Nolan. His pulse slows.

"We can go again."

"Quit playing." Nolan puts his hand up to stop Milton from getting closer. Milton slaps at his palm. They knock fists, let it go. They cut into the woods, and as they go, Milton raises his fingertips to his neck where Nolan had put him in a headlock. He's burning there. Alive with heat.

. . .

As KIDS, they had made a game of testing each other's courage by seeing who could go farthest into the woods at night. They'd shut their eyes and dart ahead as if they could beat their fear with speed.

"Do you remember that game we used to play out here?" he asks.

"What game?"

Milton steps over a thick branch downed in his way, and Nolan scrapes up alongside him, almost tripping. "Jesus."

"We used to go through here without looking," Milton says. "**Used to.**"

"Funny."

Their footsteps throw up a soft rustle as they move across the bed of leaves and sticks. Milton feels his way ahead with his feet, searching for hidden dangers. Nolan bumps against him occasionally, and Milton commits these nudges to memory along with the shape of the mountain pressing against the night sky.

"Who are you texting anyway? Abe?"

"No, not Abe. Nobody, really."

"Somebody," Milton teases. "Can't be nobody, can it?"

"None of your business, anyway, is it?"

"None of my business," Milton repeats. "Sure."

"Do you really want to know? That's weird, right? But I'll tell you if you want to know."

"If you wanted to tell me, you would have." There is more meaning to Milton's voice than he intends, but he cannot deny the truth of it or how much it bothers him. Perhaps it's that soon he'll be gone and whoever is on the other end of that phone will remain. That even when Milton's gone, Nolan will be able to speak to this other person, and so this moment may be the last time he and Nolan will walk together through these woods, among the shadows of their history. He grins, pushes at Nolan's shoulder. "Don't be so sensitive."

"We're almost there," Nolan says. Milton catches the tilt of the sky through the trees overhead. The incline underfoot pitches higher.

"Yeah."

"Man, look. You got something to say, then say it. You hate me? What?"

"Hate you?"

"I mean, you know, if you're sick of my shit, I get it. I don't think it's fair, but I get it."

"I don't even know what that means, Nolan."

"It means if you're sick of my shit, I get it. I would be."

"I'm not sick of your shit," Milton says, but Nolan isn't looking at him. He's back on his phone, scrolling.

"Sure, okay."

"Because I didn't jump up right away to go hang out with fucking Abe? Come on."

"Why do you hate him so much?"

"I don't hate him. I don't hate anybody," Milton says. They're at the edge of the woods now. The park is a series of gentle green slopes, trees, paths, and farther on, a playground of sorts. In the distance, he sees a couple of people with dogs tossing colored disks in the low light of evening. The sound of traffic from the nearby road washes in like the sound of the ocean.

"Don't cry, man," Nolan says, and Milton almost screams.

"Shut up," he says.

"Are you gonna cry about it?"

"Cry about what, Nolan?"

"Hell if I know, you won't tell me anything."

"Well, that should tell you everything, shouldn't it? What's to tell?"

WHEN THEY REACH GLAD HILL, people are gathered around an orange fire in a barrel. Music plays from a portable speaker nearby. Milton doesn't recognize anyone except for Tate and Abe, of course, and one or two others. Abe is enormous, well over six feet and bulky. He resembles a large, white bull, with a massive head and a forehead that juts forward. Tate is almost hilariously thin, reedy and short. He has crooked teeth but a good, kind face. He is neither good nor kind, however, and his favorite act of violence is to burn holes into people's clothes when they aren't looking.

Compared with Nolan, they are rough and dull. But then, compared with Nolan, anyone would seem lesser, made of inferior stuff, Milton included. Abe and Tate bring out the worst in Nolan, excite the animal part in him. The last time they were all together, smoking in the woods and drinking cheap beer, Tate gripped Nolan's arm, hauled him up, and punched him. Not a hard punch. Tate could never hurt Nolan. But the surprise of the act, the vicious courage of it, made Nolan stagger. Milton was up off the ground in an instant, gripping Tate's throat, but Nolan pushed him aside, and head-butted Tate one hard time. And then, in the evening, they were all over each other, he and Tate and Abe and Milton, throwing fists and elbows. They fought for what felt like hours, but for what must have been only minutes, biting and scratching and punching.

After that fight, Abe and Tate went home

together, shouting and shoving. Nolan reached for Milton's raw, ugly hand. The scabbed edges of their fingertips brushed once, and then no more.

Here, tonight, with the fire going loud and brilliant, Milton tightens up. Abe cracks a loose grin.

"Millie," he says.

"Fuck you, Abraham."

Abe smiles—a cold dagger in the night.

" 'Sup, No Dick?"

Nolan gives Abe the finger, which elicits a hoot. Abe slaps his hand against his thick thigh and then stands up. "Beer's in the cooler, ladies."

"God, I hate him," Nolan says with a shake of his head.

"Could have fooled me," Milton says.

"Well." There's nothing to say. They're here. Milton finds a place under some trees and squats. Around the tree from him, some skinny kid is going at it with a girl. Their wet kissing sounds to him like slugs being peeled apart. Nolan's standing with Abe and Tate, talking. He's gesturing broadly with his hands, telling some story or another. Abe's expression is placid and gentle. Abe used to be good—sweet, even. They were all in Sunday school together, the four of them. But then something had gone wrong in each of them, something turning suddenly hard and cold and malicious. A wildness in them waking up after a long hibernation.

Milton hears Nolan's voice over the music—he's making a sound like gunfire, spraying all the people around them with bullets made of air.

"Keep the change, you filthy animal," Nolan says, and more gunfire rains down on them. It's that scene from **Home Alone** where there's a movie playing, an old movie, and the man on the screen pulls out a gun and shoots someone who had come to betray him or something like that. Nolan aims his fingergun squarely at Milton's chest and fires as if he, too, were nothing more than an animal. The gesture's cruelty jolts him momentarily, and in an instant, an awful transfiguration: Nolan, the hunter, fierce and terrible, come to shoot them all down. Milton digs his fingers into the ground to steady himself.

There's a hand on his shoulder, and Milton jumps. A girl he doesn't know.

"Hey," she says, "isn't it your birthday?"

"How did you know?"

"I saw it online. We're friends there."

"We are?" Milton strains to remember where he has seen her face before. At school, maybe, or out with everyone like tonight. But she is plainly pretty, pale and blond with delicate features. He's familiar with the look, everything straightened and cleared, frosted and dyed and perfect.

"We are," she says. Her voice is musical and high. "I'm Edie."

"Milton."

"Oh, I know. Happy birthday, by the way."

"Thanks," he says. Even though he doesn't ask her to or make a gesture that's welcoming or open, she sits next to him.

"Shouldn't you be out celebrating?"

"What do you think I'm doing?" he asks, and she rolls her eyes at him.

"Some celebration."

"I know, it's great."

"Then why are you here?" she asks.

"Nolan wanted to come, and I couldn't tell him no."

"That boy," she says, and it makes Milton lean toward her.

"What do you mean?"

"Oh, I don't know. People have a hard time telling him no. Or he has a hard time hearing it, I should say." There's something resigned about the way that sounds to him, and Milton wants to press her on it, but before he can, Abe and Nolan have made their way over.

"You can't sit around here talking all night. We gotta get you high," Nolan says. Then, noticing Edie, he smiles. "Hello, Edie."

"Nolan," she drawls.

"How you been?"

"Oh, you know." She shrugs.

"How's your sister?" Nolan asks, and something mean catches the underside of his words. But Edie sighs, rises from the ground. Abe snickers to himself nearby. Edie turns her head subtly, her eyes ranging over all their faces. They are not alone. They are at the edge of the crowd. The holler and hoop of the others. The music pressing down on them all, percussive, driving in the way Nolan remembers church music to be. So solid in its presence that he had once asked his mother if it was the Holy Spirit, and she had laughed and said, **No, boy, that's just the drums**. Edie's shoulders open and she tilts her chin up stiffly.

"Better every day," she says firmly.

"Glad to hear it," Nolan says. "Praise the Lord."

"On high," she says, her voice a wavering song. Then, with a glance at Milton, a failing smile, she slides between Nolan and Abe, and then she is gone.

"What was that all about?" Milton asks, but Nolan has already turned away from him toward Abe.

"You got it?"

"Tate."

"Then I need to see Tate. Don't go any-where," Nolan says directly to Milton, who nods. He, too, leaves. Abe leans against the tree and folds his arms behind his head. Milton's digging in the ground with his shoe.

"When are you going to get it over with?" Abe asks.

"Get what over with?"

Abe smiles. He comes away from the tree toward Milton, and Milton takes a step back, roots himself against the ground, bracing. Abe leans down and whispers, wet against Milton's ear: "When are you going to suck his dick? It's getting pathetic."

"Fuck you, Ahab," Milton says, but he's shaken by it. For a moment he worries that Abe's voice has carried to Nolan, who is just a few feet away.

"Oh, it's not me you want to fuck," he says, licking his lips.

"I'm not the fag."

"I didn't say you were," Abe says, calmly, evenly. "I said you wanted to suck Nolan's dick."

"Please shut up."

"There's no shame," he says. "I mean, I don't blame you. It's nice."

"Oh, and what do you know?"

"Plenty," he says, and then steps backward. There's a small drop-off, where you slide down until you're standing under the crest of the hill. Abe vanishes. Milton follows him through the veil of gray night, down the grassy hill.

"What are you talking about?"

"You know what I'm talking about," Abe says, even as he's reaching for Milton's pants to undo them. Milton grabs Abe's thick wrists, stills him.

"What is it you think I know?"

"Oh, you have to know," Abe says. "About Nolan and those girls and me. He had to have told you."

"No," Milton says, his mouth dry. "I don't know anything about it." Abe grips him through his pants, and he's hard, against his will, he's hard. Abe starts to pump his dick through his jeans, and he smirks.

"Well, last week, he says, hey, bud, I got

this girl. She and her friend are a couple of freaks, do you want to come over? I say, yes. I come over. They're already naked, going at it, licking each other all over like a bunch of cats."

"You're lying," Milton says. Abe guffaws, soft and deep. He pushes open Milton's jeans and grips his bare cock. Abe's hand is warm and rough.

"I'm not. One of the girls gets real antsy about it. Nolan's already poking around inside of her, and she's like, no, you gotta stop, you gotta stop. And Nolan is like, let me finish, and I'll stop."

Abe is pumping him harder and faster, rough. It hurts, but it also feels good, and it's that first time that someone has wanted to touch him, has seemed to need it the way Abe does. His eyes are hungry and wet.

"So he's like, no, I'm gonna finish, and she's whining and crying, and I'm like, shut that bitch up, I'm losing my hard-on, and her friend is like, no, no please, let us go home, and I'm like, shit, man, it's not worth it."

Milton pulls away from Abe, but Abe has

gripped the back of his neck and kisses him now, hard. He pulls away again, and this time, Abe has had it, pushes him up against the hill, leans in and growls.

"What's your problem, man? You want this or not? They're gonna be here any minute."

"Want what?" Milton asks, and then, looking down, remembers his cock and how hard it is, and how damp. But there is also the hellish image of those girls in that room, trapped with them, wanting nothing but to go home, to be anywhere but there. "I don't want anything."

"Then do mine," he says, pushing his hips forward. "Come on, it's almost there anyway."

"No," Milton says.

"Come on." Abe takes Milton's hand and puts it on his dick, and after a moment, Milton does it, gives in, takes Abe into his hand, and strokes him until he comes quietly, his face nestled in the crook of Milton's neck.

. . .

TATE AND NOLAN slide down the hill and find them sitting on the ground.

"Got the shit," Nolan says. Milton can barely look at him. Nolan sits on a rock next to him, and Milton tries not to breathe because he cannot trust himself not to turn the air into words. Nolan rolls a joint and hands it to Milton. "Your birthday, you start."

Milton lights up first, even though he can still feel the joint from earlier in the day. He takes a long inhale. He hands the joint off to Nolan, holds the smoke inside, lets it build. Then he lets it glide out, slow and easy.

"What were you and Edie talking about?" Nolan asks.

"She wished me a happy birthday," he says.

"Is that all?"

"Yeah—how do you know her?"

"I don't. Not really. I know her sister better," Nolan says, and there's a not a crack in his voice or his face, nothing to suggest anything more than a passing acquaintance. Abe chokes on the joint. Nolan shrugs casually. He takes a hit off the joint. The red bead of its lit end is angry with heat, like a sore.

"How do you know her sister?" Milton asks, watching Nolan breathe smoke out into the air through his mouth and nose, his eyes closed, as if in a state of ecstasy. The calm that comes with the edge of pleasure after pain has given way to something sweeter. Abe takes the joint from Nolan, and there's a pause, a silence rising out of the smoke. "How do you know her sister?" Milton repeats, and this time Nolan opens his eyes and pins Milton with a sharp, direct look. There's confusion in his gaze, suspicion, annoyance.

"Why do you want to know so bad?"

"I don't."

"Is that so?"

"It is."

"Ladies," Abe cuts across them, making a chopping motion with his hand. He's got the joint pinched to the corner of his mouth. "Let's not get carried away here."

"Who's getting carried away?" Nolan says.

"Okay, okay," Tate says, and he makes to snatch the joint from Abe's mouth, but Abe swats him hard across the face, so hard that there's no way it's a joke, there can be no way back from it. Tate puts his palm to his cheek, slides it down to his lip, where there's already blood. Abe hisses, leans forward to inspect his hand, which must be hurting him now, the impact of it. Milton tenses, glances at Nolan, who is looking at them all as if from some vast distance, as if he's already on the other side of what is to come and is looking at them with pity. Nolan leans forward and puts his chin in his hands. Milton feels a hot, hard knot press down against the back of his throat.

"Pussy," Abe says to Tate, who is not crying, just blotting the blood from his mouth with his fingertips.

"Fuck you," Tate says, spitting.

"You can't take a lick? One little slap and you're bleeding like a pussy. Fuck."

"That's enough," Nolan says.

"Oh, that's enough."

"Abe," Nolan says.

"Abe. Listen to you. You're a bigger faggot than Millie and Titty Tate both."

Heat fills Milton's nostrils, and his vision momentarily blurs. He puts his knuckles into the bulk of his thigh and grunts.

"Just a couple of little nigger fags," Abe spits.

The light from the fire is distant and inadequate. Milton leans forward to catch Abe by his throat. Abe's eyes switch to him suddenly, widen, and then go slender with hatred. He smirks, the heft of his shoulders opening up. He's leaning toward Milton, too. Their fingers brush, but before they can get a solid hold on each other, something hard strikes the back of Abe's head and he gives a little jerk. The impact is dull, abbreviated. There and gone again, hardly discernible at all.

Milton's gut drops. Tate leaps up, breathing hard. Abe watches him, perfectly still despite having been jarred suddenly into motion. Nolan hangs over him. He's still holding the rock in his hands. It's the size of an apple. His face is pale and smooth. Then Milton sees it all happen, as if at once: Tate rushing, Abe tumbling backward, Nolan reaching out to grab him, and that horrible, horrible burst of sound, a guttural roar, and then there is blood running along the edges of Abe's face. It's hard to tell where it's coming from. His scalp? His nose? His eyes? His cheeks? Where, where is the source? It's warm and slick, sticky as it oozes out of him, gathering into torrents that fill with dirt as he moans and writhes. Milton gets his sweater off and blots the blood the best he can. He tries to get Abe's face clean. Abe's eyes dart around quickly, in fear, in flight, in pain. He's on the ground, laid out, twitching, convulsing, and the three of them are trying their best to get the bleeding under control, but they don't know where it's coming from. It's hard to know, in the dark, with their clumsy hands, where to press to stop the insides from leaking out. Abe fights them, thrashes on the ground. Tate keeps muttering, "Fuck, fuck, fuck." And Nolan's straddling Abe to try to keep him still, saying, "Abe, please Abe, stop, chill, fuck, chill." But it's Milton with the sweater trying to find and plug the source of the blood. It's Milton who eventually feels the loose plate of bone shifting under his scalp, and when he looks up, Nolan's staring right at him, his pupils wide, as if he's been suddenly thrust into the light from some vast, deep water. Abe's hand lands on Milton's arm again, his fingers stiff, his nails piercing Milton's skin. Abe's eyes widen, and his groans turn to something like the lowing of cattle. His eyes then roll to the back of his head, and he seizes one hard time, goes so still and rigid that for a moment, none of them dares to breathe, dares to do anything. They wait, holding on to Abe, as if that alone could bring him back to himself. He jerks again. Fills with motion, and they all exhale. Nolan turns to Tate and says, "Call a fucking ambulance." Milton holds his sweater to Abe's head, holds it as still as he can and tries, with his eyes squeezed shut, to imagine himself far away from all of this. From Abe and Tate, from Nolan, from his parents, from himself. Anywhere else. Anywhere else.

MILTON DOESN'T PUT the sweater with the dried blood back on. There's too much of Abe on him already by the time they load him into the back of the ambulance, groaning and gummy. Milton leans against the side of a tree at the edge of the park. He feels like he's made of something insubstantial. Nolan is coming toward him through the twilight of the cop car headlights. He's just given his statement on the matter, probably. Milton had walked away after giving his, unable to stomach the way he knew Nolan could effortlessly tell a lie. They were all standing around, and Abe must have tumbled off the side of the hill. No, sir, they weren't drinking. Freak accident. Tate had gone home, chewing his fingers raw, eaten up with nerves. Nolan, their fearless leader.

Nolan reaches Milton, looking tired, run down. He smells like blood. Like a wild thing. Like when they used to play in the woods and come home smelling like wildcats, their mothers said, wrinkling their noses. Half raised, half animal.

Nolan drops down to the ground and sits among the roots of the tree, and Milton wants to join him down there, to put an arm around his shoulder, to hold him close. Milton hands him the yellow hat from before. They're both a little shocked it's not covered in blood. Nolan lets out a snort.

"Oh, thanks."

"Sure thing."

"Jesus," Nolan says, shaking his head. Milton kicks one of the roots.

"Think he'll be okay?"

"Some birthday."

Milton's fingers are still sticky. He's got blood caked under his fingernails.

"Fucking Abe," Nolan says, a wet creak of sympathy in his voice. "Ah, well."

"You really did a number on him."

"Seems like I did."

"You all right?"

"What do you think, Milton? I bashed Abe's head in. How do you think I feel?"

"I wish I knew," Milton says, which makes Nolan sigh loudly. He picks up a loose rock and hurls it into the night.

"Man, I'm tired. Would you just spit it out already?"

"I'm leaving," Milton says.

"Well, fine. You smell like shit anyway."

"No, I mean I'm leaving this spring. My parents are sending me away."

"Fuck. Where?"

"Idaho," Milton says. "They're sending me there because I get into all this shit here, and they want to fix my fucking life."

"Maybe then you'll stop being such a little bitch," Nolan says, and there's a hint of levity in his voice.

"Oh, great, can't wait," Milton says. "Cannot wait."

"Hey, come on, Milton. It's been a terrible night already."

"I can't be here anymore," Milton says.

"What does that mean?"

"What I said. You coming? Staying? I can't be here," Milton says. But that isn't exactly what he means. What he really wants to say: Come with me. Come with me. Let's go. Let's get away from here. Let's go be by ourselves. Let's go. But he cannot ask that. And if he cannot ask it, Nolan cannot and will not answer him.

"I'll stay a little longer," Nolan says. There are still three or four cops in the distance, watching the last of the smoke trickle out of the barrels. They put out the fire. They sent everyone home. But Nolan wants to stay here among the wreckage of the night, this lost evening. There's a kind of sadness on his face, a flicker of regret, but Milton is not sure if the regret is for what's happened to Abe or because the evening's been busted up early. Nolan spits off to the side, kicks a few stones down the hill. "Maybe I'll hit you up later. We can try this birthday thing again."

"All right," Milton says.

"Or you could stay, too," Nolan says.

"No, I can't," Milton says.

"I guess not," Nolan says, giving Milton a long, slow smile that leaves Milton chilled.

Milton turns, moves underneath the black-stubble cedar and pine trees, the scent of burning paper wafting after him. He cuts into the woods, which are cloaked in a sooty mist.

Milton runs without thinking, without caring what he will emerge into on the other side. What he craves is the sensation of distance traveled, raw mileage. It suddenly seems to him, snapping twigs and getting whipped by lashing vines, that Idaho is not the worst thing that could happen to him, that even if he were to stay, Nolan would already be lost to him.

Milton reaches the other side of the woods. The night is thickening overhead. The mountain looms. He can see his house from here. His stomach turns. He retches. His throat is hot with vomit. His eyes water. In the distance, he can hear branches breaking. The woods shift with soft, hushed voices of motion. He leaves the woods entirely and steps back onto the street.

Milton thinks again of all the homes and their interchangeable lives and wishes that it were as easy as stopping at someone else's door, knocking, and switching places with the version of himself who lived there. If only he could enter into another version of his life, one in which things have not gone quite as horribly awry—if only he could pass from this world into the next or into the next, some other place without Abe or Tate, some place where he and Nolan might be as they were, though perhaps they have always been this way, full of violence and calamity.

Maybe he's had it wrong this whole time—it's not that Abe and Tate bring it out of Nolan, and it's not that Nolan brings it out of them. They're always in the thick of violence. It moves through them like the Holy Ghost might—except the Holy Ghost never moved anybody to rape a girl or ruin her life. The Holy Ghost never moved anybody to bash a boy's head in. There was some other god, then, a god for whom the spilling of blood was a prayer, an act of devotion. And they've been praying to that god their whole lives.

The streetlights glow, and bits of grass stick up coarsely from the pools of shadow below them. Milton puts the butt of his hand to his eye, which is throbbing, low and deep. The pressure in his chest intensifies, and he thinks, in that moment, of cutting himself open to let it out. **Toward home, then**, he says to himself. **Toward home.** His steps are stiff, ragged, hard, but he keeps going. One foot in front of the other until he's at his door. The lights are off. He unlocks the door and pushes it open with his hip. Then it's down the stairs, into the warm cave of the basement. He tugs on the cord and the basement is once again bathed in dim, yellow light. His mouth is sour and skunky from vomit and spit. His hand feels filmy and gritty, from Abe's come and blood and the dirt and the grass. He glances down and sees smudges on his palm, white mucosal remnants, like he's squeezed snails or slugs. There was a time when he and Nolan were boys and playing out by the creek, when they'd

catch frogs and other small animals and bash
them with rocks until they resembled nothing like themselves or anything else. And
when they got older, they shot deer and
pulled fish from the river and held them up,
grinning into cameras, smiling like **Look
what I've done**.

Milton turns and sees along the back wall
of the basement his father's work stand.
Hard, flat wood with metal rivets to keep it
in place. A string of knives hang along the
wall. Milton puts his hand against one
medium-size knife, touches its cold, silver
surface. He takes it down and holds it
against the fat of his palm. **Nolan**, he thinks.
He slides the knife up, though not breaking
skin. He presses it to the crease below his
fingers. **Nolan**, he thinks again, and he puts
the back of his hand against the table in the
corner. He couldn't cut his fingers off even
if he wanted to. Not with this knife, its edge
too dull, his bones too thick.

Bones. Milton smirks to himself. There's a
thought. What he wants is not to maim
himself but rather to pry open the world,

bone it, remove the ugly hardness of it all, the way one might take the spine from a deer or a fish or some other animal snared. Milton lifts the knife from his hand and stabs it into the table. When he was younger, he killed senselessly because the thrill of the act was like dipping his face into a clear, rushing stream. He didn't have to consider the lives he ended. It was as if they were merely parts of a game, tokens to trade with his friends. If there was any merciful part of his childhood, it was that, the cleanness of it, how the act didn't taint them, how the violence seemed to leave no trace at all. But he's older now, and the meat of the world is full of bones. Everybody's walking around all the time full of bones, full of jagged shards, flecks of hardness that need taking out and would, upon swallowing, prompt a person to choke. There's no mercy in the basement tonight.

Nolan, Milton thinks, and he squats by the table and thumbs the numb place left by the knife. He digs his nail into the thin, translucent space left by the knife until he sees the blood pooling beneath the skin. The pain abates quickly and leaves behind a memory so friable, so delicate, that it's like blowing an eyelash and making a wish.

Idaho.

Milton lies down on the floor. The oblong shapes of boxed-up boyhood toys throw curious shadows that shift along the walls and the raw, unfinished struts of the basement. They look like the muscles of some enormous animal, getting ready to leap, to strike, to snatch him down into its shadowy belly.

MASS

ALEKSANDER IGOREVICH SHAPOVALOV—
Sasha to those who loved him most in the
world and Alek to everyone else, including
himself—stared at the radiographic scans
presented to him by his doctor in the intimate corner examination room and tried to
think of what he'd tell his mother.

"There's a good chance it' s nothing," Dr.
Ngost said. "But you'll have to get a biopsy."

"A biopsy," Alek said.

"Yes. We'll take a small piece of the mass and examine it. Then we'll know more."

"But I don't feel sick," Alek said. "I just came because of this cough. I don't feel sick."

"There's a chance that you aren't. There's a chance it's just a mass that we can take out. It happens sometimes. The body is full of odd turns."

"Full of odd turns," Alek repeated— a nonsense phrase, too casual. Full of odd turns, like a clock or some other machine, routes and paths inside him swerving this way and that, and then suddenly an aberration, a deviation, a mass swelling up from below.

Dr. Ngost put a hand on Alek's arm, and Alek turned his head toward him slowly, away from the scan that showed his insides, ghostly white on a black backdrop.

"One step at a time," he said warmly. "Biopsy. Then we know."

Alek almost repeated the doctor's words again but stopped himself by biting the very tip of his tongue. He nodded firmly a couple of times, then climbed from the bench. He pulled up his jeans beneath the crinkling paper gown. The room was cool as a small cave. Dr. Ngost watched him dress, and when they shook hands, Dr. Ngost held on just a little longer: "Don't worry. It's going to be okay," he said.

ON THE BUS, Alek considered calling his brothers. Grigori was a first-year surgical resident at Mass Gen, and Igor was starting at Columbia medical school. They would know how to explain it to their mother best, how to articulate the parameters of the thing in a way that wouldn't scare her. It seemed foolish not to call them. The bus turned onto the more corporate corner of Capitol Square. All that chrome and glass against the slate-gray winter sky. Alek had a seat to himself, which felt like a minor miracle. Downtown was emptying before it began to fill again. Luminescent snowdrifts covered bike racks and lampposts.

He had pulled up the text chain with

Grigori—they hadn't texted in months, since he'd first arrived in the Midwest, to say that he'd made it. He'd sent a couple pics of the apartment he'd found. It had come furnished and felt lived in. He'd sent both Grigori and Igor pictures of the tub and the room with its decent but kind of soft mattress. And they'd texted back **cool** and **nice** and **faggot style** :).

When they were younger, Grigori's favorite pastime was to pull hairs from Alek's body. Igor held him while he twisted and tried to get loose. Then Grigori plucked out his eyelashes one at a time, fine white hairs invisible the moment they left his body. Alek remembered the little shooting stars of pain with each hair. He remembered Igor's sweaty hands holding him down. He remembered the damp odor of their panting filling the closet.

As they grew older, the punishments evolved. Soon, it wasn't enough to pull the hairs out of Alek's body. They had to burn him, too. By then, both Igor and Grigori were smoking in the alleyway behind their apartment building after and before school, when their parents weren't watching, sending up white trails. Alek caught them one day and ran to tell their parents, his body thrumming with the pleasure of finally having a secret on them, some measure of power. But as he turned to run, he didn't see their bodies growing taut with pursuit. They caught him before he even reached the end of the alley. Grigori came around first, pushed Alek up against the wall. A cigarette jutted out of his thick lips.

"Ah, Sasha," he taunted. "Sasha with his pretty hair."

Igor whistled as he came up next to him. He flicked some ashes to the ground. Grigori first pinched Alek's nose and then caught him under the chin, gripping his throat.

"What are you going to do, huh?"

"Nothing," Alek said hoarsely. Grigori had grown five inches that year, and he was terrifying. His body smelled musky, like fear itself. Grigori shoved Alek's head back against the wall, and suddenly the alley, the ground, the sky, his brother's faces, and even the very stench of the garbage swam, started spinning around and around. The dull thud of his skull on concrete filled his ears. He felt then that Grigori could have done him any kind of harm without the slightest bit of remorse. Grigori, his own brother, could have kept hitting his head against the wall until there was nothing left on his little shoulders but a meaty pulp. He was seven or eight then, and they were older and stronger. Back then, strength seemed to be the only justification anyone needed to do anything.

Grigori took the cigarette from Igor's mouth. Igor looked disappointed and angry. Then Grigori pushed its burning tip into Alek's arm. The pain was immediate and infinite, and it hurt so bad that he was sure it would never stop, that it would go on burning him forever and ever. Grigori bared his teeth as he twisted the burning cigarette into his arm. Alek didn't even scream. He couldn't muster a sound loud enough.

They were not as bad now as they were then. There had been minor skirmishes as

Alek grew stronger and better able to defend himself, and their relationship had resolved into a steady, tense stalemate. Perhaps it was always this way with brothers, a truce brokered only after an equilibrium of physical strength had been met, as if the potential for mutual destruction were the only thing that kept them from tearing each other limb from limb.

Love was not between them. He could call them, one or both. He knew what they would say. There would be a long silence at first, a curious pause, and then, **You're such a little baby, it's a cough, that's it, all you do is complain, such a whiny baby, grow up, stop being such a little faggot, stop being such a girl, little sister crying about a cough.** They did not trust him to know anything, even about his own body. They would want to speak to Dr. Ngost and then to the specialist to whom he had been referred. Only then would they believe him.

The bus didn't actually go through downtown, not to where Alek lived. He got out on the other side of the square and walked down Mifflin, toward the lake. He lived in an old apartment building, right at the head of frat row, with a guy named Mike who was from near Eau Claire. He had decamped earlier that week for fall break on his family farm, and Alek had been pleased to have the apartment to himself.

Since he'd developed the cough, Mike, who was nice in a passive-aggressive midwestern sort of way, had politely inquired as to whether Alek had seen a doctor. And, if not, would he consider doing it soon? And then he'd said, **My grandma suggests a ginger tea. She sent some ginger.** He'd even left a pack of cough drops on the kitchen counter with a note for Alek, saying **Help yourself!** But as the weeks went on, and the cough did not abate, Mike had grown irritable and silent. He didn't leave his bedroom. He didn't eat at the kitchen island anymore. He stopped offering to split the groceries with Alek, and when it came time to pay their renter's insurance, Alek had to slide his portion under Mike's door in an envelope.

The apartment was drafty, but they'd already shoved stray socks and old shirts into every corner they could find. There was nothing to be done about it. The bathroom was perhaps the best room, with its deep tub and old tile. During the more intense part of the dance season, when Alek was doing three-a-day full run-throughs and two classes, one in the morning and one in the evening, he came home with huge bags of ice, which he poured into the tub and sank himself into. Or he made warm baths with Epsom salt. He didn't have to make the trip across campus to use the rehab facility in the new rec center. He could make his own ice baths at home.

He ran the tub full of water, just short of skin-stripping hot. He tried to wash off the smell of the doctor's office, that bitter, burned hazelnut coffee smell. That smell like antiseptic. It was true, what he had told the doctor: He was not sick. He didn't feel ill. It was just a persistent cough, something rattling but not painful. He coughed and coughed, through morning ballet, through his classes, through rehearsal, through dinner, through sleep. There was nothing that his cough didn't infiltrate. He could feel the cough coming on even now in the bath, gathering at the base of his lungs like something caught there that he couldn't expel, a kind of fibrous feeling spreading out along the edges of his ribs.

His mother was going to lose her shit. He squeezed his eyes shut and tried not to think of it, but there was the image of her face. Her bright blue eyes. The stern teacher's eyebrows. He saw the play of every muscle in her face, the relaxation in her jaw that suggested grief, the fleeting alleviation of pressure in the left temple. The subtle slackening of her throat. The faucet dripped. He tried to see the space as it was cleaved by each drop, the surface rippling and then going still again. He tried to breathe.

Since Alek had started dance, he had lived in perpetual fear of disappointing his mother and father. His brothers were good at science, like their parents. His mother taught earth science in high school. His father was a plumber at first, then an engineer. His brothers had attended the advanced science and math magnet school. Alek had attended the elementary school, and had very few prospects of following them into the science and math school, but he was put into an after-school arts program by chance, and the teacher, always on the lookout for boy dancers, scouted him.

At first, his parents had only stared in disbelief. Clumsy Sasha? Hyperactive Sasha? Unfocused, lazy Sasha? No, impossible. Yes, the teacher said. He had excellent balance, a good ear for music, for timing, rhythm. He could be a good dancer one day.

Good would never have been enough for his father. If you tried your best and all you were was good, then it was time to try something else. His father believed in the optimal, and if you weren't able to get to the highest level, then you were doing something for which you were not optimally suited. Good was an insult. Good was mediocre.

And so, every lesson, Alek tried to be

more than good. Every lesson, he tried to be perfect. Every position, every line, every angle, every turn, everything perfect. If he didn't get something right, he tried harder, again and again, each time imagining himself going sharper and sharper, until he was so sharp he felt he might cut himself. It was a ferocity in him that he'd never known he possessed—a ferocity that **gave** him something—and for the first time, he felt his parents were proud of him, that he wasn't just messing up.

It was not an original story. Every ballet parent was a monster of ambition. Every ballet parent knew the terrible math. Only a few people got to be elite dancers. Everything else was just preparation for a time when dance would be something they used to do, a person they used to be. Starting ballet was like entering a second, more intense gravitational field. At any moment, an injury could end it all. Or the mind could snap and there you went, done, burned out, exhausted.

A mass in his body meant that something had gone wrong, and if that was true, he might not be able to dance again. If he couldn't dance again, what would he do? And there was the possibility that the mass meant cancer, and cancer might mean death. What would he tell his mother? What would she do? How could he tell her this, so soon after his father had died in a way that was somehow both slow and quick?

He'd be betraying her.

Alek climbed out of the bath and wrapped a towel around himself. He made a sandwich and sat on his bed. The afternoon was over. He had a view of the lake from his window. People were skating. Their voices were lost to him, but he could hear the sounds of their happiness.

THE REHEARSAL HALL was empty when he arrived. How long would it be before the evening class began? True, there were fewer people in the evening class because, unlike the morning class, attendance was not compulsory. Instead of one of the main ballet masters, evening class was led by a retired senior soloist. The evening class was mainly a way of working out things that had gone wrong during the day or had been skipped in the morning.

It was during an evening class that he had first begun to cough, back in the summer. The cough had come on slowly, small little fits of tension in his chest, an irritating heat, a scratchiness in his throat and chest. At first, he didn't notice at all, or he didn't think very much of it. In the morning he was phlegmy, spitting yolky goop into the sink or the toilet. But he couldn't get it all out. Inside he felt both wet and dry.

In class that day, though, it was something else entirely. During a five-minute break, he'd gone out into the air to clear his lungs. All night, he'd been a beat behind, his movements dragging. In summer, this part of the country was slow to darken. He watched the trees in the distance. He took a deep breath, but the air wouldn't move. It came into contact with something hard in his chest, and he tried again to breathe, to push the air down, to force it, but it wouldn't go. It was like all those years ago, when he used to sit and hold his breath. He remembered the game he used to play then, the locking down of his diaphragm, the restraint of it, the slow burn working its way up and out. But now his body was refusing him, betraying him, acting of its own volition.

Then the coughing came, and it was like choking on air itself, as if air were made of fine wool, as if it were fibrous, tickling his throat, exciting a gag reflex. Alek put his hand to the wall outside the low building that housed the ballet studio. He could feel his stomach muscles contracting, a shuddering heave up against a wall inside him, solid and unyielding. He couldn't breathe for coughing, coughing until he could taste blood, but nothing splashed the gravel below his feet. His body was still hot from dance, sore, aching, and he gripped his stomach and squeezed his body with all his strength, as if he could force the cough out. He saw spinning clots of light in front of him, stars from some inverted galaxy behind his eyelids.

A couple of other dancers stood nearby,

drinking from clear water bottles. They looked his way at first and then away. But when he doubled over, they came to him and put their palms against his back, which was damp with sweat. They leaned down to him, and he could smell their sour scent, their breath like smoke. He strained to look at them. Who was it that was looking at him? A girl, blond: Sophie. She put her small fingers around his wrist and tried to draw him up.

"Are you okay?" she asked. "Are you all right?"

He couldn't speak. She slid her palm down his forearm to his elbow and then motioned for him to sit. But he kept coughing and tried to turn away so that he wouldn't get anything on her. Still, she pulled at him, insisting that he should sit down, and he did. He slid down into the warm gravel, felt the stones through his tights, knew that their azure dust would cling to the spandex. All over, he was on fire. The sun, hazy, distant, white on the horizon, the trees, spindly fibers whirling in the distance.

Eventually the coughing subsided—it had been bronchial in nature, that hollow, echoing sound—and he could breathe again. He felt stunned, slapped, like he'd been dipped into some other world tucked just under this one and brought back too quickly. Sophie was sitting next to him, one hand gripping his, the other making circles on his back.

A bead of sweat clung to the corner of her mouth. A red clip kept hair off her face. He had always admired her, thought her talent terrifying. Sophie. She gave him a tentative, sad smile. She let him drink from her bottle. The water was flat and warm. It had a coppery taste.

"We better get inside," she said.

"All right," he said, and he let her take him by the arm again, to get him on his feet. But then he was ready to stand on his own, or else he didn't want her to think that he couldn't. She put her arm around his waist to steady him and they went into the hall, where they could already hear the music starting up again.

How long had it been since he'd spoken to Sophie? Alek sat on the floor now and began to stretch. First his legs. Then his back. He stretched to the tips of his toes, pressing himself flush against the tops of his thighs, holding the position for as long as he could. He could feel the cough gathering along the edge of his lungs, that tickling heat. He suppressed it as best he could. He counted to twenty and released the stretch, then lay on his back. The cough came quickly, loudly, and filled the empty room in the way a lonely prayer might fill a cathedral.

The last time that he'd spoken to Sophie was at the end of the summer. They were sleeping in his bed, her body tight to his. The fan drew the heavy air through the window, animated it slightly, and cooled their skin. They slept naked on top of his thin sheet. Sophie's hair writhed in the fan's breeze, and he lay there, watching her sleep.

He had sensed a distancing between them for a couple of weeks, ever since they had seen Charles at the bonfire that night after the concert in the park. Sophie left Alek's lap to speak to Charles, and he had been forced to watch it all unfurl. Charles, thick, as if cut from the side of a mountain. Charles with his decent but unremarkable technique. Charles with his curls and handsome face—he and Sophie had gone around together for as long as Alek had known them both, but Sophie had surprised him by letting him kiss her the night after the cough began. Sophie had let him put his hand on her lower back and draw her to him, had let him feel so much bigger for it, in control of both of their bodies. It was like partnering, how one only appears to surrender to the illusion of grace. And then he'd thought, perhaps, that she liked him enough, that he was enough for her. That she and Charles were done. They made small dinners. They spoke together in low voices outside the practice hall. They held hands in the casual, easy way that comes to people in relationships. Alek had begun to imagine a lifetime of such minor joys, small intimacies, which were all he could manage. They would be dancers and in love. But when she left him by the fire to stand next to Charles, he had known that the thing between them, for all its easiness and the joy it brought him, would end. And so for weeks he had watched her recede. Watched her from the back of morning exercises, from the back of the library as she looked over old choreography. Watched her over dinner and coffee, even watched her buy cigarettes from the corner store, waiting for her to turn to him and smile and shrug. Waiting and watching. The last time he spoke to Sophie was some morning, when she was putting on her clothes and tying up her hair, shrugging. He watched the expanse of her back vanish into her shirt, and she turned, kissed his palm, and said she would call him later. But she didn't.

VOICES IN THE HALL. Alek rolled onto his side, could smell the fresh polish of the floor. He pushed himself up, rolled his shoulders, and spread his legs. He leaned forward. The door slid open—Mats and Octavius came into the room. They were talking loudly about something, about someone, and Alek tried not to listen, but their voices came closer and closer until the two of them were standing over him. Octavius's purple-black skin almost gleamed. Mats was shorter than Octavius, who was a giant for a dancer, a slash of a man. They wore sweaters from East Coast colleges that neither had attended, hand-me-downs from their parents. Mats in a blue Yale sweater and Octavius in a crimson Harvard sweatshirt. They'd known each other since they were little boys and had attended the same prep schools. Their parents knew one another, belonged to the same African American Ivy League associations. Mats and Octavius were as close as one could come to an arranged marriage in this country. The two of them were in love with each other, but seemed not to know it yet, or so Alek thought. Mainly because they never seemed to be in love with each other at the same time, seemed to always be pointed past one another. In the fall, Mats could think of nothing other than Octavius, his kindness, his body, his winning shyness. But that fall, Octavius was in love with a white boy named James from one of his poetry seminars. And in the spring, Mats had moved on to Charles, and Octavius fell in love with the space left when Mats lost interest. That is, Octavius found Mats to be indifferent to him for the first time in his life, so he reacted by falling deeply in love with him. They each, in different ways and on different days, spoke to Alek about the other. **Octavius is so stupid. Why doesn't he get it? I'm in his room all the time. I'm lying here, half naked, basically wide open to him, and he does nothing, nothing. Why? Or, Mats is so cold to me these days. Why is he like this? He's always gone now. He's always out. What's going on with him and Charles?**

"Can you believe it?"

"Charlie and Sophie, you mean?" Alek asked, leaning back on his palms. He flexed his leg from left to right. Mats sat down next to him and started to stretch, too. Octavius took the spot on the other side of Alek.

"They're back together," Mats said over Alek's head to Octavius, who let out a whistle. "I mean, it was pretty obvious, but consider it **confirmed**."

"I guess some people can't make up their minds," Alek said flatly, meaning nothing at all by it, but then Mats turned to look at him with a gleaming hurt in his eyes, and he realized he'd strayed too close to the bone. "Oh, I'm sorry."

"It's fine," Mats said, voice leaping. "It's so fine. Don't even worry about it."

"About what?" Octavius said, cutting his eyes across the two of them.

"Please," Mats said, rolling his eyes, this time putting a fine point at the end of the word.

Alek coughed into the crook of his arm, and the noise overrode everything else.

"You said you'd go to the doctor."

"I did," Alek said. "I went."

"And?"

"It's nothing," he said, tossing it off as if he hadn't a care in the world. "It's fine."

"It's been weeks? Months? Is it fine?"

"I knew someone with a cough like that once," Octavius said. "Turned out to be a pretty nasty infection."

"Well, the doctor said I was fine, so I'm fine."

Mats dug an elbow into Alek's side, which dislodged some hard knot and made the coughing worse. He could taste blood again. The world blotted, shifting. He took a deep breath.

"You don't look so hot, Alek," Mats said. "Maybe you should go home."

"I've never missed a class."

"You should go home," Octavius pressed. "Do you want me to walk with you?"

"You just want to cut class," Alek said wryly, trying to smile, but there was a hard, jagged heat running down his body, and it hurt to breathe.

"Come on, let's go," Octavius said, reaching for him, but Alek pulled away.

"No, it's fine."

Mats put his palm to Alek's back, and Alek looked away from him because he didn't want to see Mats's fine features screwed up in a mask of worry. Alek was always causing so much trouble.

"I'll go, I'll go," he said. "You two stay. Cavort, whatever it is you do." He pulled himself up to a standing position, put his palms up as if to say that he had been disarmed by their care, by their love, and he gathered his things and left.

ON THE WAY HOME, he paused in the cold and dialed Grigori. Night was not yet upon them. The sky was a bowl of blue light pierced from some other, outer light glowing on the horizon. He stood outside his favorite coffee shop and thought of going in, but he didn't because it would be loud there and Grigori would complain about the noise on the line.

"Hello?" came Grigori's voice, a bellow even at low volume.

"Grigori," Alek said.

"What do you want?"

Alek paused on the line. He didn't know how to begin it, his request, if it was a request. He didn't know how to say the words.

"Hello? Sasha? Hello?"

"I went to the doctor today."

"For what? You sick?"

"I've been coughing."

"So you have a cold? Flu? What?"

"I don't know," Alek said. He could feel Grigori's irritation growing.

Grigori's voice was hard when he said: "What do you mean you don't know? What did the doctor say? Who is this doctor? Some midwestern quack? Who is this? What did he say?"

"He said I might have a mass."

"Might? What mass? You a Catholic now?"

Alek wanted to laugh and to cry, both, simultaneously, but he just coughed into the phone. He tried to block the sound of it, but he could feel Grigori's judgment. Snow was falling now. It clung to his eyelashes. The streetlight was staggering into life.

"Yes, I guess, something like that."

"Like what?"

"I don't know, Grigori. I don't know. I don't know."

"So what do you want?"

"I don't know."

"Stop saying that!" Grigori shouted, but there was something more than anger or irritation in his voice this time. No, it was something worse—something like fear, which he had never seen Grigori experience. It spoke to something in him, too, spurred his own fear into life. **Stop saying that!** was a declaration, a desperate plea to speak it out of existence, and now Alek wanted to say it back to him, until they'd both said it back to each other and would never have to say another word again.

"I'm sorry," Alek said.

"Sasha—did you tell Mom?"

"No, just you."

"Just me," Grigori said. It was the first secret they'd ever had together, just the two of them. They were standing now in a world of their own.

"What do I tell her about this?"

"Nothing," Grigori said, sharply. "Absolutely nothing. You don't know anything. We don't know anything. It's nothing."

"It's nothing," Alek said.

"Do you have an appointment? What's happening next?"

"I have a scan," Alek said. "Just to see. A biopsy. To confirm. That it's nothing."

"Okay, sounds good. Do you want me to come?"

"Excuse me?"

"Hello, Space Cadet Sasha, do you want me to come?"

Alek held the phone out from himself and regarded it. It had never occurred to him that his brother might want to come and be with him, to be in any way involved. He had never considered that possibility, and now, faced with it, he didn't know what to do with it.

"You don't have to."

"I know—but do you want me to? I can. It must be scary." There was a gentleness in his voice then, a gathering calm, and he didn't seem like Alek's brother at all.

"It's not like I'm dying," Alek said, and Grigori seemed to relax.

"Yeah. You're not. It's fine. You're fine. But if you need . . . well, you know. It's fine."

"It's fine," Alek said.

There was a silence over the line, but Alek found it comforting. There was a time when he might not have, when silence would have meant being frozen out, lined up for trouble. But tonight, on the street, in the snow, it was enough. It was enough. It was enough.

"Okay, Sasha. Okay. Good night," Grigori said.

"Good night," Alek said.

Once the call clicked off, Alek held up the phone and took a picture of the capitol, all lit up, the snow falling through the streetlights, slanted and whirling. The photo had a reddish tint to it, like a faded wine stain. He looked at the photo for a

long time, cropping out a car and the awkward corner of a building, but then he
deleted the photo. He turned in the direction of the lake and took a photo of
that instead. It was blurry, hazy from the
night and from the phone's weak zoom
lens. Grayed out, slashed through with
black and white. He texted the photo
to Igor and Grigori. He watched for a
moment, until dots appeared below it, sug-
gesting that they were typing, and then
disappeared. They appeared again and
again they disappeared. The snow was still
falling. It landed on his fingers and the
screen. Melted as the dots rose and fell.
They were like a score. He could hear a
kind of music to them. Each time they
punctured the silence, it was a different
note they played.

He walked home and sat for a little while
in the living room without turning on the
light. Igor texted him: **nice.**

Alek texted back, **thx.**

U alright?

Ok

Nice

U?

Good

School okay?

Yeah

U?

Good

Nice

Coming home?

Maybe. Expensive

Me too

Maybe Christmas?

Nice

Haha

U happy out there?

U?

Haha. Nice

ANNE OF CLEVES

ON THEIR FIRST DATE, SIGRID ASKED Marta which of Henry VIII's wives she most identified with, and Marta choked on her white wine. Sigrid repeated the question, slowly, and with a dawning chill, Marta realized that she was serious.

"I don't know much about that," Marta said, and Sigrid pressed her lips together in what looked like a condescending grin. Marta didn't know much about history. She didn't know much about dating women, either. She had recently broken up with a man named Peter, after he asked her to marry him and move to Belize. Every time he kissed her, she could feel a part of herself looking away from him, toward something else that she could not then make out. But when, after three years together, he had asked her to marry him, two things suddenly resolved into sharper focus—that she had been with him only because being with him was easier than no longer being with him, and that she'd been waiting for a moment when this would no longer be the case.

Sigrid lifted her glass and examined it, but she didn't seem like she was in a rush to change the subject. She had the sturdy, upright patience of an elementary-school teacher. Her eyes were very green, Marta noticed.

"You're not much of an Anne Boleyn," Sigrid said, and the name darted through Marta's mind like a swift silver fish. There was something there, a glimmer of recognition— or, no, maybe just a desire to have the conversation over with. She had not thought much about history in some time, in years, really. She had studied chemical engineering as an undergraduate and now she worked at a waste-processing plant in Baraboo. She might have told Sigrid this, except that the look on Sigrid's face, with its precise concentration, wedged inside her like a splinter. "Definitely not Catherine Howard."

"I don't know who they are, but I'll take your word for it," Marta said. The wine was too sweet for her. She didn't much like wine. She preferred Coors or Old Milwaukee, beer of the pale, weak variety. It may have been the result of spending all her time in college around engineers, who drank shitty beer and leaned over their notebooks and parsed their calculations long into the night. She had often woken up on their couches smelling sour and raw, with rulers stuck to her thighs. That's how she had met Peter and fallen in with him: they saw each other so much that it seemed natural that they should date, and when he asked her to the movies, she'd said, Okay, all right, sounds good. On that first date with Sigrid, she was still sad about Peter, and uneasy, and if this was how dating women was going to be, a series of increasingly esoteric questions, she wasn't sure she liked it that much, either.

"This won't work," Sigrid said, and Marta felt a little pulse of fear.

"What won't work?"

"This," she said, gesturing wildly. "You retreating, falling into silence. It won't work."

"I'm sorry," Marta said. "I don't know what I'm supposed to say or do. I don't know anything about Henry the Eighth, or whoever."

"That's fine," Sigrid said.

"You say that, except I told you before, when you asked me, that I didn't know much about it. And you kept going, so I don't know."

"It's fine," Sigrid said, and she leaned over the table and crossed her arms.

"I don't know anything about any of this," Marta said, making a circle with her hand to indicate Sigrid, Sigrid's half-eaten twenty-dollar orecchiette, her own empty bowl, which had contained a fifteen-dollar Bolognese, and their table and their bread-sticks. All of it. "I don't know how to do it. These aren't even my pants." She had borrowed the wool slacks from her roommate, Katie, and Sigrid had complimented them when they'd first met outside the restaurant. She had felt guilt then, but had also felt good. It had been a long time since someone had complimented her. Even Peter, by the end of it, had stopped telling her she was pretty. He used to do it just before he slid inside her. He'd kiss her cheeks and say, "You're so pretty," and there he'd be, the blunt end of him, jabbing at the inside of her thigh, and she'd nudge herself apart to accommodate him, the way you might make room in the next chair for a stranger at the doctor's office. But Sigrid, outside the restaurant, earlier that evening, the blue veil of late winter's twilight falling all around them, wind in her curly hair, had called her pretty and complimented her outfit. She felt itchy and anxious, like a librarian—dressed as she was in a cardigan and a nice blouse and the wool slacks—but she normally wore carpenter pants or stiff polyester to the plant. Sigrid had on leggings and a skirt and a magenta top. Marta had spent the evening admiring the slim, smooth column of her neck, the way the blouse fluttered open just a little, revealing a mole on her chest, just below her collar.

But Sigrid must not have remembered complimenting the pants, because she blinked once or twice and then smiled. Marta felt a plunging sense of dread, which had also made her smile back nervously, and it was like something cracked open.

The rest of the night was easy.

SIGRID SPENT MOST of her time in the archives sifting through documents, though she was not a trained archivist. She always added that part after she talked about her day, like saying amen after a prayer. Sigrid was hard to read sometimes. She never said, **I'm tired,** or **My boss is being a real jerkhole today,** or **Someone swiped my lunch from**

the fridge, or **My eyes hurt.** Instead, Sigrid talked about the historicity of women's diaries from the late early-modern period. She said things like, **The only thing that hasn't changed is how women are surveilled. Women were the first encryption devices.** Marta did not know what Sigrid was looking for. Indeed, the whole objective of Sigrid's work seemed to be a kind of pointless looking, organized and formalized by the creation and dissemination of increasingly complicated blocks of text. When they spoke on the phone at lunch or after dinner, Marta listened to Sigrid's smooth, warm voice as she explained why it was so important that she had found a re-creation of a re-creation of a re-creation of some middle passage from a diary of some shepherdess in Scotland.

"That sounds great," Marta would say, eating her sandwich on the grassy hill behind the plant. She could see the town, its gray, scraggly mass spread thin. It was cold in those early days, but she wanted to be alone to talk to Sigrid without being overheard. She hadn't told anyone about dating women. She hadn't wanted to explain herself to anyone—not to her roommate, Katie, not to the boys at the plant, not to any of the other faceless people who made up her life. Marta felt for the first time in a long time that she had an inner self she didn't owe to anyone. Before, with Peter, living had always felt like a constant mingling of the outside and the inside, and people had worn her out just as a matter of course in the act of living, but Sigrid, in the quiet, small time they had spent together, allowed her, for a moment or two at least, to pretend she could be her own person in her own way. Even if she did not understand what Sigrid was talking about most of the time.

Marta always signed off by sighing and saying, "Well, kiddo, I better mosey." Sigrid would say, "Oh, I'm such a blabbermouth. I'm sorry. How are you? I wasted all our time." And Marta would say, as easy as anything, "I'm doing fine. It's work, you know." And they'd talk another couple of minutes, Marta looking up at the sky, taking in a bit of the pale light, enjoying being fussed over, being told to eat her vegetables and moisturize and get some good sleep.

They had not had sex and had slept in the same bed only twice in the weeks they had been seeing each other. In part this had to do with the fact that Marta lived in Baraboo and was only in Madison a few times a week, and in part it had to do with their roommates. Katie was always home, and Sigrid's roommate, a tall law student named Thad, liked to have all his friends over, all the time. It may also have had something to do with how Marta cried the first time they went home together. She hadn't been able to stop herself. The moment Sigrid kissed her, she'd started crying. Not because it was bad, but because it was so good and so right. She'd been waiting her whole life for it and hadn't even known it, and the moment she felt Sigrid's lips on hers, she'd felt a jolt, a crack of lightning in her body. She'd cried because she'd expected it to be awful, and it hadn't been. But she felt embarrassed about the kiss, and she'd asked Sigrid if she could just lie there next to her, if it was all right just to be in bed together, and Sigrid had said, **Of course, of course**, which had felt like both an act of mercy and an act of contrition.

The first time Marta met Sigrid's friends from graduate school in a downtown bar, she was surprised by how normal they looked. They weren't in tweed and collared shirts and chinos. They weren't dressed like miniature professors. They wore jeans and T-shirts and baseball caps with logos from minor teams around the Midwest. They wore boots and sneakers. They spoke in the flat, clipped way she was accustomed to, and at first she fell right in with the rhythm of their conversation: the weather, the price of gas, the merits of cheap beer and free time. Marta, in her stretch-waist pants and scuffed steel-toes, felt at ease among them. She sat next to Sigrid along the bar, her arm loosely around her shoulders, Sigrid's arm around her waist. Sometimes they'd catch each other's eye and couldn't stop from smiling. But at some point in the night the conversation cinched in the middle, as if someone had tightened a belt around it, so that all their focus and energy had been funneled down to a point so small Marta that could barely grasp it. Something about semiotics. Something about the nature of knowledge.

It wasn't that Marta was dumb. She had been an excellent student. In Indiana, she had topped the state exams in mathematics and science. She had been selected to represent her state in a national mathematics contest, had won a blue ribbon and a full scholarship. Yet in the bar that first night she had felt out of her depth, out and behind everyone else as they talked and raced full steam toward whatever they were arguing about. She'd stood there, her finger tucked through Sigrid's belt loop, and Sigrid would sometimes look back at her with a smile, as if she were checking on a pet. She hated that look. Its knowing, gentle easiness. She hated it when people treated her like some kind of unwashed beast that needed a long leash and a slow walk.

They fought about that look after the bar that night as Marta drove Sigrid home to the Near East Side, over by Willy Street Co-op, where Sigrid worked shifts and bought ugly produce half-off.

In Sigrid's driveway, they parked and listened to the engine click. Marta clenched the wheel because she didn't know what else to do with her hands. Sigrid was drunk and tired, over it already.

"You think I'm dumb," she said. But Sigrid said, "Don't put it on me, Marta. If you feel that way, it's because you feel that way." And Marta said, "No. It's not me. It's not. I do feel that way, but it's not because of me, or not just because of it. You know that." Sigrid leaned over the center console and kissed her, and Marta pushed her away, "No, no, we are **talking**." But Sigrid just smiled and kissed her—once, twice, three times—and then she felt Sigrid's hand sliding past the elastic of her pants and pressing flat against the outside of her underwear. Marta felt hot and suffocated, but Sigrid started to massage her there, and she felt loose and buoyed up on a wave of static. She rode that wave, the friction of Sigrid's hand and the scrunching heat of her panties. Sigrid's mouth opening, slick and warm, the gentle pressure of Sigrid sucking on her tongue. And then she realized that her hands were still on the wheel, still at ten and two, just as she'd learned how to drive in high school.

"Do you want to come in?" Sigrid asked.

"Is it okay?" Marta asked back, looking nervously at the prim, white house. The light in the living room was on.

"Come in," she said. It was early April, and there was still snow on the ground, and the lakes were still frozen. In Sigrid's room, there was a pink quality to the air. Sigrid had draped a diaphanous scarf over the top of her lamp. Marta lay back on Sigrid's bed with her clothes still on, and Sigrid climbed over her.

Marta was bigger than Sigrid, taller by a couple of inches and broader through the shoulders. Her hands were tough from the plant. But Sigrid smelled like sweat and work. Her forearms were firm, and her back had slender, excellent muscles. It was from the swimming, Marta thought. She knew

that Sigrid swam five times a week, that in
her younger years she'd been a competitive
swimmer. But she'd injured something in
herself. That's when Sigrid had learned of her
capacity for reading and remembering things.
In those snowy days in her Minnesota town,
tucked away in some dank library room,
reading book after book, a cast on her arm
(or leg? Marta could not remember). Under
Sigrid's body, Marta was aware of how soft
her own body had become. She felt formless.
Thick. But Sigrid unbuttoned her shirt and
helped her out of it. When Sigrid's fingers
first entered her, Marta gasped because she
had not expected their tips to be so hard and
so kind. She gasped, and Sigrid kissed her
forehead and then her neck and then the
space below her navel. She kept whispering
kind things to Marta. She kept saying that
she was beautiful, that she smelled good,
that she was so soft, so good. Marta clenched
her eyes and knotted her fingers in the bed-
spread. She couldn't bring herself to look at
Sigrid. She tried to close her legs, but Sigrid

opened them, and it was then that Marta felt most naked, most exposed. She wanted to cry again. She almost cried again. She put her arm over her face.

"What's wrong?" Sigrid said. She could feel Sigrid's shoulders under her legs. "What's wrong, Marta? Do you want to stop?"

"No," she said hoarsely. "I've just. I've never."

"Oh, Marta," Sigrid said. She kissed Marta's thigh and then her knee. "It's okay."

"I'm afraid I'll mess it up," she said. "I'm afraid you'll see me." Marta looked at Sigrid, who was looking up at her, those green eyes.

"I see you," Sigrid said. "You're wonderful."

Marta did cry. She cried, but Sigrid didn't stop. She seemed to know that the crying meant that Marta didn't want her to stop. It hadn't been that way with Peter, Marta thought. It hadn't been like that. She had not cried with him. She had not felt nervous with him. Because with Peter there hadn't been any room for her feelings at all.

· · ·

MARTA WORKED in a cubicle at the plant. The walls were thin and covered in a kind of coarse linen fabric. She had tacked up a picture of her parents and a couple of pictures of herself from summer camp when she was a girl, when she'd had thick glasses and a shaggy bobbed haircut. One of the pictures showed Marta as a smiling seven-year-old standing at the edge of a dock, the water a deep green, the sky over the bursting hills a smooth, tranquil blue. It gave her something pretty to look at when her eyes grew tired and the columns of figures and sums swam together. Her desk was tidy except for the in-box, where people from other departments dropped their own reports, and Marta had to organize them and figure out what she was supposed to do with them. She'd been working at the plant for about five years, and the work had adhered to her like the accumulation of calcium in a pipe, until she was no longer sure if she'd always been suited for the job or had simply **become** suited through prolonged exposure.

In the plant, there was always the sound of dripping water and the dull, distant roar of surf. The hallways had flickering green lights, and when she walked from tunnel to tunnel, climbing up the ladders to inspect the tanks and take down their measurements, it was like moving through an emerald dream. Not many people worked in the plant, not on Marta's shift—maybe thirty in all. There were of course the men who worked underground, who did the real work and sometimes were burned by acid or lye, who came up the elevators screaming because they'd gotten their hand caught in a hydraulic press. The men were the thick, blunted sort whose lives had deposited them in the plant the way a sluggish stream accumulates debris. They wore gray coveralls and smelled like cigarettes and chlorine and something else, something sulfurous.

When she'd been with Peter, she had felt a rigid, formal distance between her and the men. But after Peter, something had changed, as if the center of gravity had collapsed, and their orbit around her became unstable. They spoke to her more, stopped by her cubicle, and stood there, holding their reports rather than simply dropping them and going. They looked her in the eye, and she saw in their smudged faces something faint, flickering, like hope. At first she thought she was imagining it, that it was nothing. But one afternoon, after Peter and before Sigrid, a man named Lenny came alongside the row of cubicles and stood at the edge of her desk. He was very tall but had the sullen posture of a small boy. She looked up from her computer and waited for him to ask her what he needed. Sometimes the men did that. When they didn't know where to go, when the directions shuttled into their cubbies made no sense, they came to her, and she would set them on the right course. But Lenny had never done that. He'd always been one of the bright ones.

"Marta," he'd said. "How's it hanging?"

"It hangs, Lenny," Marta had said. "What

can I do you for?" Lenny coughed, turned red. The nape of Marta's neck turned hot. "Not like that. You know what I meant."

"Of course," Lenny said. "Well, I was wondering . . ." He leaned against the cubicle wall, and it buckled under his weight. He stepped away from it. Marta felt something tighten behind her eyes.

"Oh, Lenny. We maybe shouldn't," she said.

"You know, dinner would be fine, you know, fine, dinner, we could eat dinner, you know."

"Lenny—" Marta began, but Lenny was looking at the floor, crumpling the paper in his hands.

"We could go someplace in Madison, someplace real nice. We could, the two of us, go, we could."

Marta drummed her fingers on the top of her desk. She glanced over the cubicle, where she could see some of her office mates looking back at them. When she looked at Lenny, she saw him staring at her, waiting for an answer. She didn't have it in her to say no, not with the whole world watching.

So she said yes, and they went to dinner in Madison that weekend. They ate fried chicken and potato salad, and on the way home Lenny put his hand on her knee while he drove. And Marta felt sick, flushed and sick and like she wanted to just fold in on herself. Lenny's truck smelled like wet newspaper. His big toolbox rattled behind Marta's seat. She hadn't been in a truck like that in years.

At Marta's house, Lenny walked her to the door, though she told him it wasn't necessary. She pulled out her key and put it in the lock, and she felt his stomach against her back, and he pushed against her. The world was dim under his shadow. His hand was on her arm, its coarse heat. She stiffened, like some stupid, frightened animal. She turned to him and looked up, and he was coming in for a kiss. She turned her head and his lips landed on her cheek, and she knotted her hand into a fist.

"Thanks for the evening," she said. "I enjoyed myself."

Lenny looked faintly stunned by what

she had said. She opened the door and went into the dark of her apartment, and for a moment, just before the door closed completely, she was afraid he would stop it with his hand. She was afraid he'd push his way inside. She was afraid of him.

"Yeah, see you around," he said. And she heard his footsteps go down the walkway, thudding.

The next day, Lenny was at her cubicle again. He asked her to come back to his place for a couple of beers, knock a few back. He lived not too far from her, he said, it turned out. He was close enough that she could walk back if she felt like it. It wasn't far at all. Or, hey, if she got too drunk, she could stay over. Marta said that it wasn't a good day, maybe. Lenny just put his thick arm on the top of her cubicle, stood there with his legs crossed and a look of sad, aspirational confidence.

"Didn't we have a good time last night? Didn't we? Let's do it again. Come over."

She said she'd think about it. But Lenny kept coming back, and so she went over there. Just for a few minutes. She went over there, and she brought a six-pack and she sat on his couch, which was so worn out that it almost swallowed her up the moment she sat on it. They watched a taped recording of the Daytona. They talked about the plant, about the boys. And Marta felt like she was in college again. She had not realized how few friends she had until that very moment. Or maybe she had realized it, in small bits here or there, but, sitting on Lenny's couch, talking to him about things they both knew about, about the common matter that made up their lives, she was suddenly aware of how lonely she'd felt after college. Lenny caught her looking at him in that moment. She could see his face change. It opened. His eyes widened. He stopped talking. His smile turned shy. He leaned in and kissed her, and she bolted up from the couch.

"No, Lenny. No. We can't," she said.

Lenny's face turned bright red. He looked like he was going to cry. Marta sat back down. He shook his head hard.

"Why is it always like this," he said. "Why don't anybody want me back. Why don't anyone ever want me."

Marta sat there clutching her beer can. Nobody had ever wanted her, either, except Peter. Except Lenny.

"You get used to it," she said. "After a while, you stop noticing."

Lenny chuckled bitterly. "Hell, I don't know about that."

"You're probably right," she said. "You're probably right."

She did not sleep with Lenny. But she did sit with him until the Daytona was over, and then she went home. He had been right about the walk back to her place. It was easy, and it was beautiful. She walked along the street that ran parallel to the stream, over a small bridge. She stopped to look through the trees that opened over it, and high above everything, the moon. It was cool then, and she wrapped her jacket around herself. When she got home, she lay awake in bed for a long time, and then she made a profile on a dating website. She had been thinking about that feeling she'd had when Peter had asked her to marry him, that sudden recognition of what she'd felt all the time they'd been together, the reason that she couldn't with Lenny, the sharpening resolution with which she saw herself. When the website asked her what she was interested in, she selected women and not men.

THAT SUMMER, Sigrid wanted to rent a place up north for a few days. She wanted to get out of the city and wake up to birds singing and deer in the yard. She wanted to spend some time reading for pleasure and not for work. It was difficult for Marta, because she did not have much money and did not have many days off. Sigrid kept saying that capitalism was a crime, that it robbed people of their will to live, and Marta would shake her head and think, **Someone's got to pay for all that living**.

They were thinking about moving in together. Marta's roommate had cleared off with a boyfriend, and Sigrid's roommate was getting worse by the day. Thad took Adderall to stay awake and to study. More than once—more than twice—Sigrid had found him standing buck naked in the kitchen in the middle of the night, staring out the window. She had also noticed that when she left her wallet on the coffee table, she came back to find money missing. Never a huge sum, five dollars here, three dollars there, but enough to notice and enough that, after a while, it could turn into a large sum. Sigrid didn't think about that. Sigrid didn't think about the future, really, whereas it was all that Marta could think about.

She'd come to understand their work as opposite in that way. Sigrid looked back into the past, through layer upon layer of history, trying to excavate what had been. Her new project was a scale-model re-creation of the rooms of Matilda of Scotland, and she took what she could from books like **De Gestis Regum Anglorum.** From a series of petty facts, she tried, and sometimes succeeded, in re-creating lives lived and lives lost. She was almost always looking back, and she talked with a kind of lilting nostalgia. Even when she talked about what she'd had for breakfast, she said it as if she'd never have oatmeal and toast again. Marta worked in forecasting. Taking the current levels of fluorination in the water, projecting what it would look like in ten years, in fifty, in one hundred. She worked to understand how the small, seemingly insignificant particles that filled their water and their air might accumulate over time into something dreadful and awful. Five dollars was never five dollars to Marta. It was always turning into one hundred, two hundred. All she could see was trends, losses mounting every moment of every day.

"You're like Anne of Cleves," Sigrid said one day when they were in bed and Marta was trying to explain to her why she needed to confront Thad.

"Like **who**?" she had asked, annoyed.

"Anne of Cleves."

It could be this way, sometimes. Sigrid saying things that had nothing to do with anything. Marta had learned to wait it out.

She rolled onto her stomach and propped her chin up on her hand. Sigrid was on her back, reading.

"Are you going to elaborate?" Marta asked.

"Anne of Cleves was a wife of Henry the Eighth," she said without looking up from her book.

"What does that have to do with your thief of a roommate?"

"Anne of Cleves was practical and frugal. And stubborn. But she was naive and judgmental."

"Oh, this is about that stupid question you asked me on the first night."

"It's not a stupid question," Sigrid said, and she sat up. "It's an important question. It's maybe the most important question."

"What's so important about it?" Marta asked. She was annoyed now. She had been trying to help Sigrid, and she'd been called ugly and bullheaded, and now stupid.

"The wives of Henry the Eighth were either murdered or discarded because of Henry's capriciousness. They're every woman in history. Their whole lives—everything they ever did or felt or thought—get winnowed down to this one thing about them, their marriage or association to a tyrant. Isn't that awful? So when I ask, which one of them are you, I guess, it's less about you and more about, how are we still reproducing the same awful, limited spaces for women?"

Marta thought about that for a moment. She did not see how it related to Thad's stealing Sigrid's money. She did not see how it had anything to do with her, either. It seemed like the sort of thing that people did at parties. A game, a guessing game of the self.

"So if I'm Anne of Cleves, what does that mean?"

"It means you're practical about your limitations, and you do the best you can."

"And who are you?" Marta asked. Sigrid smiled and lay back down. She closed her eyes.

"I'm Catherine of Aragon."

"And what does that mean?" Marta asked. She put her hand on Sigrid's stomach, came close to her on the bed. Sigrid turned to look at her and shook her head.

"It means I'm mad as hell."

They did get the place that summer. It was a small cabin near a river—more a shack than a cabin, really, but Marta did not mind it. The air was fresh and clear, the clearest she'd breathed in a long time. The world had a deep, saturated hue, and the tops of the trees were so green that they were almost black. They fished but didn't catch anything. They waded into the edge of the river, where it was still and cool, up to their ankles, and they splashed one another. Sigrid cut her foot on a sharp rock, and Marta bandaged it and drove her into town, where a local doctor, who had hair growing out of his ears, stitched it up for twenty dollars. At night, it was colder than Marta had thought summer could get. There were deer in the yard. There were birds in the trees. The sky was so vast that Marta felt small when she walked from the porch to the edge of the road. They drank lemonade on the swing, and Sigrid braided Marta's hair for her, weaving in blue wildflowers.

It was the most beautiful place. The most beautiful time. On their last night, they lay outside on a flannel blanket and watched the slow progression of the stars, the smooth carapace of the sky like glass.

"I never want to leave here," Sigrid said.

"You'll have to take it up with the owners," Marta said, but she knew what Sigrid meant. She wrapped her arms around her, and they shed their clothes and held each other tight as they touched each other. They didn't get off. They tried and tried, stroking and touching each other's bodies every way they knew, but as the pressure inside them rose, it dissipated just as quickly, so that by the end of it they were frustrated and hot and damp. They couldn't get traction on their desire. Every time it seemed that as they were cresting into the oblivion of orgasm, sadness drenched them. Sadness at leaving. Sadness at going back to their lives. The sadness of knowing it would never again be this perfect, this easy.

They were cranky on the drive home, and mean, waspish to each other. They sniped and fought and insulted each other, until Marta pulled them over into a roadside motel, where the sheets were scratchy and hard. And she pushed Sigrid onto the bed and pulled her pants off. She pressed her face between Sigrid's legs and kissed her against the outside of her panties. Sigrid was warm. She smelled like the field.

After that, it was easygoing. They drove with the soft, blurry focus of people in love. Sigrid, who had gotten sunburned on the last day, drowsed. Marta played a Billie Holiday song and hummed along as they moved downward through the state. The trees gave way, turning steadily into flat fields drenched in yellow and green. The air grew thicker, heavier. And then, eventually, they were back.

ONE EVENING IN THE FALL, Marta returned home to find Peter on her doorstep. He was tan and had filled out. He looked like a high-definition version of himself. He stood up the moment he saw her car. And, as she got out of it, he walked over to her.

"Marta, it's been a while," he said.

"A year," she said, leaning against her car door. "How long have you been here?"

"**Here,** as in the country, or **here,** as in town, or **here,** as in on your doorstep?"

"All three, I guess," she said.

"I got in yesterday," he said. "I came over a little while ago to see if you'd be here. But then I decided to wait."

She almost asked him what he was waiting for, but she didn't. She almost asked him inside, but she didn't. Peter seemed to be waiting for that, didn't know what to do without the offer.

"Can we sit down somewhere?" he asked, looking back toward the house.

"The place is a mess," she said. "Let's just sit in my car."

"All right, then," he said, and they got inside. Marta rested her hands on the wheel out of habit, stared directly ahead. Peter squirmed in the passenger seat. He had always driven when they were together.

"This is funny, being in here again," he said.

"It is," Marta offered. "Well, what's on your mind?"

"Oh, well. That's a great question, a real great question." He was fiddling with the center console. He lifted it, stared into its maw of papers and pill bottles, then dropped it shut. "I guess you're wondering why I'm back."

"The thought did cross my mind," she said.

"My mother's dying," he said. "I came back to see her, and, well. I wanted to see you, too. I miss you."

Marta clenched, both from the news that Peter's mother was ill and from the fact that he missed her. Peter's mother, Irina, had always been so kind to Marta. She was well into her eighties, but she had the spry energy of a seventy-year-old. She spoke with a sluggish Russian accent, and liked to finish off her sentences with a **khorosho!**, which had endeared her to Marta. All through the three years she had dated Peter, Irina had sent her cards for her birthday and Christmas. More than once she'd sent her a little gift, too, something small and delicate, intricately carved from bone or stone so that they resembled small teeth. She had reminded Marta of her own grandmother, a benevolent Finnish woman of robust health who had fallen dead at the age of ninety-nine with all the unfussy ease that had seen her through her whole life, through famine and fury and the unassailable tide of history.

"Oh, no. I'm sorry, Peter," Marta said. "That's awful, just awful."

"She really loves you, you know. She thinks the world of you."

"I care for her, too," Marta said.

"And for me?" Peter said wryly, but perhaps also seriously. Marta shook her head gently.

"Peter, you know that's done. You know that, right?"

"I do," he said. "I'm seeing someone."

"And even if you weren't," she started to say, but stopped herself. "That's wonderful."

"Her name's Katya. You know my mom always wanted me to marry a Russian."

"I'm sure she just wants you to be happy," Marta said. "I bet she only wants you to be happy."

"I am. Now I am. I am happy now."

"I'm glad to hear that," Marta said.

"And you? Are you happy? Are you seeing someone?"

If there was one thing that Marta resented, it was how those questions seemed to flow together: **Are you happy or are you alone?**

"It's possible to be happy and alone," she said to Peter and to herself, to the voice inside her.

"I get that, but you should have someone. You deserve happiness."

Marta turned to him and nodded. "Thank you, Peter." The leaves had turned bright orange and gold. All along her street, the trees were beautiful, which meant that they were getting ready to shed their leaves. She wanted to say something about that to Peter, about Irina and how the trees grew more beautiful just as they seemed to die for the season, and how that was a sign of life. Only living things got to die, after all. She had not understood that before, but now she did, and she wanted to say some of it to Peter, hoping he'd say it to Irina. That dying meant you had lived.

"Well, I better go," he said.

"All right," Marta said. Peter did not move to get out of the car.

"I heard a rumor," he said. "About you and . . . well, I heard a rumor that you're a dyke now. Is that true?"

Marta flinched. It was such a hard word.

"Don't be a dog, Peter. Don't be ugly."

"Wow," he said. "I can't believe it. No wonder. Wow." He looked at her with pity and shock. He looked at her in a way that she did not deserve to be looked at, she thought. She swallowed thickly. She set her jaw. She turned to him.

"You do not get to talk to me that way," she said. "You do not get to treat me like that."

"I'm just saying, I had no idea. That whole time we were together, you just. Wow."

"It was not about you," she said. "It was never about you."

Peter put his hand on the door and pushed it open. He shook his head sadly, ruefully.

"This will break Irina's heart," he said. "This will just break her heart."

When Peter left, Marta sat in her car for a long time. Her eyes stung. Her lip trembled. Her elbows ached. Her head hurt. She got out of the car and went into the house. She ran a tub full of water and got into it with her clothes still on. She was like that when Sigrid got home and found her.

"Baby, what's wrong?" Sigrid asked from the doorway. "What's happened here?" It was not chastising. It was not harsh. It was a gentle question.

"Peter came by," she said. "His mother is dying."

"Oh, that's awful," Sigrid said. She kneeled next to the tub and ran her hands through Marta's hair. Her expression was concerned. Marta looked at her.

"He found out about me," she said. "I don't know how, but he found out."

"Found out what?" Sigrid asked.

"About me. About us. He found out."

"Oh," Sigrid said. She looked a little surprised and a little perplexed. "I'm sorry, baby. I don't understand."

"He didn't know. He didn't know about us, and now he does. And he . . . well, he didn't know."

"That's okay," she said.

"I didn't want him to know," Marta said. The water had gone cold and her clothes were scratching up her skin.

"Well, now he does. But it's okay."

"It's not okay," Marta said, and she shivered. "He's going to tell everyone."

"Who is this everyone? Who?" Sigrid asked, kissing Marta's cheek and her forehead. But Marta felt like a part of herself was streaming into the world, spreading all over without her permission. She felt something important was escaping.

"Everyone," she said wildly, and she just

kept saying that while Sigrid held her hand under the water.

Later that evening, she and Sigrid were in bed under the covers. To Marta it felt like the first time in her life she had ever been warm. Sigrid was reading. Outside, the wind was in the trees, their jagged shadows gliding across the window. Their humidifier hissed.

"I'm sorry about before," Marta said, but Sigrid wasn't listening. She was preparing for her comprehensive exams. Marta watched her read, the slow, steady progress of her eyes across and down the page. The lamplight illuminated her hair and she appeared to Marta like one of those paintings in churches, where the head glows, denoting some minor divinity. "I'm sorry," Marta said because she felt she had to try again, and she put her hand on the book to draw Sigrid's attention.

"What's that, baby?" Sigrid smiled a sleepy smile. Her eyes were a little unfocused.

"I said I was sorry about before."

Sigrid's smile turned inward, but then she put her arms around Marta. She kissed Marta's hair. Marta put her arm over Sigrid, put her face down against her stomach.

"Don't be. That Peter's a real jerk."

"No, not that, I guess. I just meant. I'm sorry. For saying that. About everyone knowing," Marta said.

"It's okay if you don't want anyone to know, though I think it's a little late for that," Sigrid said. It was true, Marta knew. They went around together everywhere. They held hands when they went to the park. They had gone to see Sigrid's parents in Minnesota, and they had welcomed Marta the best they could with their tall Norwegian manners. All there was to know was known, by all of whom there were to know it.

"It just made me feel funny, I guess," Marta said. "Seeing him. Him knowing."

"We never are who we once were," Sigrid said.

"Did one of your dead ladies give you that one?" Marta asked.

"No," Sigrid said. "I made it up."

"I wouldn't have known the difference," Marta said. "You could have told me anything."

"And who says I haven't already," Sigrid said, picking her book back up. "Now let me read."

Marta lay there with her arm over Sigrid, thinking about that last bit, how Sigrid could have told her anything and she wouldn't have known the difference. Sigrid could have made up all of that about the queens of England. She could have made up all of that with the diaries and her elegant dioramas. She could have told Marta anything at all, and Marta would have believed her. But maybe that's what love was, she thought to herself as she fell asleep. Maybe love was that you didn't try too hard to tell the difference. Maybe love was just believing something to be true because you'd been told.

IN THE WINTER, they made latkes and borscht. They had grown vegetables in a little plot behind the house and pickled them. They opened jars of okra and peas and beans. They made their own kraut. Their house smelled like vinegar that winter, but it was the healthiest Marta had felt in a long time, maybe since she'd taken that picture at camp. Her body changed, but not in the way she expected it to. She didn't get skinny or tight all over. She didn't feel like a strung drum. But little by little, the packets of fat under her arms shrank. It was easier for her to run. She didn't look all that different, she didn't think, but when she caught sight of herself in the mirror after the shower, she did notice that there was warmth in her cheeks and the whites of her eyes were clear. The world had a vivid intensity to it, like up north, and she felt like she was moving through pure color.

After Sigrid passed her comprehensive exams, they started to sleep in on Saturday and Sunday mornings. They became lazy and easy with one another. They made love at weird times of the day, sometimes when the sun was up, which felt especially daring to

Marta. It was a strange thing to her, giving of her body so easily, sharing it with another person. It had been like adjusting to Sigrid's vegetarianism—the way Sigrid would put a hand on her back or on her shoulder, not because she wanted anything but just because she was there. It had been the reason she had not wanted to share a house with Sigrid: All that touching. All that seeing. All that being seen. But it had become the best part of her life, she thought.

When they had been together one year, they celebrated by going to London. Ostensibly it was a trip for Sigrid's research, but Marta found a way to turn it into a trip for the two of them. She had promised to leave Sigrid her own time and her own space to be with her thoughts, to commune with history's dead women. Marta just wanted to be with her there, to walk the streets of London, holding Sigrid's hand, carrying her bag if she needed it, offering her whatever support she could. It brought her happiness.

The day after they returned, Sigrid took from her bag a small deck of playing cards.

Each card was decorated with a different woman from a different historical period. Sigrid handed Marta a queen of clubs. On it, a pretty, blond woman with close-set eyes and a wry, gentle smile looked back at her.

"Anne of Cleves," Sigrid said.

"We meet at last," Marta said, sliding the card back into the deck and shuffling. As she shuffled, Marta watched the faces whip by, a parade of anonymous smiling women, all looking back at her as if across the fanning waves of time.

APARTMENT

THEY WALKED UP THE STREET TOGETHER, the three of them.

The sky was iridescent with cold. Out to their right, a shelf of white steam from the industrial park and the last of the academic buildings giving way to retail space and a few scraggly houses where the undergrads lived. To the left, the botanical gardens, Bascom's high hill.

Lionel hung back a little behind Sophie

and Charles. They were talking about the rehearsal again. Sophie seemed kinder about it now. She listened to Charles with narrowed eyes.

"It could be good for me," Charles said. "Like, really good."

"Sure," Sophie said. Their shoes scraped over the dry sidewalk. No trace of snow or ice here. The branches hanging over the sidewalk moved in the breeze from the cars.

"I'm not being a bitch. I really mean it."

"Whatever, Sophie."

"Tell me about the piece."

"I really don't feel like hearing you make fun of it," he said quietly. "It's embarrassing."

"If you're embarrassed, it's not because I made fun of it—not that I **did**. I mean, I said nothing about it, Charlie."

Charles grunted. Lionel felt a pang of sympathy for him. There were a million tiny ways to make someone feel bad about something that didn't involve saying anything directly.

"Come on," Sophie said. She pulled on

Charles's arm, but he wouldn't budge. They were passing into downtown proper then. Instead of going directly across East Campus Mall, Sophie wanted them go through the archways at the liberal arts building. Into its slanted catacombs. She pulled Charles, and while he continued to resist her, he shifted his hips slightly, pointing himself in her direction. Lionel followed, wondering still why he had let Sophie convince him that it was a good idea that he go back to her place for dinner.

She had said to him, upon leaving the café, **Don't make it weird! It'll be weird if you leave now.** Charles had said nothing, had not looked at Lionel as they went down the stairs outside and into the snowy quad. Evening was rapidly closing in on them, and because Lionel didn't want to make it weird, didn't have anywhere else to be, he had walked with them without saying he'd follow them all the way. He had said yes only in action, reserving the right to change his mind and vanish while they were distracted.

The liberal arts building was a pyramid

of nested concrete rectangles connected by an interior set of stairs rising at steep angles, as if meant to discourage a siege by unruly masses. It posed an accessibility nightmare. In the summer, students used the steep interior walls for ramps, leaping up on the railings with their skateboards and bikes. People roamed the outside layers, setting up picnics in the shade of the buildings while they watched swallows and gulls shoot from terrace to terrace.

Charles squared his shoulders to the wind that funneled down onto them. Sophie jumped up against the steep wall and walked it tightrope style, her arms out for balance, going a ways up until she had to turn back, stuttering down like a windup toy going over a patch of concrete. She darted between columns, her voice doubling, echoing, bounding back to them. Charles had hung back and Lionel caught up to him.

"Did you really have an okay morning?" Lionel asked.

Charles regarded him carefully, his curls hanging down to the bridge of his nose.

Charles wore a black puffer coat, from which the sharp end of a feather poked out near the collar. Lionel felt an urge to pluck it out, but he knew that if he did there would only be another feather, and another. Once you started pulling, the whole coat came undone.

"It was all right," Charles said. "I was late. Got chewed out a little."

Lionel blushed—Charles had been late because of him, and he knew that. A flicker of a smile at the corner of his lips, and Lionel looked away, toward Sophie. She was visible between two stone pillars in the center of the courtyard. She was spinning in a slow circle.

"I feel bad about that," Lionel said.

"Oh, yeah? What're you going to do about it?"

"What do you mean?"

"You feel bad, don't you? What are you going to do to make it up to me?" Charles puffed out his chest and looked at Lionel rather expectantly.

"What do you want?" Lionel asked.

"You tell me."

They had fully caught up to Sophie then, but they were looking at each other, Lionel with a mildly horrified expression and Charles looking smug.

"Be nice, Charlie," Sophie said. And Charles looked at her, slow, molten heat.

"I **am** nice. I'm the nicest fucking person in the world," he said. "Aren't I, Lionel?"

Lionel tried to shrug off his discomfort. "No. You're not."

Sophie let out an **Ooh**. Her mouth made a perfect, bright circle. "He got you."

Charles reached through the cold air and grabbed him up by the scruff his neck. Lionel shivered at the coarseness of his fingers, their strength. And then Charles leaned down and bit his cheek hard. A flash of moisture, the heat of his teeth grinding against Lionel's skin. The scrape of his stubble, a flick of his tongue. Lionel yelped.

"That'll teach you," Charles said.

Lionel pressed his palm to his cheek. Charles's saliva was drying quickly. The heat of the bite pulsed, each beat a warning that if Charles had wanted to, he could have torn him apart. Sophie pulled at Lionel's arm, trying to get a look at the red bruise blooming on his cheek.

"Charlie, Jesus, what are you doing?" Sophie brushed Lionel's hand away and leaned close. Her breath, its cigarette smoke, was close on him. He breathed deeply. "That's going to leave a mark."

"It's okay," Lionel said. "It's fine."

"Stupid shit," Sophie said, smiling.

"Stupid shit," Lionel repeated. Sophie took up Lionel's hand and leaned against him. Charles drifted away from them, rolling his eyes. Occasionally, Lionel caught him giving them glances, a look of concern and mild annoyance on his face. There were moments when, coming closer, he felt Charles's knuckles graze his, and Lionel instinctively clenched his hand into a fist.

SOPHIE'S APARTMENT WAS SMALL. Mismatched furniture, a tiny television in the living room, and some small white shelves that she had packed with records, DVDs, and books. The floors were covered with ugly beige carpeting speckled with stains. A radiator along the wall put out a great head of steamy air.

Charles stretched out on the couch, and Lionel knelt near one of the shelves. Sophie said she was hungry and put on some water for pasta. There was nothing of special interest on the shelf: paperbacks, some old French workbooks, a large-print edition of a John Grisham book, and three novels by Virginia Woolf.

"Are these yours?" Lionel asked.

"No—they belong to my roommate," Sophie said from the kitchen archway. Lionel looked back at Charles.

"Not me," Charles said. "She has a roommate. Miriam."

"You not much of a reader?" Lionel asked him.

"Yes."

"What?"

Charles sat up at this and sighed like it wasn't the first time his reading habits had been litigated. He crossed his legs on the couch and twisted his neck from side to side. "I read mystery novels." **Mystery novels!** Sophie cleared her throat pointedly, and Lionel tried to banish the image of Charles reading Agatha Christie, but the image, once conjured, refused to be dispelled. Not because he thought Charles was dumb or that mystery novels were bad but because it was such incongruous thought: Charles curled up in the corner of a library, the hulk of him, enraptured by descriptions of the weather and interiors.

"God, you two are so fucking pretentious. There are good mystery novels."

"I didn't say anything," Lionel said. "I'm not judging you."

"Oh, sure."

"No one is judging you, Charlie," Sophie said. She was now stirring a pot of red sauce in the doorway. Her hair was messy from the steam and the snow, her face splotchy. She stirred the pot briskly. "Mmm." Lionel could smell the tomatoes. The sauce didn't smell store-bought—it smelled musky and bitter, almost like vinegar. There was also the scent of spices in the air: turmeric, some paprika, something else, something nutty.

"Did you make that?"

"I did," Sophie said, grinning. "For the potluck last night and I had extra. I stewed the tomatoes and added a bunch of spices and stuff. No meat."

"It smells so good," he said. The sauce had a rich texture as she turned it over and over itself, stirring quickly so that a skin didn't form. The pot itself was battered and gray, probably lifted from some thrift shop or Salvation Army.

"You're welcome to have some!"

"I'd love to," he said.

Each of them had a bowl of the pasta and Sophie's tomato sauce. Lionel didn't re-member seeing any at the potluck last night, but then there'd been so many options, and he hadn't been especially hungry. He ate slowly, chewing through the whole-wheat noodles and sucking the sauce from them discreetly. He enjoyed the heat of the food, the way its flavor settled beneath the pain of his tongue burning. Chewing also made his cheek sting, and he found himself faintly aroused by the discomfort, thinking each time his jaws shifted of how Charles had bitten him.

Charles sucked down the food so fast that Lionel doubted he even tasted it. Sophie also ate quickly, but neatly. She had a small piece of fish on the side, but she hadn't offered him any. Lionel put his head down and tried to focus on the act of eating. Lifting his fork to his mouth and getting the food inside. Chewing it. Swallowing. Looking pleased and complacent. Content.

"Do the dishes, Charlie," Sophie said after they were done. She took both her bowl and Lionel's, and she handed them to Charles, who didn't even blink. He took the bowls to the kitchen and turned on the faucet. Sophie stretched and drummed her hands against her stomach. "I'm full."

"That was great," he said.

"Thanks."

"Where's your roommate?"

"Oh, who knows? She's probably in a lab somewhere. She studies chemistry."

"Cool," Lionel said. "Chemistry is intense."

"**She's** intense," Sophie said. "Way intense."

"Is that bad?"

"No, she's great. I like her a lot, but . . . well."

"I think I get that," Lionel said. He wondered if this was how people saw him. Intense. **Way intense**. If they said things like **I like him a lot, but . . . well**. The pause hanging off like something heavy with meaning.

Was it weird that he was here, that he'd accepted her invitation to come along? He was never really sure when people were being polite or when they were actually being nice. Since his time at the hospital, his life had become a series of outstretched hands, gently guiding, so it was hard, even now, to tell when someone wanted him to come along or when they didn't. Why should she have wanted him there? Surely, she and Charles had better things to do, things to do with their naked bodies. He saw, in his mind, the flash of Charles's bare skin, the intimidating solidity of his chest, the broadness of his shoulders, that expanse of dense, coarse follicles on his chest and stomach. And Sophie, smooth, faultless, a surface as pristine as milk.

"What's on your mind, Lionel?" she asked.

"Nothing," he said. "Nothing at all."

"I don't think that's true," she said. She pressed the tip of her toe against his shoulder, pressed it hard against him. He was bigger than she was, but she was stronger. She had better control of her body and, by extension, his body. She stretched her leg and he shifted back away from her. "Don't lie to me."

"Who's lying?"

"What are you thinking?" She was lying flat on her back, her leg supported by Lionel. He wrapped his hand around her ankle and slid his thumb along the underside of her foot. Her skin was warm, and her feet were hard and callused, bruised. Their muscles bulged, full of thick ligaments and tendons. Grotesque, but beautiful, too. The perfect swirl of a shell, the geometry of a rock formation, the gooey symmetry of the early embryo. He pressed his thumb against her high arch and she sighed.

"Nothing," he said. "I'm not thinking."

"Good," she said. "Don't."

She arched slightly on the couch and then sank down. There was something loose, kind of sandy, sticking to her feet. Powder and dust maybe. It came away on Lionel's hands, but he cupped her toes and then the balls of her feet, gripping more tightly near the ankles. She sighed at his touch and he felt momentarily powerful, as if he had evoked some feeling in her, pleasure or comfort, and then embarrassment. He could see himself in the game she was playing. He dropped her foot but it stayed perfectly level, taunting him. He tried to brush it away, but he couldn't make it move.

"I don't like being played with," he said.

"Who's playing who?" she asked without opening her eyes.

"I'm not playing with anyone."

Sophie left the couch and knelt in front of Lionel. They weren't in direct eye contact, but she was looking at him. He found it hard to meet her gaze. He could feel her breath on his cheeks, on his lips. She reached just past his shoulder and then cupped his head tenderly. She rested a hand on his lap, not near his dick, but on his thigh.

"You could have gone home," she said. "But you came here."

The nutty scent of the sauce, the smell of the day on her tongue. Lionel blinked.

"You told me to come," he said.

"But who told you to listen?"

Lionel flushed. He wanted to withdraw from her but didn't. It was another of those moments when he had a clear choice but chose not to act. She came closer to him then, until she was kneeling on his folded legs. Her weight felt good against him. She stroked the back of his neck, and his hands tingled, as with the feather sticking out of Charles's coat. It was like a premonition of an act. A presentiment of what he might do.

"Why are you doing this?" he asked.

"Isn't it what you want?"

"No," he said, but his mouth was dry. Her lips were on his, her tongue parting, sinking. She kissed him again on the corner of his mouth, and then on his cheek. She bit his lip, and the sharpness was a jolt.

"Are you a good boy, Lionel?"

"No." He tried to lean away from her. She swayed. She didn't need him to stay upright. She withdrew as if she'd made up her mind about him. And she climbed back onto the sofa.

"I think you're right about that," she said. She shrugged, sighed. "I don't think you're good at all."

The words crackled in the dim apartment like blue static. He saw them flare to life and then vanish.

Charles returned, his wrists still soapy from the dishes. He leaned over the back of the couch, looking down at them.

"I was trying to get Lionel to tell me what he's thinking," Sophie said. "But he won't."

"What are you thinking?" Charles asked.

Lionel stood up and cleared his throat. He wanted to be anywhere but there. They were both watching him very closely, so much so that their eyes felt like a single organ through which every one of his actions, no matter how small, was being categorized and stored away.

"I should go," he said.

"Why?" Sophie asked. "It's cold out."

"It's fine."

"You'll freeze," Charles said.

"It's okay. I don't mind."

"You don't mind freezing?" Charles asked with a bewildered smile. "Are you crazy? Sit down, Lionel."

"I should be going," he said.

"Sit down, Lionel," Charles said again, firmer this time. Something in Lionel responded to that firmness, used it as a guide as he let himself settle back on the floor. Charles smiled at him and came around the couch. He sat next to Lionel and put his arm across Lionel's shoulders. He drew him closer, inspecting the bruise.

Lionel was awash in Charles's body heat, in the proximity of his touch. He felt he'd come undone under the insistent stroking of Charles's finger back and forth across the bruise on his cheek, back and forth across that place that had been marked with a promise of violence. Lionel tried to get away from Charles's hand, but he couldn't. Charles gripped the back of his neck tightly. Lionel thought of Sophie. Looked to her. Casually, she lay on her side, watching them.

"Why are you always trying to get away? You don't like me anymore?"

"I'm not," Lionel said.

"Maybe it's because you bit him," Sophie said.

"Oh? I'm sorry," Charles murmured, and there was a soft, brushing kiss against Lionel's neck. He shivered from both the softness of the touch and the breath, the closeness of it.

"It's all right."

"Look at him, poor little fawn, shivering," Sophie said. She left the sofa again. It gave a whine of protest, the springs shifting. She knelt near them both, close enough that Lionel could feel her, would have brushed against her if he moved. He held still. "Are you cold, Lionel? Do you need a blanket?"

Lionel tried to hold himself still, but a tremor spread from the tips of his fingers back up to his wrist, to his arm, to his shoulder. He could feel something vibrate in his lower lip, the side of his face a slow-motion spasm. He tried to be still. To be easy. To be good. But they had hemmed him in. He had nowhere to go. He looked from Charles to Sophie and back, and then to the bookcase, which seemed so comically small compared to all the things it had to hold.

Charles kissed his neck again, and Lionel shivered. He hated the simple, easy mechanism of it. How obvious.

"What about last night, huh? You didn't mind me biting you then."

"I don't mind," Lionel said. "I don't mind it."

Charles flicked his tongue against Lionel's ear.

"God," he said under his breath. "Please."

"How polite," Sophie said dryly. She was close again, but she was leaning against

Charles's back, her arms wrapped around him. "So well behaved."

Lionel saw Charles look back at her, the cut of his eyes. Then he pulled his arm from Lionel and reached back to grip both of Sophie's ankles.

"Okay, that's enough," Charles said.

Sophie ruffled Charles's hair, and then pulled her feet free of him. She hummed to herself as she went down the hall. When they were alone, just him and Charles, Lionel tried to catch his breath.

"Why is she doing this?" Lionel asked.

"Doing what?"

"You know what. You're as bad as she is." Lionel heard his voice shake.

"She doesn't care, Lionel. She doesn't care at all."

"I know. That's what she said."

"Then what?"

"I don't know," Lionel said. "I don't know. I feel weird."

Charles gave him a look that was not lacking sympathy but was a little impatient. He leaned in and pressed their mouths together. He cupped Lionel's jaw and kissed deeper, more thoroughly, and Lionel relaxed under the steady gentleness of it. He thought of Sophie. He closed his eyes.

"It's okay," Charles said. "It's all right."

"What about Sophie?"

"Don't overthink it. This can be whatever you want it to be."

"I don't know what I want it to be," Lionel said. Charles kissed him again and then pulled away.

"Okay," Charles said. He stood up. "Okay."

Sophie came back. She was wearing pajamas and her face was newly washed. Lionel and Charles were not speaking to each other. He had come up against the thing that felt most frustrating about this—the inability to articulate simply what he felt or what he wanted. She sat between them—lay down between them, really, her head on Charles's lap and her feet across Lionel's knees. She stretched. She smelled like limes.

"What got up your asses?" she asked.

"Nothing," Lionel said.

"That's your favorite word, isn't it? **Nothing**."

"I should go," he said. It was not especially late. A few minutes after eight. But he had a longish trip home, and the thought of the cold air on his face and all around him was comforting.

"Why?" she asked, though she was yawning. Charles said nothing. He scrolled on his phone. "Charlie? Do you have something to say about this?"

"No," Charles said. "If he wants to go, he can go."

"It's freezing outside," Sophie said.

"It's okay."

"He can't walk. Tell him to stay. Use your common sense, Lionel." Sophie turned to him. She smiled. Her eyes were warm, caring. It was a kindhearted gesture. But then, beneath it, he sensed something else. Not meanness. But something prickly and alive.

"I can, it's okay."

"I'll drive him," Charles said. "I'll drive him if he wants to go."

"No, that's not necessary. He's staying,"

she said. Lionel twisted his scarf in his hands. Charles had looked up and was making direct eye contact with Sophie. They were exchanging some form of information. But Lionel wanted to go. He felt it necessary to leave. Sophie's head turned very slowly to Lionel. "What are you afraid of, Lionel?"

"Nothing. I just want to go home," he said.

"We have been nice to you. I let you fuck Charlie, didn't I? What's there to be so afraid of?"

Lionel felt a chill race up his spine. Sophie sat up fully then. She put her feet on the floor, but then crossed her legs elegantly. She tilted her head to the side, rested her chin on her hand.

"Do you think I'll eat you?" She snapped her teeth playfully at him.

"Sophie, leave him alone," Charles said. "You can see he's about to piss his pants."

"Don't make fun of me," Lionel said.

"Yeah, Charlie, don't make fun of him." She was still smiling when she said it. "You know the problem with you and also **you**," she said, gesturing to each of them in turn, "is that you're both selfish."

Charles stood up. He reached behind Lionel for his coat. As he was putting it on, Sophie lay back down and closed her eyes.

"I made you a nice dinner, didn't I?"

"It was great," Lionel said.

"When are you going to thank me for the rest of it?" she asked, and Lionel frowned. Charles was kneeling to put on his boots. He shook his head.

"I don't know what you mean."

"For letting you have Charlie. When are you going to thank me for that?" she asked, and Lionel flushed. His mouth went dry. And he looked to Charles and then back to Sophie. He felt ill. Charles stood up, awkwardly. He winced. Lionel thought of his knee.

"That seems," Lionel started to say, "I don't know, Sophie. That seems. Bad."

Charles put on his hat and pulled the door open.

"You don't have to," Lionel said.

"Jesus Christ. Nobody's going to make you suck their dick. I can drive you," Charles said. He nudged Lionel toward the door, and Sophie called after them.

"Lionel, your manners," she said.

HE WAS RIGHT about the air being comforting. There was so much cold black air that he could scarcely imagine a time when it wasn't this way, when winter wasn't this deep. He inhaled. Charles was stomping out ahead of him.

"I'm sorry," Lionel said. "You really don't have to drive me."

Charles stopped and turned. He wet his lips, though they dried immediately in the cold. "I don't get you," he said. "I don't get you."

"What's to get?"

Charles stared at him in open amazement, and Lionel felt a little rush of pride.

"Right," he said. Back to stomping in the cold. He could be so childish. Lionel jogged a little bit to catch up to him. He playfully bumped their shoulders together.

"Come on," Lionel said.

"Come on," Charles mocked, but he was thawing.

They were tracing the route back to campus, which meant that Lionel could see the mountain of warm air over the trees. It hadn't moved despite having earlier given the impression of moving toward them. Or perhaps this was a second mountain, a second wave of warm air pushed up out of the silos in the distance.

"Why do you keep looking over there?" Charles asked. "What's over there?"

"Oh, I like the way the warm air looks," Lionel said. "Like a mountain."

"What mountain?" Charles asked. The mountains of Tennessee. Math camp, yes, the sound of rain striking the tin of the outhouses. The perfect, succulent light of late summer in the cabins, riddled with dust motes. Running between the trees. Rain, so much rain. Their papers covered in scrawl, their handwriting silly, messy. The trim beards of the counselors. Their warm hands steering Lionel, age five, a scraped knee on the gravel path, down to the canoes, where they were forbidden to go. Ben Tovelson, nineteen, bearish, kind, green, winking eyes, showing Lionel how to write his name in the dust with piss. The damp wet of his mouth on Lionel, down there. No. Another way. Another memory. The vacations he had taken with his parents. The damp, chuffing sounds of their arguments trailing into throaty moans when they thought he was asleep. The soft rustle of the nylon sleeping bag. The cold enamel of the cups. The crack of the branches in the fire. Their car striking ruts in the road as they drove up the trail and then back out. The slow slope of the green hills, the vastness of the pine forest, the terrible distance, so far up, high above everything and everyone. That memory condensed, intensified—the rushing, clear air, the water, the call of animals, the emptiness of the perfect darkness that descends on a mountain where few people are living.

"I don't know," he said. "Some mountain."

Charles reached for his hand. Lionel pivoted away. They passed again through the liberal arts building. Their steps echoed. Charles had parked near the campus. Lionel wished that he were as carefree as Sophie. He wished that he was the sort of person to run up the steep wall and wait to be drawn back down. He wished that he could manage some careless, easy gesture. But he was not. And Charles had noticed that he was avoiding contact. There was a distance between them. A quiet that grew bigger as they walked on.

In the car, Lionel rolled down the window. Charles looked at him.

"Are you nuts?"

As they pulled out of the parking lot and into the street, Lionel closed his eyes. The cold air against his face seemed to open, leaving a cavity that was warm and hollow, deeper down in the flow of air. He pressed his face into it as if into a clear stream, and he could feel the cold rushing out and away, sliding past him. He opened his eyes, and the night was a gray smear of other lights, yellow and red and white, all of them blending until they were indistinct. He couldn't breathe. He was drowning.

He could feel the churning up of something, the movement of memory. His grandmother and his grandfather had lived on that mountain, far away from everyone and everything. They kept animals, chickens and goats, sometimes a cow. Back then, Lionel had eaten meat and thought nothing of it. Back then, his grandfather had given him big bowls of venison or fish that they had trapped and killed and cleaned themselves. His grandfather had not been tall or stocky. He had been a tracing of a man, his skin deep and black. His grandfather had taught him how to kill in the most humane way—with the straightest, cleanest line, the purest shot. There had been days deep in the ashy frost of fall when Lionel had stood with his hands deep in the cavity of a deer, had felt its body cooling, its blood thickening. He could remember how grainy blood felt after a while, and, in a more imperfect way, the gradual sense one got of the whole network of vessels and veins and arteries that kept a thing alive. When he lined up everything that he had learned on that mountain in Tennessee from his grandfather, who had smelled of sweat and tobacco, who had chased him with skin of deer and rabbits, making their fur dance, and from Ben Tovelson in the green woods—when Lionel lined all that up and peered down through it, he could see, with horrible clarity, just how he'd been able to lift the blade in the narrow room a year before.

They drove on. The cold, bright world whipped by the window.

"Lionel?" Charles asked. Lionel could barely hear him over the howl of the wind. He dipped his head back into the window. Charles was looking at him the way people did when they glimpsed the wildness in him, that part of him which was still not yet tamed, beaten back into shape. Lionel tried to smile. His eyes were teary and wet.

"I'm okay," he said. "I'm okay."

Charles put his hand on the back of Lionel's neck. He was driving without looking at the street. His eyes were on Lionel. His hand made reassuring shapes against his skin.

"Hang in there," he said. His eyes went back to the street, to the cars that were out in front of them. Lionel leaned into Charles's touch. He wanted to tell Charles about the mountain but couldn't make himself yet.

"I'm hanging in," he said. Maybe it was enough to want to tell Charles about the mountain. His life had become a series of small eruptions, minor escalations.

Charles slid this thumb against the nape of Lionel's neck, and Lionel sighed. He stretched out in the seat next to Charles, turned back to the open window. The air, which very well could have been from a mountain all those years ago, was working something strange over him and the moment itself, reordering some necessary filaments inside him. He was on the verge of speaking, saying it, finally, as he had said some of

it to Sophie in the café before Charles arrived, some edge of the truth, some bit of
what had happened to him. He turned to
Charles and opened his mouth, but his voice
was snatched away on the wind. Charles
turned to him, smiled.

"What did you say, Lionel?"

WHAT MADE THEM
MADE YOU

THE TUMOR IS INOPERABLE.

At the window, Grace watches her grandfather's progress in the garden as he makes his way toward the house, stopping to pull up stray weeds or nudge a brick back into place. Dense clouds push in from the west, and the plum trees lining the long driveway rustle. The wind combs through the screen, pulls, releases.

Her mother, Enid, has just arrived from her shift at the nursing home. She's peeling one of the oranges from the fruit bowl with a kind of pointed nonchalance. The tension in her shoulders and the stiffness in her neck give the game away. Grace knows that when the orange is peeled and set in segments upon the little plate, Enid will offer them to her as though it were nothing, a trick she learned from the other nurses. Take some for yourself and destigmatize the process. It's all so transparent. Now that Grace lives with Enid again, plates of food materialize on almost every surface. Crackers, fruit, soup, runny grits, bits of fish, or slices of low-sodium ham. It's like being haunted by some sort of hospitable ghost. She pretends not to sense Enid's desperation for her to eat.

"The bottom's going to drop out," Grace says.

Enid comes around the kitchen island, carrying the plate with the furry orange slices.

"That so? Here, have some."

Grace wants to scream, but instead asks, "Heard from Davis?"

"He's doing well, last I heard. Not that he calls like he should," she says, plucking pith from the oranges. She's across from Grace at the table now, still wearing her uniform, the deep purple scrubs under the poly-cotton white coat. Orange stains speck the hem. The plastic ID tag is smeary in the light. "I suppose you hear from him more regularly than I do."

"He wants me to try with Granddaddy again," Grace says. The oranges lie there like sad, soft worms. Sour spit fills the back of her throat, but it dries almost instantly, leaving a coppery residue on her tongue.

"He should fight his own battles," Enid says sharply.

Grace sighs. Her brother, Davis, is a third-year at Hopkins. He wants to be a cardiologist like their grandfather, for whom he is named. Their grandfather no longer speaks to Davis, however, because Davis is gay and they are from Virginia. When Davis came out, it had gone as well as it could go, which

was to say that a veil had descended between
the two of them, and Davis, like their father,
had ceased to exist to their grandfather. There
was no argument. No recitation of Scripture.
No blowup or passionate speeches. Only
instant and deep cold. It's harder to argue
with apathy.

Davis texts Grace throughout the week:

> You seen Big Davis?

> Tell him he was right
> about Marshfield being
> awful

> Remind him the pond
> needs to be restocked

> Tell him about this new
> rabbit trap

> Tell him they be
> shooting out here

> Tell him something for me

Sometimes Grace wants to weep at how pitiful it is. The **Tell him something for me** is the worst of it. She could read the text message in its entirety. It's not the words. It's not the **what**. Enid knows about the text messages. She has made her feelings known. Which is why he does not call her. Not because of the gay thing—Enid is ambivalent on the point of sexuality. What room would she have to judge, her own life having exploded so spectacularly? No. It's something else. Judgment. Davis feels **judged**, he says.

Sometimes she act like I'm trying to murder somebody. Just to be asking about Big Davis. She act like she don't care I don't exist anymore, is what Davis said the last time they spoke about it.

"She's projecting," Grace had said.

Because years ago, when they were small, Enid had shown up at this house with Grace and Davis squeezed tight to her like a shield bearer wading into a sea of pikemen. Grace's father had gotten himself stabbed outside a bar in Charlottesville—no surprise, **considering**, was what the church ladies said. It had

never been a secret how Big Davis felt about
white people, and here Enid was. The church
ladies had words for that, too. Begging. Cut
off from her own kind, like she hadn't known
what would happen. Grace wonders if Enid
sees in this needling some imitation of how
it had been years before, when they were
younger, and pushed like little pawns across a
chessboard. Sees, perhaps, some reflection of
the deceased **Junior**.

"He should be a man," Enid says.

"He's a man. Big Davis is a man," Grace
replies. "That's the problem."

"Men and trouble, like water and a grease
fire."

"We ain't," Big Davis replies as the door
bangs shut behind him. Sweat and the scent
of earth trail out ahead of him. He bends
down and kisses the top of Grace's forehead.
She rubs his back, feels the damp of him
through his shirt. His whiskers bristle against
her cheek. He's purple-black with stark
white hair, deep blue eyes.

"You are," Enid says. "Big Davis."

"Enid," he says, taking from the plate

almost all of the orange segments. She squints at him. Grace feels a flutter of relief. Leans back in her chair and lets it hold her up. The strain of maintaining her posture has left her feeling a little winded.

"I sure thank you for taking Grace in for the appointment today."

"Well, I took her fishing. I took her to school. I took her for ice cream. To the movies. I reckon it makes sense I'll take her to get well."

"All that in one day?" Enid says. Big Davis grunts.

"Don't get smart with me," he says, and though there is some playfulness to it, there is also danger. It's the edge of a temper that in Grace's father turned violent and evil. All those nights, Grace and her brother squeezed together into the kitchen cupboard while their parents screamed and broke things upstairs. All those nights of noise and tumult, banging doors and raised voices. The room vibrates with the quiet that comes after Big Davis's voice, so much like her father's that she sees her mother flinch a little. She goes whiter. But then thunder cracks over their heads, releasing them.

"Gracie bug, we better go," she says.

"Don't call me that," Grace says with more resolve than she feels. Her arms betray her, shake when she goes to push up from the chair. They both reach for her, and it is worse than the stupid name, that they expect so little from her, that she can expect so little from herself. She pulls away, feels the obscure tubing of her port shift inside her.

"Baby, rest a minute," Enid says.

"Y'all don't have to rush off," Big Davis says. "You can stay. Eat at least. I know you hate driving in the rain anyway."

Enid frowns at this. Grace folds her arms across her stomach and watches the calculation behind her eyes. It is true that Enid is wary of water on the roads. She has a pathological fear of being swept away in unseen floodwater, drowning in her car. Years ago, at the height of her terror, she had refused to drive across any bridge, fearing that it would give way and plunge them to their deaths. Junior used to make fun of her for it. One

Christmas, Enid had been driving them home from dinner at Big Davis and Mama Lil's house. Junior, drunk, high, reached over and snatched the wheel just as they crossed the bridge, and the car, with Davis and Grace drowsy in the back, swerved. For a terrifying few seconds, they were free of gravity. The whole of the car seemed to lift and turn easily, swiftly, with more speed and force than seemed possible, and they all held their breath, waiting. Then the wheels found the road again with a solid jerk and squeal. Junior's laughter broke out in the car, loud, calamitous. Enid wept the rest of the way home. He kept asking, "What you so sad for, baby? It's Christmas."

"We don't want to put you out," Enid says.

"You ain't, I got plenty. I planned for Grace anyway. We didn't know when you'd be coming by."

"I said after my shift."

"Well, but who knows—"

"I've never been late to get her."

They go back and forth this way, Big

Davis bored, pragmatic, cruel. Enid grows redder the more they haggle over her soul. Grace reaches for an orange slice, pulls the white pith from it, and makes a small pile on the table. She sometimes is struck by the irony of this new arrangement, staying with Big Davis after treatments, waiting for her mother. Somehow, at the age of twenty-five, she's reverted to her childhood self, the one who waited after school at her grandparents' house until her parents came for her. Often they were so late that the sun was going down by the time they arrived, their eyes red, faces tight and hot. She had been relieved to get away from all that once she and her brother got old enough to look after themselves, but neither ever forgot those long, hot hours in their grandmother's kitchen, the endless days of waiting to be retrieved, wondering if they'd get to go home or if they'd have to stay.

But Enid has been better these last ten years. She is not who she once was, though that version of herself remains in this kitchen, as if conjured up out of their collective memory, as if in this family one is powerless to resist its curious gravity. Grace feels a small flicker of pleasure at watching Enid shift uncomfortably.

"Let's just stay," Grace says to her mother, "it's easier."

Enid's expression is one of betrayal, but it passes. Grace puts the orange in her mouth and sucks the juice from it, as if in penance. It stings and slides down the back of her throat, alleviates some of the dryness but leaves only a sense of unslaked thirst.

"We'll stay, then, if it's no trouble."

"Good," he says.

"I'll help," Enid says. "What do you need?"

He hands her a bouquet of turnip greens, bits of dirt dropping to the floor. They are still warm from the garden. "You handle that," he says. "I got this going." The rain grows heavy, dropping into the windowsill behind her back, splattering her in fragments of cool.

"What's for dinner?" Grace asks, and they are elated. A sign of appetite, of hunger.

"Turnips and some of this roast I made

last night and some corn bread," Big Davis says, and he's proud of it. Enid is the one cutting up the greens and the turnip roots, which have always been Grace's favorite. Her brother hates greens of all varieties, and he especially hates turnips. He says they're too bitter, and Grace always has to remind him that he's thinking of mustard greens, not turnips. But Davis hates to be corrected more than he hates greens, so he does not hear her, which usually results in a protracted silence over the phone.

The kitchen is muggy with steam. She wishes she could get up and go outside, sit on the porch swing to watch the storm roll in. But she would have to ask someone, and they'd look at her with worry and pity.

In truth, if she could get up, she'd walk out of this house and keep walking. Nothing would stop her. She'd keep going and going until she got to her brother in Maryland. She'd take his hand and walk both of them into the sea, far away from here. The thought feels like a betrayal—leaving home, leaving Enid and Big Davis—but she wants to take her brother away because it seems like the only way to protect him from the inevitable hurt of their grandfather dying without forgiving, kissing and making good.

There is no reason that it should be Grace here and not Davis. When they were young, their grandfather always favored Davis. She wants to call her brother now and tell him to come, urge him to get in the car, to break any speed limit, to come home and have dinner. But she knows she can't. She's promised to work on Big Davis, to try, in small, slow ways. She has no skill for this sort of game. When they were little, Davis always beat her at checkers and chess. She was always the one to grow impatient before the game was done, to turn away and pout, sometimes to throw the board over. Davis played the long game, but he played it boldly, directly, in strong, clear moves. She was scatterbrained, collecting in small flurries of movements, tiny advancements, minor miracles of displacement. But in truth she never got far across the board before her willpower gave out. She never completed the game, begun in all the earnestness of childhood and the eagerness of believing that this time she would win.

Davis is a fool for entrusting her with this task.

Big Davis puts the plate in front of her. It's full of greens with white turnip roots sliced and spread around the plate. The roast portion is tiny, minuscule, and yet it is still more than she can bear. But it smells rich and a little musky from the vinegar.

"So, what's the plan for tomorrow?" he asks. He neatly slices his roast portion, much larger than either of theirs. Grace feels awkward, coltish, her body starting and jutting into curious directions with even the smallest movement. Enid watches her keenly.

"I'll do what I do every day—lay around until I have to hobble to the bathroom."

Big Davis grunts. "Outcomes are better if you stay active. Keep your strength up."

"I have doctors."

"Don't be disrespectful," he snaps. The fork and knife glint under the kitchen light. His gaze hardens.

"I have doctors, **sir**," she sneers. "I know what my protocols are."

"You have to keep her active," he says to Enid.

"She **is** active."

"I'm right here," she says.

"You were too easy on them kids. Look at them now."

Enid's eyes widen and go buck in exasperation. She lets out a sharp sigh.

"I did all I could. On my own."

"You weren't on your own," he says. "Them kids was here after school every day. And every weekend. And in the summer. If you was on your own, it was in some way I've never heard of."

"I never made you," she says. "I never forced you or Mama Lil to look after them. You offered."

"What was we supposed to do? With a dead pappy and a mammy hooked on that stuff?"

Enid sits a little straighter. Surprise and hurt are visible in her eyes, shame. The nape of Grace's neck crackles with electricity.

It's the sort of remark that would have prompted, in another life now, a shouting match between her parents. But here, in this house, in this kitchen, on this day, Grace sees Enid work it through. Think it over. She has worked her steps. She has taken responsibility. Enid is fond of affirmations. **Own Your Shit, Save Your Life** and **My Shame Is My Badge of Honor** and **My Feelings Are My Responsibility.** All that pretty talk, those encompassing generalities. Toothless to Grace, but powerful to those looking for something to believe in.

"That was a long time ago, Big Davis. And this is hard enough. Now, I've tried to make good and make right."

"You don't know hard," he says. "You don't know the beginning of hard."

Grace wishes she had kept her mouth shut, that she had resisted the mean, biting part of herself. Enid and Big Davis avert their gazes, look down into their plates. Grace bites into the roast, chews it through, swallows. She's let something ugly into the room, she knows. All that stuff about her parents, before her mother got clean and before her father died, all of it suddenly back in the room like departed ancestors of a common line. The spectral outlines of who they had once been. Grace has been trying to be better about letting that sort of thing go. Letting people be who they are **now**. Not holding them to account so hard, so much. Letting them change. Grow. Mutate.

"It's good," she says of the roast. "I like the pepper sauce."

"It was kind of you to offer us dinner," Enid says, quick to change the subject, to make good.

"Y'all my kin," he says.

"Davis, too?" Grace asks, because she cannot let this chance slip by her.

"Nothing stopping your brother from coming here, being here. That's his choice," Big Davis says coolly.

Grace feels like a sulky, surly teenager. She wishes that she could simply accept things as they are, not dig around. Meddle.

She wishes, too, that Davis had never asked her to. Wishes that she had more time. Then it all wouldn't seem like such a waste.

"It's not a choice," she says. "He was made that way."

"What made him made you," he says. "And you ain't that way. You're decent. Some folks is still decent in this world."

Grace laughs. It is of course a ridiculous sentiment. And anyway, if you looked at it hard enough, they were the same in a way. **That way** being that they wanted men. All the times Grace and Davis used to run to this man after being chased by the dog from down the road. Or the way they'd been chased by goats when they'd visited their cousins farther out in the country. Or the way they'd hidden their faces when they met their great-grandparents, skin like polished wood and ancient-looking, hunched forward under their shawls, smelling like astringent creams.

When she was younger and sleeping upstairs, Grace had sometimes felt a pressure on her chest or on her shoulders, holding her down, doing nothing else but that, pressing her against the bed until she was perfectly flat. She had tried to scream, to holler for someone to come and help her, but the weight on her chest had prevented it. She'd lie there all night, frozen, stuck inside her body, unable to do anything to get free. When she told Big Davis about it, he said, **What made them made you, didn't it? They don't mean you no harm**. As if some common origin could negate terror of the unknown. Because we were all made of the same fearsome stuff, nothing in the world could scare you if you looked it in the eye and saw the part of it that was yourself. It was nonsensical in the way that only wisdom could be, Grace thought. Old men and their little stories.

"What made you made **him**," Grace replies.

"You have bigger problems, little lady, than what your brother and me have between us. Mind your business."

Grace hums. Enid stares at her hard. **Now who's trouble?** she can almost hear.

It's true that, growing up, Grace had been the one they watched like a hawk. Her grandmother used to say that boys made babies and girls brought them home, dropped them like kittens at the doorstep, and then who had to raise them but the parents or the grandparents? Nothing her grandmother hated more than the sight of a loose girl, which was to say every girl. When Grace was little, she was the one whose hair they combed all Sunday morning and the one they dressed in the stiff white polyester dress with a ruffle collar before church. She didn't get to run through the woods that cut along by the cemetery. She didn't get to crouch by the pews and play cars before the service started. No. Grace had to **behave**.

Even on days when it was just her and Davis waiting to be collected by their parents, Grace would look up and see her grandmother and aunts looking out at her through the window. Their hard faces. Their mean, tight expressions. Never Davis, who tore a hole in his uniform shirt and sometimes got his new shoes caked in mud.

They never watched him that way. But for Grace, if she sweated through the neck of her shirt or got a smudge, her grandmother would pull it off her rough and say she didn't appreciate things enough. That she'd be just like her mammy, dropping babies she couldn't look after.

One time, at a family picnic, a boy cousin, tall and beige like her, had kissed Grace on the mouth. She didn't ask him to. She didn't want him to. But he did just the same, and Grace recoiled. Before she knew what was happening, though, before she could get her mind around what had just been done to her, she felt a hard, fierce tug at her arm and turned around just in time to get slapped by her grandmother. She called her whorish and fast. Grace wept and tried to say that she hadn't wanted it, but her grandmother pulled her into the house and locked her in the room upstairs.

It wasn't until she was in college that she felt she had some control over her own body. But even then, her grandmother called in the middle of the night. She called the dorm

phone, not her cell, to make sure that Grace
was in her **own bed**. Grace had once had to
run clear across campus when she realized
that it was ten thirty and her grandmother
would be calling any minute. Grace sprinted
over slick grass and hurdled stone benches,
running beneath the high, fragrant trees. She
could hear the phone ringing down the hall
by the time she got to her floor, sucking in
air, her chest burning. And she'd picked up
the phone, only to hear her grandmother's
cold voice, the crackle of her disappointment:
You been out with them boys.

But she hadn't been out with boys. She
had been out with her friends. The girls
from her floor. Who taught her to wear
skirts and how to flirt. Who showed her
how to bum cigarettes and how to burn the
ends of her braids to seal them. The girls
who taught her how to dance, how to enjoy
herself, the swing of her hips and the sun on
her stomach and thighs. Those girls had
taken her in and showed her real love and
kindness. Not watched her. She misses them
now, powerfully. Dreka, Tierra, Amina,

Asha, Brytt. She misses them and she misses that period in her life when everything seemed to fly open and she could breathe again. When she felt the strength in her arms and legs. She felt powerful. Alive.

She wasn't trouble to them. She was just Grace.

What she misses most of all is that feeling of autonomy. Being able to go wherever she wanted. Whenever she wanted. The feeling of being able to lift her fork and not have to think about what it will cost her later.

Oh, she misses it.

The carelessness of those four years.

How easy it was.

But now she misses her hair.

She misses the moisture in her skin.

She misses hunger. Not for food, exactly, or even the sensation of appetite, which remains, if much attenuated. She misses sex, the desire for sex, the capacity for sex.

Before her diagnosis, she had been fucking a white boy named Jonas. He had played lacrosse at the University of Virginia. He was tall and firm. He came from money and his family had a second house in the mountains. Her friends had tried warn her about him. Not that he was dangerous or bad, but that white men were a particular kind of hazard. She was light-skinned, they said, susceptible. But it wasn't like that, Grace didn't think. She wasn't thinking about her parents. She wasn't thinking about how she'd been watched by her grandmother and aunts, or what it meant that her mother didn't speak to her own family anymore because she'd run off with a black man. Grace was careless and free, and what she thought about was what felt good. Having been deprived of it her whole life, having spent all her time thinking about what other people thought, she'd given herself over to Jonas because he made her laugh and made her feel like she was showing him everything about his body and hers both.

With Jonas it was always so good, so easy. He was so pliant, willing to give in to her, to give way to her desires. When they had sex, she could think only of herself, the friction inside her, the gathering heat between their bodies, the scent of her hair, of her sweat and his, the rhythm of their coming together and falling apart. She didn't want a oneness with him, as she'd heard some people describe it. What she craved was the white-hot oblivion of an orgasm, riding the rim of it again and again until finally she slipped down into herself and shivered.

All of that feels beyond her now.

It seems a tragedy to say good-bye to that full-body shudder, that brief glimpse over the edge of herself down into eternity. She'd had it for only a few years before they found the tumor, before her slow withdrawal from life began. She doesn't feel angry about it all the time. Rather, it's as though she'd booked a cruise that is, at the last possible moment, canceled—or, more precisely, that her ticket alone has been canceled. The particular agony of it all is that she has to stand on the beach and watch as everyone she loves drifts out to sea without her.

They go on eating. The clink of their silverware on the good plates. The rain and

wind whipping through the trees outside.
Thunder. And the blue glow of lightning rippling overhead. They go on in their strained
quiet, and Grace watches the beautiful motion of Big Davis's hands. The way the
knuckles shift and bob like buoys under his
skin. And Enid's sharp, anxious cutting and
piercing.

They are the last of their kind, she thinks.
Her father is gone. Her grandmother. Davis.
All that remain are the three of them, and
soon these two will have nothing drawing
them together. Grace sees in their stiff awk-
wardness a premonition of her own demise,
and her vision briefly grows dim. She feels
as though she's being drawn too quickly up
the length of a well. Vertigo.

"Gracie?" Enid asks.

Grace closes her eyes, waits for the spinning feeling to abate. "I'm all right."

"You don't look it." Big Davis presses his
hand to her forehead. He hums. "You're
warm."

"I'm fine," she says, pulling away, but the

motion makes her stomach burn. She's going to be sick. She knows it the moment before it happens, that gurgling, burning retch. She presses her fingers to her mouth, bites down to hold it all in, but it is of no use. Hot acid pulses at the back of her throat, and she feels a blinding, white anger at the fact that she cannot even have the privacy of excusing herself. She must be on display even when she's about to vomit. This moment of horrible weakness belongs not to her but to them.

She hates it.

Big Davis jumps up, reaches for the red bucket on the counter where he keeps the scraps. He shoves it under her face, and the smell of it—the rotting, wet food from breakfast and lunch, the woozy smell of grease and stale bread, the soggy, sad grits—draws the vomit out of her, and she empties herself into the bucket. Her stomach clenches. Her chest clenches. Fire spreads through her veins.

She leans back, her vision all splotches

and luminescent squiggles. Enid presses a wet cloth to her forehead. Grace reaches, holds her hand and sighs.

"Just call him," she says. "Just call him, please."

"Now isn't the time, Grace," Enid says.

"You have to call him. He's afraid of you. But you have to call him."

Big Davis drops the bucket on the counter. Braces himself.

"You better worry about yourself."

"Call him," she says.

"And say what?"

"Tell him the truth. Tell him you love him," Grace says.

"If he doesn't know that after all this time, that I love him, then that boy is worse off than you."

Grace sinks low in the chair. Enid is blotting her brow.

"Well, that we can agree on," Grace says.

"You need rest," Enid says. "You overdid it."

"She has a room," Big Davis says.

Enid nods at this, loops Grace's arm

over her shoulder, whispers reassuring
things to her about strength and patience
and balance. Grace feels embarrassed for
her, the way she sometimes feels when she
can hear Enid praying in the next room in
that tiny apartment of hers. Some things
you should get to keep to yourself.

GRACE SITS by her room's wide window,
from which she can see the deep green
pond. The old forest rimming the property
line. The sleepy fields. The house is full of
sounds, night music.

Enid sleeps in the adjoining room that
had belonged to Davis. When they were
little, the two of them would spend a portion of each night passing back and forth,
leaving small things for each other. Sometimes, Davis pranked her. Or left frogs
under her bed. But that night of the picnic
all those years ago, when her grandmother
had slapped her and locked her in this very
room, Davis had come in from his side.
Grace was on the ground sobbing, her face

hot from her grandmother's palm. She'd been banging at the door, begging to be let out. It hadn't even occurred to her that Davis's side would be open, but when she looked up, there he was. Her brother. He handed her a small kitten. It looked so young that it might not have even been weaned yet. Its fur was soft gray, and it had a pink tint to it. When she asked Davis why he'd brought it to her, he had only shrugged and said he'd grown bored with it, that he'd found it in the woods and played with it until he got tired of it, and he didn't want a cat, anyway.

All that long summer, she carried the kitten around with her, stroking it and petting it and saying that she loved it. Giving the kitten everything she didn't have. Until her grandmother got sick of seeing her loving up on the kitten and pulled it from her hands and flung it out the back door. She said that girls had no business holding on to things with all them fleas. And cats would make a girl hot, and Grace was already fast enough. She never saw the kitten again.

It was the last summer they stayed with their grandparents. The last summer that her father was alive.

So much had come to an end that summer.

Grace should move to the bed, but she is so tired. She's got one of her grandmother's old blankets tossed over her legs. The window emits a cold chill that turns the room bluish in its light. She will regret falling asleep in this chair. Her body will torment her in the morning. But her legs refuse to cooperate. Her arms too heavy. She sinks low in the old chair and closes her eyes.

She will rest a moment. Just a moment.

She dreams of a boat going farther and farther into the distance. One of those rickety white boats out back, the kind she and Davis had taken across the pond, shouting and squealing so loud, they scared all the fish away. Such a boat had no purpose on the sea or a river, where the water was too wild and would rend it to pieces. She dreams of a boat going farther and farther into the distance, disintegrating all the way, leaving behind a trail like a comet, the shrapnel that a life leaves behind as it burns itself out. And now she feels herself beneath the weight of the invisible world, stuck. After all these years, stuck. She might have known it would happen, might have known to prepare herself for this, but she did not.

Beyond the periphery of the dream, though her eyes are still closed, Grace feels suddenly that she is not alone. There is some sort of presence in the far corner of the room. Some barely there shift in the room's air pressure, the impression of space being taken up. She cannot make her body move, cannot get her eyes to open. Instead, she turns the whole of her concentration toward the presence in the corner. It reaches back toward her, as if it were using her concentration to pull itself hand over hand in her direction. A sensation, heavy, dragging up the length of her leg, the quilt rumpling under this unseen force.

She forces her eyes open with all her willpower.

What is this, what is this, what is this,

she chants to herself. The presence has always been amorphous. Her tongue is stuck to the roof her mouth, her throat full of static fuzz. She floats beneath the surface of her skin, staring at the ceiling, the white globe of the lamp overhead.

The door creaks open. There is a change in the shape of the darkness as it lightens fractionally, insignificantly, but perceptibly, if only just so. There is another presence now, coming on from the distance, coming across the void toward her. She swallows thickly. Something is reaching for her, and there, suddenly, contact.

Warmth like a human hand.

MEAT

THEY WERE LYING IN LIONEL'S BED again, facing each other.

"Where are you from?" Lionel asked, and then, because the question seemed too personal, even though they had just fucked, he said, "Not that you have to tell me."

"Bangor," Charles said. "Maine."

"What's it like there?"

"Cold. Wet. Empty," he said. "It's kind of a bleak place."

"That seems dramatic."

Charles didn't say anything after that, and Lionel was afraid that he had been too sharp. He put his hand on Charles's chest and moved closer to him beneath the blanket. The bed's complaint under his shifting weight drew his attention to the fact that he was yet again sharing this lumpy mattress with another person. So remarkable was the thought that he could not hold it still, and it slipped down out of his awareness. It was just as well.

"Sorry," Lionel said.

"What are you sorry for?"

"You got quiet."

"If I'm quiet, I'm quiet."

"Okay," Lionel said, "sorry for being sorry."

Charles flicked the bruise on Lionel's cheek with the same casual gesture he'd used to spin his fork around last night. Lionel could still feel the indentations of Charles's teeth. The skin was swollen and a little tender from the hickey. But it was nothing, really. By morning it would be gone. It seemed sad that it would fade or that things had to end. When he was a child, that had depressed him. When his mother read him stories, he'd bawl at the end even if the little duck found its way back to its mother or the bears and the girl became friends or green eggs and ham were eaten. It didn't matter if the story had a happy ending or if things turned out okay and all the scary things were put away. He hated that vertiginous feeling of things ending. That sense of the world dropping off under his feet. It had been the same at math camp. Everyone rolling up their sleeping bags, putting away their clothes for one last time. Saying good-bye, or pointedly **not** saying good-bye. There was, too, something unsurprising in all that. After all, his father had left them suddenly. Or it had **seemed** sudden, at least to Lionel. One day, his dad had packed up for a trip the way he always did. But then weeks went by, and when he asked his mother where his father had gone, she turned to him and said, as if describing the weather forecast, that he wasn't coming back and that Lionel should get used to it.

It seemed impossible, though, with Charles's hand coming to rest between his thighs, that he'd wake up tomorrow and be alone again. Yet it was true. That was what would happen. Charles twisted some of Lionel's wiry pubic hair. The skin over his pelvis grew taut when Charles pulled. They were connected by that single fiber, that single black thread of hair. He imagined the place down far in his skin where the hair was rooted. He could graph in his mind the function that would perfectly describe the growth of hair over a period of time. And then he could see the derivative of that function. Nested inside each other, the calculus of his changing form. And, too, the function that would describe the application of a force at a radius the length of a public hair. It was a comfort to him, this math. This easy, direct calculus. All of life was shifting equations.

But then Charles pulled so hard that the hair came free of Lionel with a burning jolt, and he yelped at the surprise of it.

"There you are," Charles said.

"What do you mean?"

"You kind of spaced on me. You were just zoned-out there."

"I was thinking about functions to describe biological processes," Lionel said.

"Was that your project? Before?"

Lionel laughed and Charles pulled three more of his pubic hairs free. Lionel tried to get loose, but Charles pushed his shoulders flat and rolled on top of him.

"Why's that so funny, tough guy?"

"I'm not much of a modeler," Lionel said. "That stuff is so dry. It sounds cool, but it's really tedious. Imagine spending your life picking nits out of eight million lines of code. Modeling is so awful."

Charles blinked at him slowly, and though they were physically touching, Lionel felt far away from him. It was not merely the difference in their chosen fields. It was a difference in the very constitution of their minds. Lionel felt lonely there under Charles. He had made a poor choice. He should have stayed with the host last night. There was some shared language there.

"You should get back to Sophie, I guess."

"I don't have to be there."

"Are you sure?"

"Yes, I'm sure," Charles said, mocking Lionel a little. "Do you want me to leave? I can."

"No," Lionel said.

"Good." Charles sat back on Lionel's legs, and Lionel gasped. It was the pathetic, involuntary sound of his body giving in without his permission, opening itself. "Oh, little baby wants."

"Yes," Lionel said, because the light had come into Charles's eyes again.

"Little baby." Charles pressed his fingers into Lionel's mouth. "Suck, little baby." The tips of Charles's fingers were chalky. Lionel could feel the whorls of the fingerprints as they slid across his teeth and tongue. Charles watched carefully, and it was the watching that made Lionel hard. The seeing. The witnessing of what he was doing to Lionel. Charles pressed his fingers deeper, and Lionel tasted his knuckles and the spaces between his fingers. Lionel could taste himself and Charles and everything that Charles had touched, a whole world sliding into his mouth, down his throat. Charles worked his fingers past Lionel's lips, back and forth, in and out, fucking Lionel's mouth with his fist. Down to the knuckles and back. Lionel's teeth scraped his knuckles, and then there was the coppery taste of his blood. Lionel shivered beneath him, breathed hard through his nose.

"Good. Greedy little baby." Charles pulled his fingers from Lionel's mouth, and there was a terrible, gaping emptiness inside him.

"No," Lionel mouthed. "No." He wanted it back, needed it back.

"**Shhh**," Charles whispered. Then Lionel felt it, the slick heat of Charles's fingers inside him. There was an awful heat, and then more pressure. Charles was opening him again, with the wet from his own mouth, wearing thin the membranous boundary that kept the world out.

"Yes," Lionel said. "Yes."

"Good," Charles said.

.   .   .

LIONEL HAD NAILED a pillowcase over the broken window. He'd tried to make it as taut as he could, but there was still a little give in the fabric that let in the cold air when the wind blew particularly hard. Charles was leaning over the sink inspecting Lionel's work. He stuck his finger through a gap between the window and the pillowcase.

"Some handyman you'd be," he said.

"I'm a discredit to my dad."

"Oh yeah?"

Lionel had taken the carafe from the fridge and was pouring cold water for the two of them.

"My dad was always good about that sort of thing. I'm sure I did about ten things wrong."

"You might have gone with plastic. Or called your landlord."

Lionel didn't want to say that even the idea of calling his landlord and asking him to replace the window made his stomach hurt. Just using the phone to call the department secretary to cancel his proctoring a couple weeks ago had almost put him on his back. It was another of the things that seemed easy for other people, as if they were born knowing how to use the phone without having their throats close up and forgetting all their words. He tried to handle everything with email. Or text. Even face-to-face wasn't as bad as the phone.

When his parents split up, his dad used to call him every Thursday and on weekends. But Lionel didn't know what to say to him, and they'd spend a couple minutes on the phone in total silence. Then his dad would ask to speak to his mom, and Lionel would give the phone over to her. Lionel wasn't sure what you were supposed to say to other people over the phone. That time last year, when his dad came to see him after he'd tried to kill himself, had been the first time they'd seen each other in years. And what had his dad said? **You look homeless.**

"I'll send him an email," Lionel said.

Charles hooked his finger over the top of the pillowcase and pulled. It was looser than

Lionel first thought, and the nails wedged into the wall squeaked.

"I don't think you secured this," Charles said. "Is this just plaster?" Charles tapped the wall with his knuckles and frowned.

"You've made your point."

Charles lowered himself to the floor. He was wearing a gray sweater and just his underwear, no socks. He stretched his legs out under the table and brushed Lionel's ankles with his big toe. He rested his head against the cupboard doors and closed his eyes. Then he started to hum, and his toe switched back and forth over the knobs of Lionel's ankle bones in time to the humming.

"Is that what you're working on?"

Charles shook his head, but the humming grew louder, and he smirked a little. He was having fun at Lionel's expense.

"Very funny."

"You don't know Tchaikovsky?"

"Did Bach write that?" Lionel said.

Charles laughed loudly, and it was like that sound from last night when he'd stood on the porch and howled.

"Is Bach the only composer you know?"

"I know about Chopin," Lionel said. "He's a composer."

"Well, with Bach and Chopin, you could probably fake your way through a dinner party."

"Is that what you do? Fake it?"

"Don't you?" Charles asked.

Lionel felt stupidly hurt by that. Not because he objected in principle, but because it implied that the two of them sitting in Lionel's kitchen was fake. Not real.

"Sure," Lionel said. "I'm a big faker." He left the table and sat next to Charles on the floor. Closer to the window, he could hear the wind kissing the narrow gap at the top of the pillowcase. He reached up and back, his shoulder pinching a little, and pulled the broken halves of the ruler down. On the back, the blue marker had faded to black. He'd written his name there and the year he'd gotten it. Charles took the ruler from him and put the two halves together.

"This has seen better days."

"Yeah," Lionel said.

Charles made to throw the ruler into the trash across the room. Lionel reached for it.

"Don't do that."

"It's busted," Charles said, holding the ruler out away from Lionel. "What's the deal?"

"It's not yours. You can't throw something out when it's not yours." Charles turned toward him and pushed him onto his back. Then sat on Lionel's stomach. He held the ruler over his head, out of Lionel's reach.

"Your boyfriend give you this?"

"No," Lionel said. "No."

Lionel closed his eyes so he didn't have to see Charles mocking him. But then Charles started to drum on the kitchen counter with the ends of the ruler. It was the music he had been humming. Charles squeezed his knees tight to Lionel's sides.

"This isn't funny," Lionel said. "It's not a joke." He reached up for the ruler, and Charles caught his wrist, held his arm still. His first thought was that Charles was going to tickle him, and he flinched in anticipation for it. The extension of this horrible game. But Charles did not tickle him. No. He did something much worse. He leaned down and looked closely at the keloids. His breath was close on Lionel's skin, warm, damp. But it was the brightness in his eyes that made Lionel look away. He didn't want to see Charles seeing him.

Lionel tried to pull his arm free, but Charles was stronger than him. They both knew that, and it made Lionel feel more pathetic for struggling as he did.

"Don't," Lionel said.

Charles kissed the keloids, and Lionel almost jumped out of his skin at the shock of it.

"You don't know what you're doing," Lionel said.

"Watch me," Charles said. He kissed the heel of Lionel's palm, and then moved down the tributaries of his veins, down the whole length of his arm. Kissing him again and again, until they were face-to-face. It was an ugly, cruel thing to do, Lionel thought. It was as mean a thing as he could have imagined. He couldn't look at Charles, not after Charles had done what he did.

"I wish you hadn't," Lionel said.

Charles got off him then, and Lionel sat up. Blood had pooled in the back of his head, making him dizzy. He rested his back against the legs of the chair. And he took the pieces of the ruler from Charles. He felt safe with them there. A part of his old life, who he used to be.

"Why'd you do it?" Charles asked, and when Lionel did not answer, he added, "It must have hurt like hell."

"You know how sometimes an animal will chew its arm off to get loose if it's desperate enough?" Lionel turned his arm over and looked down at the scars there. They were mute. Whatever wisdom or clarity they had given him was gone. What he saw was a mass of tissue stitched back together. What he saw was only evidence of his body's history. And to try to discern old moods, old insights, was just chasing shadows.

"Be serious, Lionel."

Lionel wanted to laugh at that, being accused of not taking his own suicide seriously enough because he had tried to tell the truth about it. There was no **why**. No coherent theorem. It had been all gesture, as empty an idiom as the references from the potluck last night. When you tried to explain it, all the meaning went out of it. But Charles was looking at him with the expectation of an answer, and Lionel did not have one. Not a satisfactory one anyway. He felt as unprepared now to answer the question of **why** as he had when his mother first asked him last year. **Why** was an anachronism.

"You only ask why if you've never tried it," he said.

Charles took Lionel's hand in his own. Lionel saw Charles's eyes flick to the particular array of scars. The hashwork of them. Nothing systematic or intentional about it.

"I think you're very brave," Charles said with a degree of sincerity that made Lionel wish he could take back everything he had said. Sincerity was a condescending emotion. People went around calling you brave when you tried to kill yourself and failed. They called you brave when you went limping through your life, as if the very difficulty of it were a sign of moral courage or valor. But there was nothing noble in suffering. There was nothing brilliant or good about the failed endeavor to exit one's life. There was nothing courageous about the persistence of life, the prolonged project of living. People called you brave for going on because it affirmed their own value system. They considered their own life worth living, and so they considered **every** life worthy.

But it had to be true that life could be discarded when it was no longer of use. It had to be true that a person could ball their life up and throw it out with the trash if they found they had no desire to go on. Some lives, Lionel thought, had to be ordinary or ugly or painful. Ending your life had to be on the table. If you were the one really in control, and you were in it for yourself, then ending your life certainly had to be an option if you wanted it to be. But people called you brave for going on. They called you brave even if you only lingered in the world because you'd lost your real courage at the moment it mattered most.

"That's what people say when they're uncomfortable," Lionel said.

"What?"

"I'm not brave."

"Don't get worked up," Charles said.

"Man, whatever."

Lionel lay down under the table. Gray spiderwebs and caught dust billowed in the corners of the legs. He could see the pencil marks of the carpenter who had made the table. He reached up and brushed the faded blue numbers. He scratched the wood with his nails. Charles crawled under the table, too. They lay on their backs, head to head, looking up into the blank underside of the table as though it were the night sky.

"You ever feel like your life is getting away from you, Lionel?"

"Yeah. All the time."

"If I don't get this thing at PNB, I think that might be it for me."

"As a dancer?"

"Yeah. Maybe you can put in a word for me at your proctoring thing."

"Absolutely. You bet."

"A dancer only gets so many years. And that's if they're brilliant."

Lionel knew better than to say that Charles was brilliant. It would have been insulting. Charles sighed.

"I'm going back to the program in the spring."

"If I had another three years of **this**," Charles said, waving, gesturing to Lionel's life, apartment, world, whatever. "You had this little blip. And you'll get to go back."

It was true, Lionel thought, that he'd return to his life. That had been the thing he wanted most. But listening to Charles, it sounded childish. It sounded simple and easy. It was another form of condescension.

"You're kind of self-pitying right now," Lionel said.

"All I'm saying is, you've got this nice setup. And I'm here with a bum fucking knee, about to suck some old guy's dick so maybe he'll arrange an audition for me. So that **maybe** I can get another two years out of doing the thing I love most. You tell me who's self-pitying. You're the cutter."

Lionel almost gasped at the fluidity of the remark. The way it snapped off at the end.

"I think it's possible for my life to be shitty and also for your life to be shitty. Maybe you should keep your eyes on your own paper," Lionel said. He was grateful then that he hadn't said more to Charles, that he'd recognized the pitying, facile nature of Charles's regard for him. For what he'd gone through. He was grateful he hadn't betrayed himself by feeling more than he'd let himself feel.

"I didn't mean that," Charles said.

"You're selfish."

"Yeah, probably." Charles turned and reached for Lionel. But Lionel moved away. He slid from beneath the table, and Charles followed. They sat up together. It felt like a game. Every time Lionel moved, Charles followed. They were locked in a round of Simon Says.

"Stop it," Lionel said, but Charles just assumed his posture. Lionel huffed and spun around, and Charles did the same. Charles's ability to copy not only his actions, but also the attitude each action contained, was uncanny. Lionel had the feeling of watching himself in a mirror, though on a delay. After a while, he forgot to be angry at Charles. They sat facing each other, doing mirrored gestures.

"This is one of the first things I learned to do. You learn to watch people. Imitate. Improvise."

"You're really good at it," Lionel said.

"No. I'm not. The best people make you feel like **you're** copying **them**. This isn't even close."

Their palms didn't touch, but Lionel could feel the static from Charles's skin. The human warmth of him. When Lionel sped up, Charles sped up. Except there was no gap between Lionel doing the thing and Charles adjusting. It seemed that they decided upon what they would do at the same moment. Lionel reversed direction, but there was Charles right in front of him. No matter what he did, there was Charles. They made a circuit with their hands, a figure out. Then more complicated sinuous patterns.

"We're all just selfish assholes," Lionel said. "Just like Sophie said."

After a few minutes, Charles said, "I need a haircut."

"You do," Lionel said, but he was only half paying attention.

"You weren't supposed to agree," Charles said, a little pained.

"But it's true. You're kind of shaggy."

CHARLES SAT in the chair with a towel draped over his shoulders. Lionel got the trimmers from the bathroom. He didn't like electric clippers. The buzzing irritated something fragile in him, and the vibrations sometimes stayed stuck in his head for a long time. But ever since the hospital, he

had been too anxious to use manual razors—
as if a part of him worried that, with
sufficient opportunity, he might try again.
He found that he could use the clippers on
the lowest setting. Mostly, he used them for
his head because his facial hair was far
from formidable. He reconsidered this as
he looked at Charles's broad head, shaggy
like a large, friendly dog's. There was also
the fact that Charles had white-people hair,
which was a unique complication in this
endeavor. White-people hair was smooth
and slippery. He didn't know how it would
react to the trimmers. His own hair was
woolly, fibrous. It came away in clumps,
little balls of light brown fluff. It was easy to
shear him.

"Okay," he said, turning on the clippers.
"Let's do this, I guess."

"That does not inspire confidence,"
Charles said.

"I'll have to take it all off. I can't do anything else." There was a pause. He could feel
Charles turning that thought over in his
head. He thought he could suggest that

Charles take care of the front and instruct him on how to do the back or the sides. He bit the tip of his tongue.

"That's okay," Charles said. "Do it."

"All right," Lionel said, and drew the trimmers back through the first, delicate layer of Charles's hair. He enjoyed running his fingers though it again and again as he buzzed it all away. It seemed like such a shame to do it to hair this good, this beautiful. It hadn't even started to thin the way his own had. Charles had the kind of face that was suitable for any kind of hair, but the curls suited him most, brought out the boyishness in him. Without them, he would be too severe, too intimidating, too much like a man. But it was too late, all gone. Charles caught whatever hair he could and piled it in a little mound on his lap. Lionel slid his fingers against the fuzzy scalp that was slowly emerging from beneath the hair. He occasionally scraped too close, and Charles hissed at him, which made Lionel hard. The reprimand reminded him of how they'd fucked.

It was done in about twenty minutes, and Lionel was proud of how even it all was.

"You look good," he said, appraising him. "You look really good."

"Let me see," Charles said, and went to the bathroom. He stayed in there a long time. Lionel could hear the water running. He was sitting on the edge of his bed, rocking his feet back and forth, testing the strength of his ligaments. He was chewing the edge of his lip raw. He could see falling snow through the window over the bed. It fell through the blue light of the street lamp, drifting sideways in the wind. It was accumulating on the sidewalk and the windowsill. He let the window up, and cold air blew in on him, clear and perfect.

"I like it," Charles said from the bathroom. "You did a great job. I feel tingly all over, raw." He came from the hallway, rubbing water into his hair. He had been rinsing away the loose bits. His face had lost its softness. There was still warmth in his eyes and in his brow, but now there was also sharpness, clean, cruel lines.

"You look different," Lionel said, and Charles frowned at him.

"Bad? I thought you liked it."

"I do like it," he said. "I do. You look great."

"I don't believe you," Charles said. His feelings were hurt. Lionel got up from the bed and gathered Charles's hair into his hands.

"We have to burn it," he said.

"Why?" Charles asked.

"So that birds don't take it and make you crazy. It's something my grandma says."

"Okay," he said. "Let's do it."

CHARLES MADE a small circle in the snow, a place that he excavated with his bare hands. When he was done, his fingers were red and numb. He put them under Lionel's shirt and held them there against his skin. Lionel shivered, but he didn't move or make Charles take his hands away. He could do this, could give his heat, at least. Then Charles set the hair down in the middle of the circle and tried to light it, but it wouldn't stay lit. A couple of strands turned bright orange then immediately burned themselves out. The ground was dampening the other hairs, making them hard to burn. Lionel went back into his apartment and came out with a small pot. He set it on the ground and put the hair inside. He took out a sheet of paper and handed it to Charles.

"Try this," he said. Charles smiled at him and crouched over the pot. He lit the paper and nestled it into the hair. The smell was awful, as the strands turned to fire, like little worms writing as they burned themselves out. Their light was insufficient to illuminate anything, but for a while, it was beautiful to watch.

Charles put his arms around Lionel, and Lionel leaned back against him. The wind was at their faces, the smoke rising toward them, then above them, and then away. Lionel felt he might fall asleep right there, standing up—drift off and never come back to his body. The snowfall was even and slow.

"Let's go inside."

ACKNOWLEDGMENTS

Thank you, in no particular order, to Meredith Kaffel Simonoff, Cal Morgan, Claire McGinnis, Sophie Missing, Jimena Gorraez, Zeljka Marosevic, Catalina Trigo, Jacey Mitziga, Sylvie Rabineau, Antonio Byrd, Derrick Austin, Sarah Fuchs, Natalie Eilbert, Christopher Sprott, Verrazzani Mitchell, Hux Michaels, Lan Samantha Chang, Deb West, Jan Zenisek, Sasha Khmelnik, Philip Wallén, and Lyz Lenz.

Thank you to the editors who took these stories on in other forms:

Michelle Tudor at Platypus Press, who published a version of "Potluck" as "They Belong Only to Themselves."

Alex McElroy, who published a version of "Flesh" at **Gulf Coast** as "God Is Not Flesh, But Air."

Adeena Reitberger, who published a version of "As Though That Were Love" in **American Short Fiction.**

Michelle Lyn King, who published a version of "Proctoring" as "French Absolutism" in **Joyland.**

Meakin Armstrong, who published a version of "Anne of Cleves" in **Guernica.**

Sarah Lyn Rogers, who published a version of "What Made Them Made You" as "Grace" at **The Rumpus**.